The Elfin Brood

For just a moment Thrett paused, looking directly into Profundus' eyes. He knew Vastar was a master of poisons, and he assumed Profundus to be equally skilled. Then, quickly, he grasped the goblet and drained it.

Profundus watched Thrett carefully, finally saying with mounting excitement, "You have made your choice, and I have made mine. For many years I have awaited for an answer to a riddle that has taunted me all my life. I trust few men—in that I am not unlike my brother. The Vergers, the Beastums, the Querques are all doomed by an evil visited upon them in the dark past. Then, from the sere grasslands, a stranger comes with balm for our wounds, with hope when we have already abandoned ourselves to despair. I rule tired men in a time-wracked land. My dominion is blighted, my people infertile. Perhaps, new land means new vigor, the resurgence of the once-mighty Vergers. And if there is gold, so much the better. You have brought us hope in the gathering darkness. But you—what am I to do with you?"

And as Profundus spoke, Thrett slowly felt more and more tired, and as he grew weaker, too weak to resist, he realized that the wine was poisoned and that he was dying. So this is how it ends, he thought...

The Elfin Brood

by

Orville Wanzer

Commonwealth
Publications

A Commonwealth Publications Paperback
THE ELFIN BROOD

This edition published 1997
by Commonwealth Publications
9764 - 45th Avenue,
Edmonton, AB, CANADA T6E 5C5
All rights reserved
Copyright © 1996 by Orville Wanzer

ISBN: 1-55197-312-X

This work is a novel and any similarity to actual persons or events is purely coincidental.

Cover Design by: Patrick Earl

Printed in Canada

Part One
The Journey Northward

varying in any individual Elf according to the season, according to changes in temperament and according to his surroundings, but all were green, for that was their nature. Man, before his decline in the ancient past, had attributed the power of invisibility to the Elves, but that, of course, was foolish; the Elves, being as green as their habitats, were difficult to see, a difficulty of which they took advantage to escape the fatal curiosity of Man even during his tenure of nobleness. But being green served a more profound purpose than acting as camouflage, for the greenness of Elfin skin was a source of energy and strength; an Elf was able to convert the rays of the sun into the substance of life just as the plants around him did. To bask in the sun, to absorb the energies radiating from the father of life, to feel the warmth of being was one and all to an Elf whose only religious impulse was the adoration of the mighty sun. On cloudy days and at night, the Elves supplemented their need for life-giving energy by eating the insects and fungi of the mesquite thickets, feasting thus on nature's bounty, and protecting the mesquite trees and bushes to which they claimed kinship. For in all directions, the mesquite was the dominant tree, covering the great flood plains of Prosopia in dense, almost impenetrable undergrowth, a natural barrier to all who would enter the Elfin lands. Fiercely thorned, the mesquite grew most abundantly along the river edge and in the numerous arroyos feeding into the Rhus. In small, open areas within the thickets, the Elves made their homes by judicious pruning and thatching.

And as Man was large, so the Elves were small, at least among the Prosopian Elves, for they knew of no others. Seldom did an Elf stand above three feet. Elfin hair was worn long, except for the elderly, and varied in hue from the most common light brown to rich, dark brown, with female's hair becoming boldly red at the tips during her periods of fertility. Elves were beardless and their bodies were without hair quite unlike their nearest neighbors, the Dwarfs, who were very hairy with rich, full beards in which they took great pride. Elfin ears were pointed, and their red eyes were much larger than the beady eyes of Man, thus their hearing was very keen and their eyesight was as sharp as the eagle during the day, and the owl at night. In all things, Elves honored proportion, their bodies being prime examples, for unlike Man whose multitude of shapes defied description, and unlike Dwarfs whose heads always seemed too large for their bodies, Elves prided themselves on having limbs that were never too short or too long, not bellies too vast or shrunken, nor muscles too prominent or not at all, for Elves all was in balance, all parts harmoniously fit together, and if an Elf was thin, his features, his arms, his legs, his body were also thin; if he was stout, then all of his parts were stout. Endurance, agility, and speed were also Elfin traits, for these skills enabled them to survive in a hostile, Man-ridden world, and these traits became the substance of all their contests and games, their pleasures and pastimes. For the Elves were a joyous lot, given to great exuberance and gaiety, their laughter gladdening the endless mesquite thickets and often annoying, even causing rage among the men across the river Rhus who envied the joy and contentment of the Elfin Brood.

On this, the longest day of the year, Elves from all the many villages of Prosopia were to meet in a mighty conclave in the hamlet of Prosopia, the home of Styrax the King. The Elves had named their land and their capital village Prosopia which seemed confusing to creatures other than Elves. For Elves were wary of names and used as few as possible thus Styrax was the son of Styrax who was the son of Styrax; and Canna was the daughter of Canna who was the daughter of Canna. To an Elf, a name was a dangerous thing, for as names proliferated, self-aware beings gradually began to accept the name as substance rather than that which it represented. Each year, at this time, the elders met in solemn forum to study and discuss the Man problems of the Elfin world the foremost of which was the frequent attempted incursions of Man the destroyer. But all was not solemn, for only the elders and the King sat in serious council. By far, the greatest number of Elves met for feasting, sporting events and musical enchantments, for Elves are great lovers of music, believing they were created originally from the music of the celestial spheres. For many days, the women and children of Prosopia had been preparing a noble feast, catching a myriad of fat insects, especially the frisky grasshoppers and cicadas which were in great abundance in this season and which the women of Prosopia were famous for their savory concoctions, particularly when roasted in mesquite honey and smoked in tamarisk wood. The children wandered far, collecting bark fungi, black toadstools, and amanita mushrooms which they then shredded, mixed together, and boiled in a rich broth of thornapple, a happy drink that made Elves laugh and have pleasant dreams, though this very same mixture drove men mad before they died in great agony. The Elfin men, meanwhile, prepared the courses for racing, jumping, crawling, and swinging, a true test of an Elf's speed, dexterity and courage. The racing paths were so made that they ran through the densest mesquite thickets with passages so small a careless Elf could easily tear his flesh deeply on the cruel mesquite thorns; then they ran in more open areas where the contestants had to leap long distances to avoid stumbling on sharp rocks; and finally the paths moved off the ground into the arching limbs of the greater mesquite trees where each Elf had to leap and swing from limb to limb until he found himself again at the point from which the race began. Though seemingly dangerous, few were ever hurt and then but slightly scratched and bruised. Both young and old, men and women competed together, for, unlike Man, Elfin women were easily as fleet and as brave as their mates, and the old were often faster than the young because they were wise in the ways of mesquite undergrowth. Next, they built circular targets made of massed osier reeds and densely packed leaves, for Elves were masters of the blowgun and poisoned dart, their only weapon and one that was rarely put to use. Many were so skilled they were capable of striking a mantis at ten yards.

While these preparations were being made, King Styrax and his constant companion, doughty Thuja, were patrolling the Prosopian border along the Rhus as they did most every day. Styrax, tall and reed-like, led the way, pausing frequently to ascertain that no breaks in the dense mesquite would allow a Man to enter the sacred Elfin land. Thuja, short, stocky, and mightily strong, followed closely, talking frequently with the chaparrals, quail and herons who lived along the river banks. The friendship of Styrax and Thuja was adamantine since the time of their childhood a century ago when Styrax drove off a pair of scrubble bears that were about to kill young Thuja who foolishly thought his strength a match for the fierce bears who were merely protecting their cubs. Thuja was still foolish in many ways, but Styrax knew that beneath this mask of foolishness lay a noble heart and the wisdom of the wild. For of all the Elves, and all Elves could understand the creatures of the wild, Thuja was the most conversant with the animals of the Prosopian wilderness.

Finding a rocky ledge jutting into the Rhus, both Elves contentedly lay down to bask in the warmth of the summer sun. As they rested and absorbed the sun's energy, Ulmus the chaparral, a particularly large and fierce bird and a special friend of Thuja, sped quickly to where they lay. Standing upon Thuja's chest, Ulmus spoke quickly and emphatically, "Cooo, cooo, coo-ah, coo-ah, cooo, co-ah." Then, spying a lizard retreating beneath a jimson-weed, he was gone.

"What did Ulmus want?" Styrax murmured lazily.

"He is angry, for he saw three men trying to cross the Rhus, just downstream from here. The swift current drove them back, once again. They were mounted and armed."

"I fear they are the same ones that have been haunting us of late, though, it seems, they have not yet found a crossing into Prosopia." Styrax paused in worried thought, then continued, "if they go much further north, our troubles will multiply, for at one place the river is wider and less deep, and the mesquite has been torn open by spring floods. Damn them! Can they not stay among their own kind?"

"I should think not, my friend. I should think not." And Thuja slipped into a charmed sleep.

But Styrax could not sleep. He knew how persistent Man can be; he knew that sooner or later, Man would find a way across; and he knew that blood would be spilled, and that appalled him. The spilling of blood, any blood kindred or not, was loathsome to Elves, and even in self-defense, an Elf would prefer to simply run away or, if that failed, to stun his foe. The darts he shot from his blowgun were dipped in poisons of varying potency, some so weak as to merely incapacitate the enemy, some more potent to stun the enemy, and some so deadly as to kill most living things in a matter of minutes. The Elfin prohibition against killing anything was so intense that an Elf apologized to the mushrooms he ate by saying aloud that he must do what he must do. Styrax sighed sadly, knowing that the council must consider Man's latest attempts at intrusion, and knowing also that the council would postpone any decision until they knew more or until Man had entered the sacred lands. What should I do? What can I do? He had only one answer, and he feared its consequences. Should I summon the Wanderer? Can I trust him? Has the time come? He hoped not. Oh, how he hoped not. And then the warmth of the sun's nourishing rays proved too much, and he slipped into a troubled sleep.

Queen Canna, slender but strong, busily roasted the grasshoppers and cicadas in her earthen pans, adding just the right amount of mesquite honey and wild herbs. The sun was well into the west; the heat of the day was waning; and Prosopia was becoming crowded with Elves from distant villages. Canna loved this midsummer holiday more than any of the other feast days; how happy it would be to eat and sing and dance until the moon rose and the musicians gathered for the evening's enchantments. She hoped that she and Styrax would be done with the inevitable council meeting early enough to join in the festivities, for

Canna found little joy without Styrax. Since childhood, since the many years of schooling, she and
Styrax had been lovers in truth and harmony, in
body and in spirit. As yet, they had not children,
but soon their time would come. As she stirred
the savory favorite of the Elves with one hand, she
brushed her light brown, silken hair with a thistle
brush. Looking down at her trim legs and rounded
belly, she laughed to herself as she remembered
Styrax telling of Man's foolish practice of covering
his body with strange cloths and skins of other
creatures. How strange, she thought, to hide
oneself from the light. Elves, of course, wore no
clothing or other bodily ornamentation and saw
no reason to hide themselves. How ugly the Man
creature must be to cover himself in such a fashion, she thought, and then dismissed the image of
Man from her mind, not caring to think of that
which was malevolent. As she looked up from her
reverie, she nodded to the first of the elders,
Acanthopanax and Callistemon, as they sat upon
the benches placed in front of the home she shared
with Styrax.

Acanthopanax was the eldest of the elders, a
teacher of great renown and a mighty voice in council. His age showed but slightly in the greying
fringes of his closely cropped hair and in his deliberate manner of walking, as though he thought
of each step he was about to take. Elves did not
age as did Man, for on sensing the coming of
decrepitude, they simply returned to their ancestors, as Acanthopanax must soon do. His companion, Callistemon, was much younger, hardly
beyond her 300th year, and she was still a handsome woman, her hair still the vibrant dark brown
of her youth. Her teaching was so respected
throughout Prosopia that she traveled from village

to village, when not busy with her own students, earning the honored title of 'Gentle Philosopher.'

The home of Canna and Styrax was made from living mesquite limbs that had been bent and pruned into a domed shape which was then thatched with tamarisk branches. The interior was small, with a leaf-softened bed, a fire pit, and hundreds of colorful stones which ornamented the lower walls and kept the floor dry. The colored stones in reds, greens and yellows were gifts from other Elves, for Elves from ancient times valued anything permanent and colorful. The act of giving was sacred to the Elves, and the stones Canna would receive one day, she would give to others at a later time.

Now it must be told that all elders were teachers, and teachers were elders, for in the Elfin world and in Elfin logic, it could be no other way. Unlike the world of Man, even in his ascendancy, the Elfin Brood held teachers in the highest esteem, for to an Elf it was obvious and unquestionable that the ones who knew the most, and were gifted in imparting what they knew, must inevitably and rightly lead the rest. Each village had its own teacher, though each teacher often traveled to other hamlets to enrich and vary the learning to which the young were exposed. For exposure was the sole method of teaching throughout the happy land of Prosopia. No one was required to attend the village schools nor was there anything to complete by attending classes. The teacher simply was there; the things to learn were there, the pleasure of learning was there. Elfin learning concerned itself almost wholly with understanding processes rather than individual things. Rather than give names to everything, the Elf concentrated on the relationships, the harmonies that unified nature, for to

an Elf knowledge meant only the realization of the
harmony and balance inherent in the process of
life. Thus, though the Elves were kind, gentle and
loving, they seldom spoke of kindness, gentleness,
or love. Many young Elves stayed at school but a
year or two, others for longer periods and others
for all of their lives. Some attended not at all.

Elfin learning was two-fold. First and foremost
was the learning of Elfin ways: what an Elf was,
where he came from, and how he could enrich his
life and the lives of others. Herein the teacher spoke
of the Elfin place in the world scheme, his freedom and his obligations that were inherent in the
nature of that freedom, his ancestry and the ex-
ploits of notable Elfin heroes and heroines, and
the skills necessary to the continued happiness of
Elfdom. In all of this, memory was the sole guide,
for the Elves had no written language and intentionally avoided developing one for in a written
language they saw the bane of Man, the terror of
knowing more than anyone needed to know, and
the shame of using engraved words for self-aggran-
dizement, the horror of using learning for an end
beyond itself. For it must be understood that the
Elves had no creed, no religion, no body politic,
no yea and nay for the sake of yea and nay, and
no illusions of self-importance. By far the most
beloved of studies was music, or Elfin-song, a study
that had a beginning but no end, a subject that
enriched the mind and body and gave pleasure to
all.

The second form of learning for the Elves was
the study of the works of Man, primarily to understand their timeless enemy but also to enrich their
own lives by understanding the joys of their relentless foe. In this learning but few of the Elves
participated, for it required learning the ways of

Man by reading his most revered works, at least the few books that the Wanderer had given to the Elfin tribe. Most of the elders had read all of the books of Man that they possessed and lent them to those who also desired to read this strange lore. Styrax and Canna together had read all the books available, and though Styrax feared the coming of the Wanderer, he also looked forward to the coming of new books to read.

As the first cool breath of evening blew by and the last golden whisper of the sun had passed, Styrax and Thuja came bounding into the throng of Elves gathered in the village happily awaiting the night's festivities. Styrax greeted all he met with warmth and cheer, and they returned his kindness. But no special forms or terms of address were used to greet Styrax the King, for to be a king in Prosopia meant little in the passage of days, and only in times of trouble did being king matter. Thuja immediately rushed to the great banquet table heaped with delicacies, and Styrax, after greeting his many friends, strolled purposefully toward the gathered elders seated and chatting in front of his thatched home. Canna was already there, serving coreopsis and jimson tea to the assembled teachers. All were quite content, for the evening sunset had been exceptionally vivid in blazing reds, the color most beloved of the Elfin fold, for it was common in all Elfin hamlets to pause each night to celebrate the sunset. Greeting each elder individually, as was his custom and his pleasure, Styrax sat beside Acanthopanax. It must now be noted that Styrax sat among the elders because he was their king; he himself was not an elder; the elder for Prosopia was his younger brother and dear friend Lupinus who was seated with Callistemon. As their king, Styrax participated in debate but was not asked to vote when a vote was needed, which was seldom for rarely were decisions called for or made. Generally, decorum ruled, and the sense of the discussion and debate was carried out without further ado, perhaps covering as simple a problem as the need for more brazen instruments for musical groups. Though no specific recommendations were made and though no one Elf was assigned any specific task, the brazen instruments would appear by the time of the next seasonal gathering. Without being told to do this or that, the hamlets nearest the smithies of the Nibelungen Dwarfs in the caves of the Pinus Mountains would acquire that which was needed, expecting neither recognition nor thanks. Generally, this was the way of the Elves. None even inquired into what the Dwarfs were given in the exchange. But on this night, heavier matters were facing the elders.

Acanthopanax, as the eldest, was first to speak. "Elders of Prosopia, greetings on this midsummer eve. May you all have great joy on this festive occasion and may there be many more like it." A murmur of approval echoed about the gathering, just barely audible above the happy chattering of the thronging Elves surrounding, but oblivious to, the more composed group of teachers.

Acanthopanax continued, "I fear that we have grave concerns to burden us this night, for ravaging Man is haunting the mighty Rhus, though as yet he has found no ford to enter our sacred lands. This very day, three armed and mounted warriors attempted a crossing, but the mighty Rhus drove them back to the grasslands. Now is the time for King Styrax to speak. I have finished."

Styrax stood and spoke quickly. "Elders, for eight days Thuja and I have observed these three men scouting along the Rhus, slowly moving ever northwards, probing for a crossing. Ulmus, the bold chaparral, first among the roadrunners, warns us that further north where the Rhus widens, Man on foot or horseback can cross, and that still further north the spring floods have washed a great gap in the mesquite barrier. These men are many days from finding the crossing for they move but fitfully and it will be many more days before they reach the gap, but they will eventually reach it, I have no doubt."

All sat in thoughtful silence as Styrax finished but remained standing, awaiting questions. After a moment, Buxus of Mesquitana, the Elfin outpost nearest the Pinus Mountains and Dwarfland, rose slowly. "King Styrax, forgive me if I question the reliability of Ulmus, for chaparrals are crafty birds."

"Buxus, my old friend, I have Thuja's word for the sincerity of Ulmus."

"Then, Styrax, I will accept the observations of Ulmus, for we all know of Thuja's skill. But now I must bring up a thought that has hovered about my mind these many months that Man has been threatening our territory. Not since the youth of your father have we had a meeting with the leaders of the tribes of Man in fact, we do not even know the name of the tribe now scouting the river's edge. Granted, the past has given us strong reason to fear Man, but we all know that the past, as we conceive it, is often misleading. Perhaps, and I speak with full knowledge of the evil ways of Man, but, perhaps, we might with proper arrangements be able to meet safely with their king. If nothing comes of it, we might still gain insight into their schemes and we certainly will gain time. I have no more to say."

Numerous elders raised their right hands to signify that they agreed with Buxus.

"I agree with Buxus. His thoughts are wise," said Styrax who was still standing. "But before you decide in conclave, I must yet bother you with another problem that has been vexing me. We have been warned of the coming intrusion of Man by the Wanderer. You all know that I fear the Wanderer, for he seems to be one of their kind, though he has ever been a friend to us. If we place him in a position that requires him to choose between the Elfin Brood and Man, can we expect him to go against his nature to side with us, or will he, perforce, abandon his Elfin friends? After all, it is only natural and right for one to side with his own kind."

Callistemon rose, brushing back her lovely tresses. "The Wanderer has ever been loyal and true to us, and I have never shared Styrax's fear. Styrax is too Elfish. But I do feel that we must ascertain the Wanderer's position in this possible confrontation, for, truly, we assume it to be harmonious for Elf to seek Elf and Man to seek Man. We are laboring in a state of confusion and would be foolish to meet with our enemy until we determine the Wanderer's loyalties in this matter. He is my dear friend, but in this case I cannot speak for him. I strongly suggest a meeting with the Wanderer, for our sake and for the sake of his long devotion to friendship with Prosopia. I have finished."

Styrax started to leave the elders, turning to speak as he took Canna's hand. "These are heavy matters, befitting the elders alone. I will be ruled in all things, as was my father and grandfather, by the wisdom of the council. Callistemon speaks boldly and wisely. I will wait your decision, and until then Canna and I will partake of the merriment surrounding us. Harmony upon you."

Seated at the great banquet table, sipping the thornapple and amanita brew called Fool's Delight, both Canna and Styrax were about to join the next mesquite race, but Canna, sensing unease in Styrax, asked, "My love, are you displeased with the elders?"

Styrax flushed yellowly, a sign of embarrassment, though he realized that his thoughts could not be hidden from his beloved. "Displeased? No. That would be unseemly. But worried I am."

Canna waited, knowing that he would continue.

"I do not worry about Man, for I know him to be what he is. I worry about the Wanderer, for I know him not. And further, I fear that Callistemon has been too close to this outsider, friend or not. He is not an Elf."

"Nor is Ulmus, but you trust him. Come, my love, you are too narrow in your thoughts, too prone to suspect others simply because they are not Elves. Is not this a touch of pride, a touch of Elfishness, as Callistemon has said? Put aside your fretting, I wish to drink until the stars spin, and race until the dawn kisses me."

Styrax put his arm around Canna's waist, and his worries were gone.

The second race was furious with Canna leading the others until she stumbled while leaping across the stones, only to see Styrax fly by laughing. But his laughter was short-lived, for in leaping he missed his handhold, stuck a limb, and tumbled into the sand as youthful Hebe, Canna's closest friend, flew past and gained the victory. Back at the banquet table, Thuja joined Hebe, Styrax, Canna, and many other Elves in a victory toast, hailing the shy Hebe as the swiftest of the swift. Thuja then poured the gourds full again, toasting Hebe as the loveliest of the lovely for in truth Thuja was smitten by the enchanting and petite Hebe. And, finally, Hebe overcame her shyness and toasted Thuja as the slowest of the slow, and happily all joined in at merry Thuja's cost.

The blowgun contest was intensely competitive as dart after dart flew to the targets. Carefully, each Elf, male and female, knelt, took careful aim with his blowgun, and then with a burst of lungpower the dart flew swiftly to its goal. By process of elimination, the final match was between Thuja and Lupinus, Styrax's younger brother. Thuja shot first and his dart stuck dead center, seeming to ensure his victory. But Lupinus, smiling, then shot five darts so perfectly placed that they surrounded and touched Thuja's dart. A great cheer went up for Lupinus for the only way to beat a center dart was to engird it, and this Lupinus had done. As champions, both Lupinus and Hebe then gave gifts of brightly colored stones to all those they had defeated, and Lupinus saved the most brilliant carnelian for Thuja.

Having had too much to drink, at least for continued racing and blow-gunning, Thuja and Hebe, and Styrax and Canna walked arm in arm to the clearing where the musicians were gathering for Elfin-song. Lying on the warm sand, still sipping Fool's Delight, they listened as many Elves sang alone, in duets, and in trios, but most of all they listened to Ipomoea the Golden-Voiced, the most honored of Elfin singers, as she sang of the drove, "Oh, she who sings gladly in the saddest of tones, to sing of joy in sounds of woe." For Elves loved the seeming contradictions of life and love. And after the singers had finished, the instrumentalists gathered with their brazen horns and mellow reeds, their strings and drums to symphonize beneath the stars. The wooden instruments, the flutes, the deeper reeds and the strings were made by Elfin craftsmen for Elves were masters of wood-work, and the brazen horns and drums were made by the Dwarfs, masters of the forge and metal-workers without peer. Now all were silent as the instrumental music soared and faltered and soared again, evoking all the harmonies that were so dear to the Elves and expressing that which haunted all Elfin hearts but could be voiced only in music. May it never end was the feeling of all who were gathered there.

But end it did, and the Elves in pairs vanished beneath the sheltering mesquite bowers. Styrax and Canna wandered toward the Rhus, followed by Thuja and Hebe who carried the Fool's Delight and the drinking gourds. By the river, beneath the stars and the waning moon, they built a small fire against the morning chill. Hebe, still full of energy and emboldened by too much Fool's Delight, danced with Elfin grace around the fire as Thuja tapped a rhythm upon a hollow cottonwood log. Soon Canna, unable to resist, joined the graceful Hebe. The hearts of Styrax and Thuja exulted in the perfection of their young bodies as they moved in harmony and physical unison, giving up their self-consciousness to the ecstasy of the moment and to the enchantment of the night and their lover's intense gazes.

Later, as Canna lay peacefully within the strong arms of Styrax, and Hebe within those of Thuja, Canna felt the need to speak. "See the soft light in the east. Midsummer night will soon be gone."

"How sad," sleepy Styrax answered.

"Oh, no, no. Not sad. Oh my love, never sad. Just that it is over, over and gone. But never sad.

Chapter Two

The grasslands were sere, for rain came but seldom during midsummer. All day, along the Rhus, the three men had hunted without success, and their hungers were fierce, as were their natures. Dressed in wretched rags and tattered hides, partially covered with fragments of armor, and mounted upon worn and decrepit horses, the three men dismounted by the Rhus to slake their thirsts and that of their feeble steeds. Graspar, the King of the tribe called Beastums, threw himself bodily into the current, and his henchmen, Thrett and Strang, instantly followed, while the horses drank discretely at a distance upstream. After a few moments of splashing about in the swift flow and after gorging themselves on water, they sat upon the bank and relaxed in the temporary coolness of their wet skins.

Graspar, large and strong, his face, arms and legs covered with scars from endless combats in which he maintained his authority, gruffly shouted for he could only shout at Strang, a much smaller Man who fawned at his lord's feet, "Strang, you idiot, you told me we would find game here. I must eat, and soon. But I don't even see rabbits. I see nothing to eat anywhere. Is it your wish to die?"

Strang answered in a high-pitched voice, "But, my Lord, I saw them this morning, many of them, but I fear they hide from the midday sun and won't come out again until after dark."

Graspar angrily poked his long staff against Strang's stomach, forcing him backward, "I can't wait till dark, you fool. I must eat soon or you shall pay dearly."

Thrett, who stood apart smiling as his King tormented the cringing Strang, stepped forward and spoke in a strong voice, "My Lord, give me Strang for a short while, and I will return with game enough for us all."

"Take him! Take him! I am disgusted by his presence," Graspar barked.

Thrett, a strong Man and master of the bow and arrow, led Strang toward a small hill covered with dense clusters of twisted greasewood and yucca, indicating that Strang was to thrash about within these thickets, beating the dry shrubs with his club. Thrett, meanwhile, craftily stationed himself in a wash on the far side of the hill. Within moments, gaunt jackrabbits rushed in terror from Strang's violent bush thrashing. Quickly and with unerring skill, Thrett shot three arrows and killed two jackrabbits.

On returning to Graspar, Thrett gave him the larger rabbit, keeping the other for himself. Immediately, both men chopped off the rabbit's heads, split open their stomachs, peeled back the hides, and began eating voraciously while Strang nibbled as best he could at the severed heads. They ate as ravening beasts such was their hunger and such their manner, their faces and beards dripping with gore as they tore the fragile rabbits to pieces. Strang hovered about gleaning that which was cast off. As they finished, they stumbled back into the river washing away the blood and cooling themselves in the clear waters of the Rhus.

These, then, were the foes of the Elves; these were the wildest and crudest remaining vestiges of what was once the noble race of Man. Yet, they themselves knew nothing of the honored past; they knew not that they had a past; they knew only the endless struggle for food in barren lands beneath a searing sun. Graspar, his tribe of Beastums, Strang and Thrett still possessed some of ancient man's capacity for craftiness, and much of man's strength and courage but little else of Man remained with them.

The camp of the Beastums, who numbered fewer than 300, sat upon a knoll of dead and dying cottonwood trees and was little more than a large cluster of shapeless thatched shacks and shabby tents. During the day, the camp was largely deserted while the inhabitants were afield scavenging for anything resembling food. The men hunted for rabbits, ground squirrels, rats, mice, lizards and snakes, while the women and what few feeble children they had dug among the sere grasses hoping to find dry tubers and other edible roots. Other tribes of Man, many better but none worse, still existed but under less distressing conditions, but they were scattered far and wide beyond the sterile plains. In the evening as the Beastums returned to their camp, the people immediately began struggling and quarreling over the day's meager supply of food, as the stronger took the most, and the weaker argued and fought over what little remained. Only seven horses were left to the tribesmen, for when there was nothing to eat, they ate the oldest and most wretched of the remaining horses. In the past, the tribe had been stronger and the horses had been far more numerous, and when the game became scarce, the tribe moved on to better hunting grounds. But in recent years, they found no better hunting areas, for there were none to find on their side of the Rhus. Thus, as a last resort, they had camped by the river, knowing that across its fast-flowing current within the vast mesquite copses and beyond in the hills and the Pinus Mountains was abundant game and good hunting. To cross the river was their last and only hope.

They were also aware that the shores across the river were inhabited by strange creatures who were rumored to be green, small and harmless, like rabbits, though much more cunning. In times of extreme stress, the Beastums had become cannibalistic and had eaten their own kind, frequently those slain in battle with other tribes; thus the Beastums thought little more of the Elves than as something new to eat, something as common as rabbits but larger and, to their thinking, easier to catch and kill. These thoughts had come to the Beastums from their Shaman Vastar who had caught a fleeting glimpse of stout Thuja running along the shore with a chaparral.

That evening Graspar held council with Vastar, Thrett, Strang, and two of his wiliest hunters, Grudge and Bastard.

Peeved, Graspar was the first to speak. "I have this day almost starved because you damned asses have forgotten how to hunt. We must find a way across this cursed river, or we will begin eating each other again until we are no more. We must find more substantial food than rabbits and mice, and even they are harder and harder to find. Vastar, speak, and speak wisely, for starving warriors have little use of a Shaman."

Vastar, who in comparison to the others was

truly wise, spoke slowly and firmly, knowing how secure he was and how dependent Graspar was on him, "We all know where the food is and where it is not. We also know that each day we remain here the weaker we become. Thrett, you have been farthest north along the Rhus. What have you discovered?"

Thrett, who truly knew no fear and held Graspar in loathing, drew a line in the sand and pointing with his stick, spoke, "We are here. I have gone this far north; but we must go still further. For when I climbed the highest hill, I saw in the far distance a widening of the shores."

"Speak to the point, you fool, I care not for your rambling," grunted Graspar, who needed but feared Thrett.

"If the shores grow wider, the water must be less deep and must flow more slowly. Is that not right, Vastar?"

"Assuredly so, Thrett. This is the good news I have long expected, a crossing into virgin lands. But how many days travel on horseback?"

Thrett pondered the question a moment, then he answered, "Four or five days if we have feed for the horses."

"Then this is my plan," Vastar said quickly, knowing they had to agree. "Graspar, with Strang, Grudge and Bastard, and with adequate feed for the horses—"

Graspar angrily interrupted, "Where in Hell are we to find adequate feed when we hunger ourselves, you dolt?" He stood and walked around the fire. "If we had feed, we would still have many horses. If we had horses, we could attack Profundus and the Vergers. But we have no feed for horses or men."

Thrett then rose and spoke boldly, "Take the

roots and grasses gathered today by the old and the weak; they will probably die soon anyway or die in the crossing. Besides, if we find a ford, the old and the weak will lighten our load."

Graspar thought for a bit, then spoke to Strang and Bastard. "Go, kill the feeble, and gather all the food you can, enough for at least six days. Then feed the four strongest horses, and return here as soon as you can."

Strang and Bastard left at once while Vastar continued, "You four will hasten to this widening in the Rhus. Cross if you can. Go east and regain your strength. And when you find a suitable site for our new camp across the river, send one of your number back, and we will follow."

"Is there nothing else, Dotard?" Graspar growled.

"Yes, my Lord, I would go with adequate armament, for we know not these green creatures that live on the far shore, though from ancient lore I seem to recall legends of green people called Yellfens who were very strong in magic. They are called the first born and are exceedingly clever. I know no more, but it is ever wise to be heavily armed."

All then were silent. Graspar agreed with the plan though he disliked Vastar for conceiving it. At first, he thought of the abundant food across the river, but then he thought of the Yellfens and their magic. This he did not like. For though Graspar felt himself a match in strength for any creature, he lived in terror of anything that dealt in the magical. His fear of magic was the very source of Vastar's power over him.

Graspar broke the silence. "And if these Yellfens, or whatever you call them, have magic, what am I to do?"

"Fear not, my Lord. I will give you a charmed powder of great strength; you need but cast it on them and their power will be gone." And as Vastar spoke, he smiled inwardly at Graspar's gullibility, for in truth the powder he planned to give his Lord was little more than dust.

Graspar stood, saying, "So be it," and the council of Beastums was ended.

* * *

As Thrett walked toward the river to cool himself, he noticed Vastar furtively following him. By the Rhus, Thrett turned and called out, "Hide not, Vastar. I know you are there."

Vastar came forward out of the shadows, "I am ever cautious in these times, for none are to be trusted when men starve and are governed by senseless brutes."

"What do you want of me?" asked Thrett, knowing that of all the men he knew, Vastar would be the last he would trust, for Vastar was not a Beastum but an exile from the land of the Vergers who were ruled by Profundus the Guileful, the elder brother of Vastar. None knew why Vastar had joined the Beastums nor why he had left the Vergers.

"Did you not question why I excluded you from Graspar's forced march on the morrow?" Thrett nodded, saying nothing as he waited for Vastar to continue. "Graspar will fail, for his strength is of use but for brawling with his own kind. Your tribe is doomed unless we get fresh horses and fit warriors. I fear that but few would survive the crossing, if one is found."

"All this we both know," said Thrett, anxious for Vastar to get to the point. "What is it you want of me?"

"What I tell you now, none of this tribe knows

and must not be told. If you agree to these terms, if you swear to hold your tongue, I will speak further."

"I agree but get on with it."

"Far to the east, beyond the grasslands in a mountain fortress called Greydome live the Vergers, a mighty tribe, ruled by Profundus the Guileful, my brother in blood. Between us is great loathing, but Profundus is no fool and knows when hatred must be put aside. I have not the strength to attempt such a journey, nor would my brother be glad of my presence. But if you were to go to him with a letter from me, written in words beyond your ken, he would give you the aid we need to conquer the far shore, the land of the Yellfen."

"And why should this Profundus believe me any more than he would believe you?" Thrett asked coldly, masking his curiosity.

"For my brother and the Vergers have but one passion—to possess the yellow metal called gold, a metal they believe has the secret of granting them power over all other men, for it had been so in the ages of Man's greatness."

"I know nothing of other ages, nor of Man and his greatness, nor of gold and Vergers. I see no greatness in the beasts we are. Do not play me for a fool, Vastar." Thrett spoke warmly, for he wanted Vastar, as was his nature, to say more than he intended.

"But you are a fool, Thrett. In your ignorance, you know not that Man—yes, Man who was made no differently than you—that Man was once able to fly in great metal machines as if he were a bird, that Man built and lived in houses larger than mountains the ruins of which can still be seen in the land of the Querques. that Man had weapons of such power that he could destroy his enemies and entire cities while still many leagues away. Know also that these times of power and glory can come again. If we find new lands with abundant game and if we learn to till the soil, we can then begin to breed fruitfully new lands, new food, and we will again have many children to build a strong army. But enough of that, the men I speak of have long since destroyed themselves, though I know not how or why they are no more. But, in this letter, I will tell Profundus of the mighty store of gold hidden in Yellfen land, and that I alone can lead him to it."

"And is there such a store of gold? Have you seen it? Does it really bestow power? And if there is no gold and the Vergers come to know it, will they not slaughter us for lying to them and misleading them?"

Vastar was ready with an answer, "I will direct Profundus to send but ten warriors and twenty horses. He, distrusting me, as he should, will send twenty warriors and forty horses. Once across the Rhus, I will bribe some to join our cause and the others I will poison, for as you know, I am wise in the ways of poison. Then we will have fresh horses and new warriors to conquer the Yellfen and all the lands across the river."

"All that you say intrigues me, Vastar, but I do not know why you have chosen me."

"I know you, Thrett. I know that you despise Graspar but you fear a confrontation with such a brute. I know that you are waiting for the dark night when he sleeps too soundly for his own good. Have I not hit the mark, Thrett? But think, think of what your actions would gain you. You would be our King, perhaps, but a King of a dying tribe— too feeble to survive here and too exhausted to ford the river. Now think of my plan. You would still be King, and I would be your Shaman, but we will have fresh horses and warriors on the far side of the Rhus, and with food available, we can build the Beastums to their former strength when we feared no one."

Thrett spoke not. He walked away for a space of ten paces, squatted by the river's edge, running his fingers through the flowing water. Vastar walked up to him and stood there waiting.

Thrett, still squatting, looked up into Vastar's intense gaze, and, after a moment, spoke, "I like your plan, Vastar. I think it is wise, and I think it might succeed. But I trust you not."

"In that you are shrewd, Thrett, for I trust no one. Our plan forces us upon one another. We need each other but we need not trust each other. I will be honest but for a moment do not turn your back on me. Do not trust anyone."

Standing, Thrett looked directly into Vastar's face, "These are terms I can understand, and I too will be honest. I will kill you when I no longer need you."

"But you will need me, lest you degenerate into a wretch like Graspar. For no tribe can long exist without a Shaman to guide it. The Beastums are brutes and will die as brutes, unless you and I lead them to better things."

"I am with you, Vastar but beware of me, for I was born a Beastum."

"Give me your hand then, and thus we seal this fiendish pact." For a long moment they stood, firmly grasping each other's hands. Then they parted as Vastar spoke the final words, "Be prepared to leave shortly after Graspar has gone northward. I will prepare the letter and a map to guide you."

Thrett, excited by his conversation with Vastar,

walked further downstream, occasionally staring up at the star-burdened sky. All his life he had struggled for food with the other Beastums. But unlike the others, Thrett had a vision of life as more than an eternal quest for the next meal. He knew little of Man's past, but deep within his being smoldered dreams of better days, of escape from bestiality, of a richer and more powerful life. Soundly he slept that night, amid dreams of being King.

Chapter Three

Styrax and Canna returned to their hamlet as the sun reached the meridian of the cloudless sky. They had left Thuja and Hebe by themselves, still sleeping by the Rhus. Acanthopanax was seated before the thatch home Styrax and Canna had built.

"The elders and their people have returned to their villages," Acanthopanax said as Styrax sat beside him. "We have decided upon a course of action."

"Was the council long? Did you have time to attend the Elfin-song? Canna and I drank too much Fool's Delight, and we spent the night stargazing by the Rhus."

"I envy you your youth, Styrax, for at my age I can no longer escape the cares that haunt me even in the mists of Fool's Delight. Sadly, I missed the concert. But I am glad in the pleasantness of your evening, for now you have burdensome work to do. We have decided to beckon the Wanderer; the signal fire will be lit this evening. Callistemon will bring him to your village in three days. Naturally, your presence is required."

"I will be here, of course. Much is to be discussed, and I must sound deeply the Wanderer's position and must know more before I trust him in all matters."

"Do that, my friend, for your own sake. I have great faith in him. I must tell you, though, that there are things he is not free to reveal without permission from his Lord, the Aged One."

Styrax was surprised, "I thought he was alone, that he answered to no one. Who is the Aged One?"

"That I cannot answer other than to say he is the oldest self-aware being in this world. Perhaps a hundred years or so before your birth, he came to us, already a Man of great age, wrinkled and bent but with great energy. He spoke little but seemed to know what it was we were about to say. It was then that he told us to use the Wanderer as his agent in all things. Many questions have I asked the Wanderer that he could not or would not answer, saying only that it was not within his province to speak of certain matters and that only the Aged One could speak of these things."

"And where is the Aged One?"

"I know not. I know only that his kingdom is in the farthest reaches of the north in the land of perpetual snow and ice. You are also directed by the council to make no attempt at meeting with the leaders of the tribe across the mighty Rhus. They know little of us, I'm sure, and that is in our favor. First, you are to seek advice from the Wanderer; meanwhile, you are to watch the enemy closely, for he means us ill."

* * *

Upstream, Nyssa the quail was foraging in the shade of a tamarisk grove, its branches laden with pink florets swaying in the gentle summer breeze. Having no thoughts but to eat, Nyssa was shocked into alertness by the sounds of horses' hooves beating on the stony far shore. From the shade of the grove, she saw four mounted men plying their way northward, moving with determination and in silence. After they had passed, she hurried downstream to the sunny bank upon which Thuja was still sleeping alongside lovely Hebe.

"Pit, pit. Pit, pit, ka, ka, kow. Ka, ka, kow. Pit, pit," she spoke again and again into Thuja's ear until he finally sat up.

"What, my pretty? What are you jabbering about?" Thuja said, rubbing sleep from his eyes.

She repeated her message with a touch of annoyance at Thuja's slowness, for, after all, she had left her feeding, something she was loathe to do, for Thuja's sake. She cared little what evil men were doing.

"Oh, my little one, you must forgive me," Thuja apologized, gently stroking her feathers. "We Elves are not as fast to wake as Nyssa and her kin. Thank you, pretty Nyssa. Now you can return to your feeding."

Thuja woke Hebe, and after washing in the river, they headed for their village.

Thuja found Styrax gathering dead wood from beneath the mesquite. He carefully selected dead stumps and branches, never touching the living wood that Elves believed pulsed with the same life as their own. Thuja quickly relayed Nyssa's message, happily recounting Nyssa's annoyance at his sleepiness. Styrax and Thuja then gathered their blowguns and darts which they carried in pouches tied to their waists. Gently, they bid farewell to the lovely Canna and Hebe.

Later that day, Styrax and Thuja caught up with the four men as they continued their journey northward. The Elves had no problem in keeping pace, for they were tireless and were hidden in the shade, and though the men moved steadily, they moved slowly, not wanting to tax their enfeebled horses.

"They do not pause; they do not survey the land," said Thuja, ever observant and penetrating.

"How right you are, my friend," said Styrax. "They know where they are heading; they must know of the crossing."

"Their horses are weak and must be rested frequently," mused Thuja. "They cannot make the ford before the fifth day, perhaps the sixth, but certainly no sooner."

"True, true, and that will give me time to meet the Wanderer and still be at the crossing before they get there, for they cannot be allowed a foothold on our side."

Styrax and Thuja walked in silence, for they both knew the knotty challenge they were to face and dreaded to give it voice. To Elves the greatest of all evils was to kill for any reason other than to eat or protect oneself and one's loved ones. When killing grasshoppers or others insects, the Elves suffered a sense of guilt, and all Elves, to assuage that guilt, whispered to themselves, "It must be so; it must be so," again and again. Yet Styrax was not a fool and knew that a time for killing inevitably came, as when he slew a rabid coyote that threatened Canna, for in that moment he made his choice instantly and with his blowgun shot a poisoned dart into the coyote's neck. Many a sleepless night he suffered thereafter even though he knew he did what he had to do. But to kill a Man, a reasoning creature, no matter how debased, caused his gorge to rise, weakened his purpose, and made him question the seeming necessity of doing what he must. In his reverie, he thought it would be better to simply hide and let Man enter Prosopia. The land is vast enough, he mused to himself, for us to move back from the river toward the mountains. Perhaps, this tribe of men would move on for they seemed by nature to be nomadic. But, then, if we retreat, they will follow and sooner or later we must face each other to the death. No, no, he thought, better to face them now, but even as he accepted the inevitable, the terror of having to kill continued to perplex him. He knew that his foe suffered from no such uncertainty; he knew that Man could kill with joy in his heart. That these men should die bothered Styrax but little, for he felt deeply their deaths were deserved, that their return to the earth was in the nature of their violent lives. But that he, or Thuja or any other member of the Elfin Brood, that he should strike a blow, that he should kill with his own hands was anathema to him, an evil the consequences of which would haunt him eternally. For Styrax had read the books of Man, of Man in his ascendancy, and he knew that somewhere, somewhere deeply buried within even the vilest of men, were thoughts not unlike his own, thoughts that rebelled against the necessity of butchering other beings. "But it must be done; it must be done," echoed in the chasms of his mind.

"What will we do?" Thuja asked, himself a victim of the same thoughts.

"We will wait and see."

For the Elf had a quality, unique to his kind, of instantly dismissing that which troubled him, of putting it from his mind, of allowing fate to seem to determine his course. Man, in his pride, believed that he alone determined that which was to be, that he alone could control destiny, that nature was subservient to him or, perhaps, that he held nature in thrall. Not so with the Elf, though not a stranger to the urgings of pride, who, though often erring, knew finally that it was he who was subservient, and that all matters within and beyond his ken were controlled by eternal laws of harmony in which he was as nothing.

Later, that same day, as the Elves continued to follow the unceasing northward movement of the four men, they found themselves climbing a rock-strewn hill above the Rhus. Here they paused, attracted by certain stones that gleamed readily among the grayness of the great mass of rocks. When either Styrax or Thuja found one of outstanding quality, he would put it in his waist pouch. For these were stones much prized by Elves and by Man, often called carnelians. They were semi-crystalline, red to reddish orange, and with a luster that seemed to glow from within. The stones made them happy, for now they had lovely gifts for their friends, the giving of gifts being of great importance in Elfdom. Among the stones Styrax picked up was one of dull yellow and of great weight for its size. He showed it to Thuja who looked at it and felt it with little interest.

"Do you know that this drab yellowish rock is considered of great value by men?" Styrax asked, surprising Thuja who found that particular stone to be readily forgettable. "It is a stone for which they kill, a stone they worship and hoard as a rat hoards seeds."

"Why? What good is it? It isn't beautiful. It isn't even pretty. I would be ashamed to give it to a lizard. And what does it mean to hoard something that has no use?" Thuja was disgusted by having even to think of this worthless yellow rock.

"If a Man has many of these stones, then he is considered mighty among his fellows, and they in

Chapter Four

The Wanderer was clad in a long, sweeping hooded cloak of the lightest of grays, and as he followed Callistemon along the Elfin path through the mesquite he seemed like a holy Man from the ancient past. He moved slowly, carefully, bending frequently, pushing branches aside, for he was tall, even for a Man, and had trouble in the dense and thorny shrubbery following an Elf but half his size. When he reached the clearing of Styrax's village, he straightened up and drew back his hood, revealing a strongly-featured face crowned by flaxen hair. His eyes were soft blue and had the penetrating power of a mountain cat. Both Styrax and Canna bowed slightly as the Wanderer came toward them.

"Hail Styrax. Hail Canna," said the Wanderer in his deep voice as he returned their bows.

"Hail Wanderer. Greetings, Callistemon. You are welcome to my home."

After all were seated and coreopsis tea was served, the Wanderer was the first to speak. "Callistemon has told me of the problems faced in council, of the encroachment of the barbarians, a feeble and dying tribe that calls itself the Beastums. Their leader, Graspar, is a powerful brute and a tested warrior, but, fortunately for Prosopia, he is a fool."

"I have seen him from across the Rhus. He and three others, all armed mightily, are headed for the crossing three days to the north," Styrax said, measuring the distance in Elfin terms, for an Elf can travel at twice the pace of Man, even on horse-back.

"And what is it you want of me, my friends?" asked the Wanderer, knowing in his heart that Styrax was unsure of his friendship.

"I know of no way to stop them except to kill them, and that I am loathe to do. Is there no other way?"

"No, there is no other way."

"But once the killing starts, I fear that Elves will be slain," Styrax said softly.

"Either you kill them or they will kill you," the Wanderer replied, "You must realize that Man has always solved his problems by killing. In his prime, Man justified his killing through complex laws which governed his tribe. Now, in his decline, he kills without either justification or law. Men are beyond reason; harmony they can never know."

"This sears my soul, Wanderer, for I am King, as was my father and his father before him, and the heavy burden of slaying is my responsibility. Yet to kill is the ultimate evil justified solely by necessity. But, first, I must understand the necessity of what I am to do. And as the Warlord of my Brood, I must question deeply all that I am told. For if all men are evil, and unchanging, then I must also question your concerns in this tragedy. Are you not one of them? Are you not a Man?"

"Styrax, please remember that the Wanderer is our guest, and a loyal friend, many times proven," Callistemon said strongly, feeling that

Styrax had spoken inhospitably.

"I am sorry if I offended, Callistemon, but it is I who must do the killing. You are a Man, Wanderer. Are you not?"

"I am not offended, Callistemon. Styrax has good reason to question my loyalties. Have I not questioned them myself? But I cannot answer as simply as he has asked, for, as yet, there are matters of which I cannot speak. This much I can say. To say that all men are evil is to oversimplify. Most men are weak and allow themselves to be ruled by evil for they cannot stand alone. They must be led. Perhaps, we had better walk to the river, for I have much to say, and the Rhus will not abide untruth or vagaries, and the river will allow my thoughts to flow."

Seated on the banks of the swift flowing Rhus, the Wanderer began his tale. "I have been and ever will be faithful to the Elfin Brood though, as has been said, I am of the tribe of Man but that is my misfortune for me to bear alone. I serve but one master, the Aged One whose name cannot not be said, but is written thus." And in the sand, the Wanderer wrote with a stick the word HWHBRNGSTHND. "He alone can answer all that you can ask. I, meanwhile, will speak of that which I have the authority to convey, and that must content you for the nonce."

All sat in silence, waiting for the Wanderer to continue, though for a moment he spoke not, as if daunted by the task before him.

"The Aged One is also a Man, a Man who has lived beyond our normal reckoning of the years, a Man whose span is better imagined in centuries, he is that ancient. Of wisdom, he has no peer: he sees all; he knows all. He dwells amid the great ice sheets that cover the most northern territory, a forbidding and lifeless land. For many hundreds of years, I have done his bidding without question, for he has that which commands obedience and awe. Originally, I was a Man amongst men, and I rode with that ravaging horde, destroying all that opposed our will, and more besides. I stood foremost among my tribe, whose name has been erased from the slate of life. I was a fierce warrior who knew no match. But in my success, in my warlike achievements, in the very might of my being came doubt. For in my conquests, in my glories, I perceived that something was awry, for all around me were the ruins of previous ages of Man, and these very ruins so far excelled anything I had ever thought to achieve, I began to question the worth of my life. I built not. Instead, I took, I destroyed, I annihilated, I burned, I left ashes and nothing more. I spoke of this with my companions—I could not call them friends for at that time I did not know what friend was and they laughed childishly, and the more I spoke, the more they laughed and thinking I was growing weak began to plot my downfall. For I ruled through strength; they followed through fear. In my last battle with another tribe as ferocious as mine, I lost all heart in what now seemed pointless and foul. My own men surrounded me, hatred in their eyes, and as they rushed to slay me (I was so downtrodden that I simply fell to my knees and covered my head with my arms), I was suddenly blinded by a fearful light, brighter than the sun, but colder than the most wintry of winds. I opened my eyes, and all before me was the Aged One, seeming to glow from within, his crimson robes shimmering with light. In a high, cracking voice, the voice of old age, he said, 'They have killed each other to a Man, eh, eh. Only you survive. Come with me, eh, eh.'

And thus I went, feeling terror for the first time in my wretched life. I cannot speak of what I saw, of what I learned, of how I became what I am."

Styrax wished to speak, but paused, seeing the Wanderer in pain from the telling of this tale, and feeling a sense of awe for this lonely Man. They all sat staring at the rushing current. Finally, Styrax spoke out, "But what of us, the Elves? What have we to do with this woeful world? How did you come to us?"

"You call me the Wanderer; my real name is this," and in the sand he wrote RMRFTHRTHNDS, "which means much the same thing. After my enlightenment of which I cannot speak I was assigned the mighty task of traveling throughout the vast world, ever seeking that which I found here in Prosopia, that which is written thus," and again in the sand the Wanderer wrote HRMNFTHSPHRS and BDNGLVFLL "It means happiness, contentment, and love of equity and balance. I have visited the lands of the Shee, the Gwyllion, the Salvenelli, the Skogsra, the Tuatha De Denann, the Tylwyth Teg, the Fay, the Stillevolk, the Trolls, the Nibelungen, the Wichtlein; I have traveled the lands of Asgard, Midgard, and Niflheim, ever seeking that which the Aged One wanted me to seek, and ever to him I spoke of the wonders and terrors of my endless wanderings; I have sailed upon the mighty oceans and met with people who spoke strange and alien tongues. But wherever I wandered, I found Man ever the same, bestial, restless and greedy. How many years these travels lasted I can no longer tell for I have ceased to age, but my journeys came to an end in Prosopia, amid the enchantments of the Elfin Brood. I returned to the Aged One and told him of the Elfin World, thinking that this might bring him happiness, but to my chagrin, he only smiled feebly, informing me that he knew of Elfdom from the beginning. Though I ever held my master in awe, I was angry and asked him why I traveled over this endless world to find that which he knew of in the beginning. He answered, 'For in the finding of it, you have learned to know it for what it is. How else were you to know unless you saw it all?' And in the many years since I first heard those words, I have come to understand his wisdom, for in all things he is ever right. And thus I have become the friend, the ally, and the guardian (to the limits of my power) of the Elves. The Aged One calls you this," said the Wanderer as he wrote the following word in the sand, THLFNBRDTHTFNDSLSTNGHRMY.

The Wanderer rose, relieved to have finished telling his story, though he suffered in relating it and walked to the edge of the river, taking a drink of the cooling waters. Standing, he turned to his Elfin friends, smiled and said, "The Rhus gives me the strength to carry on."

"Your tale is of great sadness," said Callistemon. "My heart weeps for your suffering. My fondest hope is that you may find that joy Man has lost and that you find it here among the Elfin Brood."

"And I offer you my hand as a brother," Styrax said warmly. "I no longer think of you as one of them, but as one of us."

"But what I cannot grasp," said Canna, "is what happened to Man to have fallen so greatly. We have read many of the books of Man you have given us, and from these works he seems the noblest of creatures—wise, gentle, loving. What is the curse that has been placed upon him? What has caused his degradation?"

"You ask the very question that has ever haunted me, a question that only the Aged One can answer fully. Man knew too much but understood too little. Beyond that I cannot speak."

"Will we ever know the answer?" Asked Callistemon.

"I do not know. Perhaps, you will be told; perhaps, not. Perhaps, there are things better not known."

"Have you no woman? No children?" Canna asked.

"I have a mate whom I call SHE; her name cannot be spoken; but it is written thus," and again the Wanderer wrote in the smoothed sand, SHWHSNSSLLTHNGS. "She is the only daughter of the Aged One, but she never leaves the Hill of Light, the Aged One's home. I have no children."

"The evening is upon us," said Styrax, "and I must determine what to do about these men who are approaching the northern crossing. What should I do, Wanderer?"

"That I cannot say, Styrax, for you must make your own decision in this matter and in all things. I am restrained from killing my own kind unless it becomes necessary. Yet, I will support you in all your actions, but you alone must determine what they will be. Graspar is the least of your problems, hardly a fitting adversary. Defeat him and the Beastums will dissolve quickly into the grasslands."

"I do not understand. Are others to come? You speak as though this was just the beginning."

"And so it is, my friends. These few men about to attempt crossing the Rhus are but the cast-offs of the horde to follow. In a sense, Graspar and his men are the enfeebled scouts of a great wave ever moving toward Prosopia, a great tide of men ever pursued by an echoing sense of doom. For there are many tribes of men as numerous as ants but they are scattered across this vast land of which Prosopia is but a small part. The Beastums are men on the verge of dissolution; they have run their course. But beyond the sere grasslands are numberless tribes all lusting for new land rich in game. Yet even as we speak, these forces are on the move though cursed by constant warfare amongst themselves and continuing infertility, for something has gone awry in man's ability to reproduce."

Callistemon, Canna, and Styrax sat as though transfixed. Little had they guessed of what was to come, for they knew of no other men than those they feared just across the Rhus. The Elves by nature were not warlike, nor were they given to acting in a great mass, in a collective way. For Elves shunned too much closeness, living in small and widely scattered villages in which each dwelling was far removed from the next one. Their sports were all individualistic, for they never developed the concept of team activity. In music alone did they form collective groups, but even in music, each Elf was prone to go his own way. The only great gatherings of Elves any of them could recall were the seasonal holidays, like the midsummer and midwinter festivals, times of great happiness, of individual pleasures among the throng. Styrax, ever the King of his kind, was overwhelmed, stunned, for only hours ago he thought his great problem was four intruders, a problem to be faced and solved, and thus to be lost forever in the churning seas of the past. But now, now he was to face an endless horde of men in a savage conflict for survival, a conflict in which his people, win or lose, would suffer and die.

"I know I have brought evil tidings. I did not come because Callistemon signaled for me to do so; I was already on my way. I was bringing this tragic news and a recommendation from the Aged One. Graspar will be taken care of, as you will see, but before more warriors come, you must prepare yourself as you have never done before, in a way you never imagined before. Thus, you, Styrax, are summoned to the Hill of Light in the frozen reaches of the far north, for my Lord, the Aged One, wishes to speak with you."

Styrax stood facing the Wanderer. With deep sadness, he asked, "Is this a command?"

"No, Styrax, this is not a command. The Aged One invites you to his home in the ice forest. You are free, and must ever be so, to do as your reason dictates. With all my heart, I advise you to do as you are asked. I will accompany you and will be your companion until the end. But you must come alone."

"Why alone? Cannot Thuja, my right arm, attend me as he ever has? The Aged One places unreasonable restrictions on me."

The Wanderer paused a long moment before answering. He knew how much, the world itself, depended upon the answer of this Elfin King. Finally, he spoke, but in a sterner manner, "King Styrax," the Wanderer's voice became intense with gravity as he spoke, "King Styrax, hearken to what I say, for the strands of existence tremble upon your answer. Many years before you were born, when your father was still a youth, the Aged One came here to Prosopia and spoke of somber things to your grandfather, King Styrax of yore, things so profound and awesome that your grandfather took those words to his final rest without ever revealing what they were. What the Aged One is to say can only be said unto you, and you, like your grandfather, must decide if they will ever be spoken again. Hear me, King Styrax, for that which will be revealed, the Aged One will pay the heaviest of prices, beyond your present imaginings, arcane lore of the end of things, and you alone, of the great Elfin Brood, will decide how far this secret knowledge will go. Lastly, I say unto you that what you learn might mean your death, for few can stand before the press of this burden. You have been chosen, my friend, because you are the son of your father and his father before him."

Styrax looked at Canna, seeing love in her eyes; he looked at Callistemon, seeing devotion in her eyes; he looked at the Wanderer, seeing terror within his eyes. He stood and walked methodically around the others, thinking of his father and his grandfather, trying to fathom this great sea that suddenly seemed to engulf him. Finally, he stopped in front of the Wanderer, looked deeply in his eyes, and said, "I must speak with my grandfather. Will you wait upon me?"

"As you wish," answered the Wanderer.

Styrax took Canna's hand; their eyes met for a moment; and then he was gone, his lithe figure flying into the densest mesquite thicket.

He traveled at reckless speed, rushing toward the tallest mesquite on the outskirts of his hamlet. In front of the tree, he stopped, looking up at its vast expanse, for it truly was a huge mesquite. Then walking beneath its arching limbs, he twisted and crawled to its center where its many trunks fanned outward. Silently, he sat there.

This mesquite tree was the grandfather of Styrax. For when an Elf grew aged in spirit (an Elf never grew old in body) he found a mesquite tree with which he was in harmony and laid down in its center, and there he expired, as simple as that. For Elves did not know death as men did. As Man aged if he was not slain in the continuing state of tribal warfare and if diseases did not shorten his span he became weak and helpless, a burden on the living and was often dispatched by his own children. The Elf aged in his mind, his body retaining the vigor of youth, and at some point, the individual Elf elected to join his ancestors. To die, an Elf simply closed his eyes and willed a cessation of his being and in time death came peacefully. His essence, his being, his soul entered into the being of the selected mesquite and lived on as long as the mesquite survived, and when the mesquite died (the mesquite is a plant of great age) the Elf also died. In Elfin lore, it was believed that life as an Elf was a continuing attempt to understand and become part of the harmonies governing life entirely, governing the life of all things. Yet as an Elf, active in living a personal life, building a home, raising children, doing one's allotted tasks, allowed but little time to become one with the essential harmony of all things, of life itself. Thus, in the second and final phase of Elfin life, the Elf would enter into the being of a mesquite tree wherein he would sense and know all that was to be known, and would come to be one with nature, fused with the life force itself. His first death would be peaceful, and the remains of his body would later be buried at the foot of the chosen tree by his kinsmen. In this way, the very thicket that surrounded an Elf's village was imbued with the spirits of his ancestors, explaining why the Elf revered the mesquite, for in each and every mesquite tree lived the fathers and mothers, the grandfathers and grandmothers of his tribe.

Styrax placed his hands upon two of the stoutest trunks, grasping them firmly, and, with his eyes closed, he spoke aloud, "Oh Grandfather Styrax, revered King of Prosopia, it is I, Styrax, your grandson, King as you were King, seeking your wisdom in this, the evilest of times. Oh, beloved Grandfather, can you hear me?"

The mesquite seemed to sway in a breeze that did not blow.

"You alone spoke to the Aged One, my grandfather, and you alone know if I must do as you did. Is it right that I leave Prosopia for the far north? Is this the path for Styrax the King?"

Again the branches swayed, their tips seeming to tremble.

"Hast thou found harmony, oh Grandfather? Has my Father found peace?"

* * *

Later, Styrax found the Wanderer, Canna, and Callistemon drinking tea in the shade of his home. Canna ran to him, and arm in arm they stood quietly before the others.

"Has King Styrax, your Grandfather, spoken?" asked Callistemon, for the Wanderer would not dare to ask about something so sacred to Elves and something of which he had no understanding at all.

"He has spoken. He holds the Aged One in high reverence, and is surprised that he is still among the living. He spoke to me of the music of the earth, the water and the sky, and wished me peace beyond my understanding. His last thoughts were that I should carry his joy to the Aged One and that I should listen with my soul to the counsels of the Aged One and then decide what is the right path for Prosopia."

That night as he lay in bed, Canna asleep in his arms, he became afraid as if the entire world were rising up against him. His weariness tainted his reason, allowing his fears to soar. On the morrow, he was to leave Prosopia, his beloved home for the first time and he was to enter a world he knew naught of, a world immersed in the blackness of Man's soul, in pain, in suffering and in death. His terror mounted until he suddenly noticed a great horned owl perched upon his thatched roof, calling into the night, "Hoo, hoo-hoo-hoo, hoo; hoo, hoo-hoo-hoo, hoo." The sound of the owl soothed his torment, and soon he slipped into a deep sleep.

Chapter Five

The following morning, Styrax rose before the sun to prepare for his journey to the crossing. The Wanderer had left the night before, simply wandering off into the dense thicket; where he went, where he lived, how he knew when to come, these things Styrax did not know. Styrax wished to ask the Wanderer many questions about himself, but, as yet, he still felt shy when in the company of this lonely Man. He knew now that the Wanderer could be trusted and trusted profoundly, but he was still afraid to know too much of his new friend, as though with his own deep problems, he cared not to take on those of the Wanderer. Carefully, he selected two blowguns, one short for close range within the dense river growth and one long for striking the foe at longer ranges, and a plentiful supply of amanita powder which he mixed with equal parts of mesquite ash. He took nothing to eat, for Elves had the ability to easily live off the land, gaining most of their strength directly from the sun. He bid the still sleepy and beautiful Canna a fond good-bye, for he knew not how long he would be gone. He knew that Thuja was still tracking the four Beastums, and he knew that the Wanderer had promised to be at the crossing.

Within three days, he was at the ford. Thuja was already there, having built an impromptu camp on a knoll that jutted high above the river, giving a long view both to the north and to the south. Thuja informed Styrax that the men were but a half day behind and would surely reach the crossing on the morrow. They had been slowed down by the collapse of one of their horses, a portion of which they had eaten, leaving the rest to be plucked and torn by the carrion birds.

"Has the Wanderer been here?" Styrax asked as he placed his blowguns against a jutting rock.

"No one has been here except Ulmus who has come to help with but little encouragement from me." Thuja pointed to a large tamarisk in which Ulmus was perched.

"The Wanderer promised to be here, though he will be of little direct help, fearing, as he must, to shed kindred blood. You and I must be the bearers of death."

"Then it is settled?" asked Thuja, knowing in his heart the sad answer.

"It is settled, friend Thuja, it is settled," Styrax answered woefully. "We must kill them, or they will kill us, and enter Prosopia. That we cannot allow."

Thuja grasped Styrax's hands in his, squeezing firmly, and their eyes met in resigned sadness. Boldly Thuja stood and said, "We shall do what we have to do."

In the morning, Styrax and Thuja scouted the banks of the Rhus, finding but one place suitable for a crossing, just below the knoll on which they were camped. The sky was clouded, promising, perhaps, a rare summer shower. Thuja gathered handful after handful of grasshoppers and fungi for them to eat, for without the sun they had to supplement their need for energy in the coming struggle. King Styrax carefully prepared his weapons. The blowgun darts were made of dead mesquite for weight, trimmed with quail feathers and pointed with an ocotillo spine. Carefully he snapped a tamarisk limb, letting the sap flow freely. He coated the point of each dart with the sap, then rolled the sticky spine in the amanita and ash powder. One problem that Styrax was aware of was that the amanita poison took a few minutes to down a bear, and as these men, now approaching from the south, were nearly the size of bears, he knew they would not die at once. How strange, he thought, that Elves eat amanita daily, loving its tart flavor, even though it was a deadly bane to most other living creatures.

Just after the sun had passed its peak, Thuja espied Graspar, Strang, Grudge and Bastard in the distance. Strang was afoot; the other three were mounted. As they had planned, Styrax crawled forward to the edge of the knoll, and Thuja and Ulmus descended to the swift river. As Styrax lay waiting, he wondered where the Wanderer was, never doubting that he would come.

Strang, who was scurrying ahead of his mounted companions, was quick to find the crossing, wide and shallow, just below the knoll. He splashed and ran in the shallow water, falling and laughing in the swift current. Then, he signaled the others, and they rode up quickly, dismounting as they arrived.

"It is no more than three feet deep in the middle and much less deep near the shores," Strang informed his fellow Beastums. "I have seen no one on the far shore."

They all sat upon the river's bank, resting and preparing to cross.

"There's a small clearing over there, but I don't see any break in the thicket beyond," Graspar said as he splashed the cooling water on his sweaty limbs.

"We may have to go still further north to find a large enough break in the mesquite, but at least we will be on the other side," said Bastard who was rabidly eager to cross the Rhus.

Styrax, lying concealed, slowly and carefully aimed his long blowgun at one of the horses. At that distance, he knew his chances of hitting a Man in the neck, the most vulnerable place, was minimal, but he knew he could strike the large body of a horse. He inserted a dart that had been only slightly covered with amanita powder, for he no intention of killing a horse, a creature enslaved by Man. Taking a very deep breath, he blew with all his might. The dart flew unerringly and pierced the horse's rump, causing the steed to jump and whinny.

"What is the matter with that stupid beast?" Graspar yelled, but in a moment the animal settled down. The poison would act slowly, Styrax knew, and in a few moments, the horse would weaken, then collapse into a deep stupor.

Meanwhile, Ulmus, on Thuja's instructions, had flown across the river. There he found a small rattlesnake hidden in the grass, grabbed it by its head, but did not crush it. Carefully, Ulmus the chaparral skirted around the seated men, and then with a great burst of speed he ran through the horses' legs, dropping the snake near their hooves and then flying back across the river. The horses bolted in panic, two running off while the other, already poisoned by Styrax's dart, collapsed. Grudge ran up, his sword drawn. He hacked the snake to pieces but could do little else.

"A snake has bitten your mount, Graspar. The others have run off. Should we go after them?" Grudge asked.

"Damn the horses. They were near dead anyway. We don't need them now. Arm yourselves. We will cross." As Graspar thus spoke, he stood up and drew his mighty sword.

As the men entered the river, they suddenly heard a voice from on top of the knoll.

"Stop! Stop, I say. Go no further if you value life," Styrax shouted, hoping against hope to frighten the men before they went further.

"Who speaks?" Graspar shouted back in his booming voice. "Show yourself so that I know to whom I speak. I am Graspar, King of the Beastums, and I fear no one."

Styrax stood up in clear view of the men. Graspar ordered Bastard and Grudge, both skilled bowmen, to shoot the stranger as he finished speaking.

"I am Styrax, King of Prosopia, as was my father and his father before him. I am here to deny you entrance to our sacred land."

"May a serpent devour you and all your kind," Graspar yelled back. Then he said to his men in a muted voice, "Goree, he's no larger than a child. Shoot him!"

The arrows flew truly, but Styrax was too quick and leaped aside, back into cover. Thuja, meanwhile, had crept to the edge of the Rhus, placing himself much closer to the approaching men.

Graspar, tantalized by the smallness of his enemy, plunged into the river, followed immediately by Strang with his spear and Grudge and Bastard, both carrying bows and arrows and sheathed swords. They found their progress slow, for though the waters only reached their waists, the current was fierce, making them struggle on the rocky bottom to keep their balance. Halfway across, a dart flew from a dense thicket, striking Grudge in the shoulder. He wrenched the dart free, held it up for the others to see, and shouted laughingly, "your darts have the sting of honeybees." The four men struggled on against the surging waters, confident in victory. But only moments later, Grudge cried out in agony, grasped at his throat, stumbled forward, struggling as the river swept him away. Another dart flew toward Graspar's chest but bounced off his metal breastplate. The men were approaching the shore when one of Styrax's darts caught Strang full in the neck, knocking him down. He rose quickly, losing his spear, for he knew that the darts were poisoned.

"Graspar! Help me! They use poison." And in his panic, he leaped forward grabbing Graspar's massive right leg.

Without a second's reflection, Graspar swung around, and with a sweep of his great sword beheaded the floundering Strang. "Worthless fool, the poison can't hurt you now."

In a rage, Graspar reached the shore and rushed headlong up the knoll. Bastard rushed toward the thicket in which Thuja was hidden. He spied Thuja loading a dart in his blowgun, and quickly drew his bow aiming the arrow at Thuja's exposed chest. Then in a mad flurry of feathers and talons, Ulmus flew into Bastard's face, causing the arrow to go awry and giving Thuja the opportunity to blast a dart into his neck. Bastard, flailing at Ulmus who flew away, stumbled backwards, fell into the river, and was swept downstream, recovering his footing just as the poison was taking effect. Thuja rushed to the river's edge to see Bastard's final feeble death throes, and then only the river.

Styrax, standing in the open on the knoll, awaited Graspar, his blowgun ready. He could hear the roaring cries of Graspar as he crashed through the dense brush, his savage curses coming ever closer. Then as a flood burst through a dam, Graspar broke free from the thicket. From across the bare knoll, they saw each other, Kings and enemies to the death.

Graspar, gasping for breath, decided to parley before he squashed his tiny foe. "Are you the King of the Yellfen, Little Man?"

"I am Styrax, King of the Prosopian Elves."

"But you are all alone, Little King. Where are your armies?"

"I have none," Styrax answered.

"Then prepare to die, for I am Graspar the Mighty who yields to no one."

Graspar started running toward Styrax. Styrax launched his dart, but to his surprise Graspar quickly held a brazen shield in front of his neck and the dart glanced away. Quickly, Styrax placed another dart in his blowgun, but, again, Graspar, who was exceedingly fast for so big a Man, blocked the dart in flight. Styrax, who no longer had time to load another dart, was about to run for cover when, suddenly, the Wanderer leaped between the onrushing opponents. Graspar stopped abruptly, stunned by the sudden appearance of a Man as big as he.

"Who are you to deny me my prey? Be gone, or you shall fall to my sword," Graspar growled.

"Do you know me not, Graspar? I am Ravager, who drove the hapless Beastums from the highlands so many years ago."

Squinting as he hearkened back, Graspar's blood boiled as he recognized his ancient enemy. "Then die, Ravager," he shouted, raising his sword and rushing toward the Wanderer.

The Wanderer threw back his cloak, raising his right arm as though to stop Graspar, his hand within a great black glove set with so many dazzling stones that it seemed to radiate beams of blinding light. Graspar stumbled to a halt, mesmerized by the brilliance of the glowing glove. He lowered his shield, holding his free arm across his eyes. And at that moment, a dart pierced his neck on the right side, followed by another on the left side. Styrax and Thuja had both hit the mark. Graspar dropped to his knees, his sword and shield falling noisily to the ground.

"Am I to die at the hands of these little green creatures, these Yellfen? I am Graspar who knew no peer in battle." Graspar gasped for air as he spoke.

"You die by your own grasping hand. Your time is no more," the Wanderer said softly, as he looked down at the dying warrior.

"Can you save me, Ravager? For we are men and I know not what they are." Graspar's voice grew weaker.

"They are Elves, the bane of men. And you are about to die. Make your peace."

Graspar twice attempted to rise, but slowly his strength ebbed, and he fell forward on his face. His life had flown.

* * *

The Elves and the Wanderer hefted and rolled Graspar's huge body to the edge of the knoll, then over, letting the carcass careen down the slope into the river. They hoped that when the bodies floated past the Beastum's encampment, the remaining Beastums would be discouraged from any further attempts at crossing the Rhus. The Elves had the added pleasure of knowing that the bodies of these men would not defile Prosopian soil.

As they sat, resting from their exertions, the Wanderer quietly spoke, "You have done well, my friends. And you too, Ulmus." Ulmus had joined the group and was perched on Thuja's shoulder.

"I feel less disturbed over what I did than I expected to," said Thuja. "I have killed men for the first time. May it be the last."

"There will be many more, so many, in fact, as to darken the grasslands. The killing has begun. Steel yourselves, for the men who will follow Graspar are mightier and wiser. The Rhus will yet run red," observed the Wanderer.

"You speak with the voice of doom," said Styrax, "as though there were no other path, no alternative way, as though you were speaking of the inevitable, the rising sun."

"And so it is, Styrax. This great conflict is destined, for Man, as he now is, and, perhaps, always was, and the Elfin Brood cannot share the land. Man, by his nature, is expansive; he must always move onward from the lands he has exhausted; he must ever search for more and more and more."

"Are there so many of them? You speak as though they were as countless as leaves upon the trees," Thuja said sadly, for not having heard the woeful words the Wanderer had spoken to Styrax, Canna, and Callistemon, he thought that Man numbered no more than the small tribe of Beastums. He thought the battle won; he thought the war was over.

"No, friend Thuja, there are great hordes of men living beyond the grasslands. They do not number as they once numbered, for with each generation, they have fewer and fewer children, and they constantly war amongst themselves, further reducing their numbers. Perhaps, in time, they would vanish in the course of things, but now that they know of Prosopia and other new lands beyond Prosopia, they will make peace amongst themselves, for the time being, forming great armies to descend upon these unravaged lands. The gentle folk, and there are many others besides the Prosopian Elves, must also unite, and if they do not, they will then perish."

"Speak more of the other gentle folk, for I know of none but the Dwarfs in the Pinus Mountains," said Thuja.

"I can say no more until Styrax and I have returned from the distant north, until we have the counsel of the Aged One. Then Styrax can tell all that he deems fitting."

"Where I am going, Thuja, you, my right arm, cannot come, for I am to learn things that only a King can know. You, my trusted companion, must return to the village and assist Queen Canna, for she rules in my stead. Be wary, watch the far shore, and do that which must be done." And as he spoke, he grasped Thuja's hands firmly, not knowing how many days or months before he would see his friend, his beloved Canna and his people again.

That evening, after Thuja had started back to Prosopia and as the Wanderer and Styrax sat on the knoll by a small fire, Styrax withdrew from his waist pouch the yellow stone he had found earlier with Thuja. He looked at it closely; then he passed it to the Wanderer.

"Is this not gold?" Styrax asked.

"Aye, it's gold. Where did you find it?"

"Just south of here, on a small rise but I have seen many such stones in the arroyos." As Styrax spoke, the Wanderer passed back the yellow stone. "What I cannot understand is why Man values it as he does. It seems to be rather drab and uninteresting, not fit for a lizard, as Thuja said."

The Wanderer laughed at Thuja's sublime indifference to gold. How Elfish, he thought before he spoke, "Not only Man, but the Dwarfs also value gold highly, though for different reasons." The Wanderer took the stone from Styrax, and again he studied it closely, turning it slowly in his hands.

"But of what value is it? Thuja and I were both mystified by Man's obsession with what seems to be a thoroughly worthless and ugly rock."

"To Man, even from the most ancient times, gold has always been a basis of power. He who has gold in abundance is ever obeyed and honored and envied intensely. For somewhere in the mists of time, this drab stone became man's most valued possession for with it he commanded others; he became master. And the more gold he amassed, the mightier he became with endless servants and slaves who worked laboriously while the master tended to his gold. In itself, it has no value. The Dwarfs also adore gold though they think of it solely as ornamentation, shiny metal that is easily worked. The Dwarf is a creature of the dark; he shuns light for it burns his flesh and injures his vision, and that is why the Dwarfenfold lives in dark and gloomy caverns. But the Dwarf is wise and knows the sun to be the father of life even if it harms him. Thus, the gold they smelt, refine, and fashion is a symbol of the sun's creative powers, their link to the essence of life. Gold is the sun of the Dwarfs bringing them brightness in its sheen with warmth in its color."

"And I find it ugly," Styrax said emphatically as he stood and threw the stone into the Rhus.

"If Man had known of this gold, he would have been here long ago, digging in the earth like a termite. Even as I felt the stone, I still sensed the exquisite joy it once gave me. And that I once killed for it, now covers me with shame and loathing both for myself and for my kind." The Wanderer spoke softly and looked at the ground beneath his feet.

"And you still suffer for the crimes of Man, my friend." And as Styrax spoke, he rose and walked to where the Wanderer sat, putting his small green hand on his friend's shoulder.

Later, while the Wanderer slept, Styrax sat on the edge of the knoll looking down at the river, brightly reflected in the moon's rays. He was weary, but his mind was active. Today, he had killed men. Today, he had slain, for the first time in his life, a self-aware being, a creature who knew what death was. All of his life, he lived in terror of having to kill, but, now, as he watched the pearly reflections of the Rhus, he had become a murderer and slayer of men. His mind was deeply troubled not because he had slain but because he felt so little remorse in the act of slaying another being. Where he expected great shame, he now felt the urgings of pride. In the struggle, he had had no fear of death, no awareness of it, nor any sense of guilt on giving death. He had been numbed in the necessity of doing that which he had to do. He had conquered a mighty warrior forearmed with a massive, death-dealing sword. He, a tiny elf, had slain a mighty warrior. Though he felt slightly ashamed, he knew the shame was a reaction to his not feeling the terrible guilt he had come to expect.

As he prepared to sleep, he thought to himself, "It is easy. Killing is easy." And then he was horrified at himself and at the knowledge that the killing had just begun.

Chapter Six

On the fourth day of their journey northward, days in which they had struggled through mesquite thicket upon thicket, a task that was painfully difficult for the Wanderer as large as he was, Styrax and the Wanderer came upon a towering gorge at the bottom of which the Rhus cascaded wildly in a rocky canyon, flowing toward the land of Prosopia to the south. At the base of the gorge, they rested, having walked relentlessly these four days.

"We have come to the northern border of the Prosopian land," observed Styrax. "Beyond this point no Elf has ever ventured and but few have ever come this far."

"Have you not been curious as to what lies beyond?" the Wanderer asked.

"No. Should I be?" Styrax replied innocently.

"No, my friend, not you, not an Elf. But for a Man the question would be idle and childish, for Man is consumed with foolish desires, the silliest of which is the longing to know what lies beyond the next hill, and the next, and the next. Even if he knew that nothing of value was beyond this gorge, he would still proceed; he would go on and on, driven by an impulse so ancient and demanding that he would never think to question it. If

Man were in Paradise, he would still want to know what was beyond the gates. In this, the Elf and Man are as alike as the eagle and the trout."

The following morning, they climbed the steep walls of the gorge, issuing forth on a plain with occasional clusters of pinion and juniper trees, beyond which stood vast tracts of tall timber stretching to the horizon in the surrounding mountains. The Wanderer insisted that they stay on the western side of the river, the Elfin side, to avoid any contact with roving tribes of men. The days passed methodically, and the bond of friendship between the Wanderer and Styrax became stronger and deeper. They were both Kings who were alienated from their own kind, for Styrax knew that by taking this journey, by joining the Wanderer, he had separated himself somehow from all the other Elves.

One morning, as they crossed a small rise, Styrax was stunned to see before him a fantastic and far-reaching land of ruins on both sides of the Rhus. Some of the structures, though in disastrous ruin, still towered higher than anything Styrax had as yet seen. Though overgrown, he could still trace the geometric patterns of pathways that once were busy streets. In this moment, he began to grasp what the Wanderer meant in speaking of Man in great hordes, for all of the Elves in Prosopia would hardly fill a small section of the sea of ruins that lay before him.

"You see before you the melancholy remains of a happier age for Man, a time when he little suspected that all he took for granted would soon collapse beneath his feet. To think, my friend, that at one time these ruins were a thriving city, teeming with life and activity. Men then drove strange carriages that were swifter than the finest steeds, and they flew in the air in great metal machines." The Wanderer spoke with stern aloofness beneath which Styrax sensed profound despair. "In another thousand years, nature will completely hide this mark of shame."

"Is it without life? Have they all gone? The men? The machines? It is so vast, so grand, that I cannot imagine what could have destroyed it."

"No, it is not without life, but the machines are long forgotten. Some few thousands of wretched men still live among the ruins they understand no more than you do. It was destroyed by the very forces that built it. You will learn more when we reach our destination. But now we must be wary, for the Querques, the tribe that still dwells there, are ever hungry. We must cautiously skirt around this evil place, and even then we must have eagle eyes."

Slowly, they edged around the ruins, trying to stay within the cover of the cottonwood and elm trees that abounded on the fringes of this once great city. As they left the decayed vestiges of man's golden age behind them, they began to walk faster and less cautiously. Little did they notice a rustling in the deep grasses, nor did they see the huge yellow eyes that peered at them from within the dense undergrowth.

As the sun drifted further into the west, they found a clearing near the river and settled down for the evening. Having built a fire, the Wanderer removed his cloak and laid down by the small blaze. Styrax, as was his custom, climbed a nearby cottonwood tree to rest among its limbs. The night descended quickly as it always does when the sky is cloudless. For many moments, he lay among the branches, looking up at the stars through the cottonwood leaves. So many stars, he thought, gleaming mysteriously through the darkening night, so harmonious, so peaceful, so unlike the world he was entering.

Styrax was woken from a deep sleep by a strange scent in the air, a pungent odor, strongly reminiscent of decay, and then he seemed to hear the sound of raucous breathing, a sound that had to come from something very large. Having excellent night vision, as do all Elves, he scanned the area still dimly lit by the dying fire. Then, from behind a mound of dead trees and limbs jutting into the river, he saw a huge creature creeping on all fours toward the sleeping figure of the Wanderer. Behind it crept another creature, much like the first but larger still. Its skin appeared hairless, black, and shiny in the darkness; it crept on feet that seemed more like talons than paws; it had a large mouth and fierce, pointed teeth and was slavering abundantly. Ever so slowly, the two creatures approached the Wanderer's sleeping figure.

Styrax quickly loaded his blowgun, blasting the poisoned dart deeply into the shoulder of the beast nearest his friend, but the creature crept onward oblivious to Styrax's dart. Not knowing what else to do, Styrax shouted as loudly as he could, "Wake up, Wanderer! Wake up! Something is upon you."

But even as he shouted, the first creature pounced upon the figure by the fire while the second beast rushed to the foot of the tree in which Styrax was situated. Horrifying screeches issued forth from these ugly creatures, filling the night with terror. The first beast was tearing at the Wanderer's cloak, ripping up talons full of straw and screeching all the louder; the second and larger creature leaped at the trunk of Styrax's tree but was incapable of climbing it or even standing on its hind legs. Styrax, in terror for his friend, launched dart after dart into the fierce beasts but, seemingly, without effect.

Then, as though from nowhere, the Wanderer sprang into the middle of the camp. His right hand was within the great black glove encrusted with radiant jewels that emitted brilliant multicolored rays of light; his left hand held a glowing sword on high. Both beasts turned around, screeching louder and tearing at the ground that had been muddied by their slobber. They paused but for a moment, then leaped toward the Wanderer, but in mid-career their bodies were caught in silvery enshrouding nets that fell from the sky, and the more they struggled and the more they screeched, the more deeply enmeshed they became.

"Come down, Styrax. Your darts will now take effect. The beasts are helpless," shouted the Wanderer, as the ghastly noises of the creatures began to subside.

"What are they?" asked Styrax as he ran up to his friend.

"They are Grendels, creatures that never should have been. You did well with your lethal darts, but these monsters are so large that the poison takes much too long to achieve its ends."

Styrax walked around the huge carcasses but soon backed away because of the beast's stench.

"They are as evil as their smell. It was the stench that forewarned me, but I said nothing as you were safe in the cottonwood."

Moving to his friend's side, upwind of the Grendels, Styrax asked, "How did you cast those silken nets?"

But before the Wanderer could answer, the tree canopy was filled with happy laughter, as of young girls.

"What is that?" Styrax muttered, looking all around.

Then, like rainfall, tiny creatures, half the size of Elves, dropped to the ground from the high branches above. They were bright silver with glowing green eyes and were slender in form, and had no sooner hit the ground when they were scampering about the Wanderer, each grasping his large hands in turn, laughing incessantly.

"Welcome, Wanderer, welcome. It has been long, too long, since you have honored us. Welcome. Welcome." The little creatures shouted in high pitched voices.

Styrax was dumbfounded. He wanted to ask who these creatures were, but their happy chattering gave him no opportunity. Then he noticed one particular figure in the bouncing throng, a bit taller than the rest with a small crown of white crystals that sparkled in the night. Strange, he observed to himself, they are all female.

The hubbub slowly subsided, and the crowned figure spoke over the others, speaking and laughing at the same time, "Who, my old friend, he-he-he, have you brought with you on this lovely night, he-he-he?"

With a slight bow, the Wanderer answered, "I have brought my boon companion Styrax, King of the Prosopian Elves, a fitting guest for the ever-happy Shee."

"Step forward, he-he-he, King Styrax. Be welcome. Be of good cheer, he-he-he, for you are among the Shee, he-he-he, the people of laughter, the people of the moon."

Smiling, though still confused, Styrax stepped up to the crowned figure, holding out both his hands. "You must forgive my confusion, for you seemed, for a moment, to fall from the sky."

This immediately caused more laughter as each and every member of the Shee ran up to grasp Styrax's extended hands, and as each one held Styrax's hands, she burst into renewed laughter and covered her pretty face with her hands.

"I am Fon-du-Fon, he-he-he, Queen of the Shee. You have come with the Wanderer, he-he-he, you are ever our friend, he-he-he. But let us not stand here, he-he-he, befouled by the Grendel stench, he-he-he. You must come to Sylvium, he-he-he, our enchanted glade."

And as the Wanderer nodded his head in agreement, the Shee scattered so quickly that in a moment Styrax and the Wanderer were standing alone, as though they never had visitors. Only the silken nets around the bodies of the Grendels attested to the Shee having been there.

The glade of the Shee, Sylvium, was but a short distance from the death-site of the Grendels. The glade itself was a small island of solid land situated in a bosque of reeds, osiers, tamarisks and cottonwoods which could only be reached by wading through soft and treacherous mud, a natural deterrent to any invader. From a distance, Styrax noticed that the Shee's silvery skin actually glowed, actually emitted light, not unlike the glowworms that amused Elves in Prosopia. How dangerous, he thought, to be so obvious in the dark.

"Is it not foolish to glow that way? The Shee would be easy targets for darts and arrows," Styrax observed as he and the Wanderer struggled through the mud.

"Dangerous? No, not for the Shee, for they glow only when they wish to, mostly when they are happy and secure. After all, they crept up on us without our knowing it. Their nets surprised me as much as they did you. They leap so effortlessly through the tops of trees that they seem to fly. They do not struggle through this muck that we are floundering in; they simply leap from limb to limb like wrens. Man seldom bothers them, for they are creatures of the night when men are most helpless."

"Why? They would seem an easy prey for Man. What weapons have they besides the silken nets?" Styrax spoke uncertainly, for the Shee seemed hardly an adequate foe for so brutal a creature as Man.

"First of all, do not belittle the silken nets, for they are more deadly than your most potent darts. The Shee spin the fibers from their bodies much as spiders do. The net, when cast, wraps around its prey, gradually tightening, crushing to death whatever lies within its folds. If the Shee do not release the victim, then death is inevitable. Remember that men suffer from endless fears, especially fear of what they do not understand. They are a superstitious lot, and the fact that the Shee appear at night as if from nowhere and glow when they desire has made Man especially frightened of these little females. Their only weapons, other than the remarkable nets, are a small arrow that they launch with a sling and the daggers that they carry in their hair. They are extremely accurate and are aimed at the eyes of their enemies with such success that even the metal helmets of men afford but poor protection. This tactic works for the Shee, as most men would rather die than be blinded. But, like your people, the Shee do their utmost to avoid confrontation, for they prefer to live privately, amongst their own kind, and in peace."

As they slowly pulled themselves up on the dry land of Sylvium, Styrax quietly asked, for he wished to offend no one, "Where are the males of the Shee?

I have seen only females."

"That question you had best ask Fon-du-Fon," the Wanderer answered softly.

A feast of mushrooms, toadstools, insects, frogs, lizards and snakes had been made ready by the Shee, and these tasty foods were enhanced by a fermented drink made from mistletoe. Styrax ate heartily of the mushrooms, toadstools and insects but could not be persuaded to taste the frog, snake, and lizard meats, though he thoroughly enjoyed the mistletoe concoction. The Wanderer drank water and ate the frog, lizard and snake meat, telling the Shee and Styrax that mistletoe was poisonous to Man. As they ate, the Shee scurried about, never seeming to settle down and always laughing as they frolicked around their tiny fires. They asked many questions of Styrax, about his land and his people and mostly about Elfin pleasures. At first, Styrax was intimidated by the constant laughter, fearing, perhaps, that the laughter was at his expense, but as he became accustomed to this unseemly levity, he asked the question that had been haunting him.

"Where are the males of the Shee people?"

This caused an even greater eruption of laugher, and many of the Shee rolled upon the ground, he-he-he-ing louder than ever.

"We have no males, he-he-he," said Fon-du-Fon. "Though we know how strange it seems, he-he-he, to other peoples we, simply, have no males, nor do we think of ourselves, he-he-he, as females. We are only Shee, he-he-he; we have no sexes."

"But what of children? How do you keep your clan alive? How is the next generation made?" Styrax spoke in awe, not even sure how to phrase his questions.

"He-he-he, how confusing we are to King

Styrax, he-he-he. But children are no problem, he-he-he, when our numbers diminish from old age and uncertain death, he-he-he, we simply build nests and lay eggs, he-he-he, like all our feathered friends, he-he-he."

"You lay eggs?" Styrax muttered, and the incredulity of his voice started the Wanderer laughing, something which he rarely did. Whether it was the mistletoe or his general discombobulation, Styrax himself began to laugh.

Amid the general laughter, more mistletoe was poured, and many of the Shee began to dance with frantic grace, twirling and leaping high in the air while others sang in shrill, piercing but always melodic voices. Fon-du-Fon was particularly taken with Styrax, finding that her new green friend's spirit was attuned to the Shee.

"Do your people have children, he-he-he, in the same way as Man does?" Fon-du-Fon asked when the happy sounds had subsided a bit.

"I think we do. We have both males and females, and we form pairs for the joy of raising young Elves, but I am not fully acquainted with man's breeding habits." Styrax turned to the Wanderer, asking, "Are Man's reproductive ways like those of the Elves?"

"Physically, you and Man breed in much the same manner, though Man now has great difficulty in having children—something has gone wrong with his ability to conceive, and even when he does, the children are often malformed and die at birth or in their infancy. The only other difference that I know of is that Elves seldom have more than two children, usually about ten years apart, for Elves always consider the problem of whether the land will sustain more mouths, so that there will not be too many of them. Elves breed with their reason—the object being to produce a child to continue the flow of Elfin life. Man breeds through sexual passion, with no other goal than self-gratification. Children are by-products, mistakes of his sexual madness. Man, before his ever-growing infertility, bred haphazardly, having as many children as he pleased regardless of his ability to maintain them. At one time, Man bred at such a rampant pace that the world had five times as many men as it could support, causing upheavals and madness which are still the very condition of Man as we now know him."

"We have but rare meeting, he-he-he, with Man, and most of those meetings, he-he-he, have caused us great injury, he-he-he. Man is always at war with himself, he-he-he, or other creatures, he-he-he, or with the earth or the elements, he-he-he. If his powers are on the wane, he-he-he, then the Shee are the happier for it, he-he-he."

"Have you noticed any recent changes in man's ways?" the Wanderer asked.

"The Querques, for that is the name they go by, he-he-he, have had many visitors from the east, he-he-he, all splendidly attired, stronger, and more vigorous than the Querques, he-he-he. Their numbers are ever growing, he-he-he, and they seem to be preparing for some great task, he-he-he."

"They and others are planning to invade the lands of the Shee and the Elves, and all the virgin lands to the west. You, Fon-du-fon, and Styrax, and your peoples must prepare to face the coming onslaught." The Wanderer spoke in his most earnest manner.

"Face them, he-he-he? Surely you jest, Wanderer, for we will just move to another glade, he-he-he."

"There will be no other glades, my friends." The Wanderer knew the Shee were dauntless when cornered, but he also realized that the traditional Shee approach was to move on whenever danger threatened. The Shee had no attachment to any given segment of land. If Sylvium were attacked on the morrow, the Shee would simply disappear into the trees and reappear elsewhere, and that would be their home until forced to move again.

"You mean that Man will allow us no peace, he-he-he, that he will harass us continually, he-he-he, to the death?"

"Yes, that is precisely what I mean. Styrax and I are now on our way to the Hill of Light to see what the Aged One recommends. But I am sure we must fight to survive. It is our hope that the Shee will join us in this struggle." The Wanderer spoke sternly to counteract the continuing Shee laughter.

"Well, Wanderer, he-he-he, if we must fight, we must, he-he-he, but if we fight, it must be on Shee terms, he-he-he. We are hardly fit to meet man's warriors in the field, he-he-he." Fon-du-Fon spoke happily, dismissing the problem of Man for the moment.

Styrax and the Wanderer slept that night as the Shee did, in hammocks woven of silk, suspended high above the ground within the canopy of the trees. They slept soundly, feeling both happy and secure among their new friends.

Early the following morning, they bid the Shee good-bye, saddened to leave so soon, but the Shee laughed and laughed, even as Styrax and the Wanderer walked off into the distance. But before they departed, Fon-du-Fon said to Styrax and the Wanderer, "If war comes, he-he-he, we will join the Elves, he-he-he, for Styrax has won our hearts. You have but to summon us, he-he-he, and we will be there."

* * *

For two days, their travels were across somewhat desolate high plains that stretched great distances on either side of the narrowing Rhus, but on the third day the ground began to rise into scrubby foothills and rocky outcroppings beyond which towered lofty peaks, some still snow-capped. The Rhus had become less broad, swifter and deeper, flowing more wildly over great boulders that crowded its course. Walking became more difficult and tiring, as they ascended steep gorges misted by cascading falls.

They spoke of many things, but especially of the Shee. Styrax was bewildered by the continual laughter of the silvery people, wondering if they ever knew sadness.

"They always laugh," the Wanderer observed. "I have seen them struggling for their lives against men or Grendels or scrubble bears, and even as they were injured or slain, they laughed."

"Are there many of them?"

"A great many, but scattered far and wide; like the Elves, they do not seem to congregate in great numbers."

"Have they no homeland, no soil that is sacred to them?" Styrax asked.

"None, for they move constantly, requiring little more than shrubbery and trees within which to hide. The Shee are night hunters. You noticed their silvery skin that absorbs moonlight much as Elves absorb sunlight, and you also noticed, I'm sure, how their argentine skin is almost invisible at night. When an enemy is attacked by the Shee, he seldom knows they were there until he counts his dead and by then the Shee are long gone.

* * *

On the following day, they reached the headwaters of the Rhus, where the main stream divided into numerous rills that splashed down precipitous cliffs which seemed almost unscalable.

"We must now make the first ascent," the Wanderer said, "and above these cliffs we will find a vast, deeply treed valley leading to even greater mountains. Be on your guard, Styrax, for the valley belongs to the Shags, great Man-like creatures covered with coarse hair as thick as a bear's. They are brutes—savage and ever hungry."

"And what lies beyond the valley?"

"Beyond the valley, after the second ascent, we will enter the Aged One's realm, the land of perpetual snow and ice. But what lies between the Shags and the land of snow, I know not, for I have never come this way before."

The ascent was slow, for the cliffs were full of loose stone, and unsafe handholds and footholds. At times, they had to climb hand over hand to reach safer trails where they slaked their thirsts from crystalline waters that seeped from rocky seams. The Wanderer, spying an eagle's nest, made a long detour to avoid disturbing the king of birds, but Styrax, also seeing the aerie, made straight for it. As he approached the nest, he noticed it had two eaglets, just as the male eagle returned to feed his young. Surprised by the Elf near his nest, a creature he had never seen before, the great eagle prepared to attack. Styrax quickly called out in high squeals, "Scree, scree, elt, elt, scree." The eagle paused, calling back in a similar fashion, though now less alarmed and with less belligerence. Styrax modulated his calls, moving from the screeing to the softer mewing of the eagle at peace. The eagle cautiously landed on its nest, carefully inspecting his young while trying to understand the intentions of this unexpected guest. Thuja had taught Styrax eagle speech and that the eagle was the most rational of all birds, excluding only the great horned owl. Shortly, the female eagle returned, having heard the alarm cries of her mate, but she too became calm as Styrax continued mewing softly. Soon the male bird, having fed the eaglets, moved closer and closer to Styrax, finally perching on a rock adjacent to the one Styrax was clinging to. In softened tones, they spoke with an occasional "scree" or "elt," and soon Styrax was able to caress the eagle's neck. The female joined the male, and the conversation grew animatedly intense, the eagles often seemingly surprised by their Elfin friend's daring.

When Styrax met the Wanderer at the top of the cliffs, the Wanderer immediately asked his friend, "How came you by eagle's speech? Were you not afraid? Eagles are not the friendliest of birds. What did they say?"

"I learned to speak with eagles from Thuja the friend of all birds. They said many things, the first of which was that they had no quarrel with Elves but were glad my Man-friend had skirted their aerie; they do not like Man. They warned me of the Shags, telling me to climb directly up the center of the valley, for safety is to be found behind the stone walls. They know of the Aged One, whom, though a Man, they revere for his wisdom. The male's name is Cleetus; the female Reia; they call themselves the lords of the scarp, and they will watch me carefully, meaning they will watch over me. They asked me to stay, but I had to excuse myself because there were limits to how long I could cling to those treacherous rocks. Finally, Cleetus told me his tribe numbered in the thousands and were ever ready to assist their friends as though he knew of the bad times to come."

"Not only the eagle, but all of nature senses the coming of an upheaval of man's new attempts to master the world." The Wanderer paused as he sipped the cool water seeping from mossy rocks. "For in his prime, Man tampered with natural law alienating all who lived within nature's vale. Even the grasses and the trees shuddered at the works of Man, and the great struggle began. Man disrupted the harmony and in so doing disrupted his ability to create life, his ability to have progeny, his ability to see beyond his generation. All of nature now shuns Man, a creature who has attempted to divide the world and in the process achieved little more than dividing himself off from all other living things."

"Certainly, Cleetus and Reia sense the evil in Man," Styrax replied.

"You have made mighty friends," the Wanderer said, still amazed at Styrax's courage, which had seemed more like foolhardiness but moments before. "There is a cave beyond this outcropping, a likely place for this evening's rest. Tomorrow, we must face the Shags until we reach the stone walls Cleetus spoke of, whatever they might be."

As the sun set, they sat securely by their fire, well within a large cave that looked back upon the land they had traversed. Styrax busied himself with his darts, dipping the barbs numerous times in the amanita poison so that they would be exceptionally potent. The Wanderer took off his cloak and from within its complicated folds he drew out a short sword, the like of which Styrax had never seen. Barely two feet long, it was a carved crystal, the blade of which was as clear as a tarn, catching and magnifying even the feeble light of the fire; its handle was of black stone so intense that it seemed to absorb light. Next, he withdrew a large hunting horn of gold, intricately shaped and engraved with floral patterns.

"This is the Horn of Fear, a gift of the Aged One. Its sound is that of legions, so brazen and loud as to frighten the very stones of the mountains. I have not had reason to use it as yet, but tomorrow we will need it, I fear."

Styrax, setting aside his darts, picked up the huge black, begemmed glove that the Wanderer had worn at the battle with Graspar and during the struggle with the Grendels. It was of great weight to Styrax and the gems seemed at that moment to be lusterless, little more than colored stones. Slowly he put his small hand inside, and in a moment he yanked it out, dropping the glove to the ground.

The Wanderer smiled, saying, "It becomes extremely hot and has no power for anyone but myself. Here, watch what happens when I don it."

The Wanderer picked it up and slowly put his right hand inside. Immediately, the gems started to glow, growing ever stronger in intensity until bursts of radiant light in a multitude of colors shot forth from each gem. The rays of light were so intense that when they struck the walls of the cave, pieces of stone burst from the surface of the rock. The Wanderer quickly withdrew his hand, the radiance dying almost instantly. "My glove is too powerful to be worn within a cave."

"With your weapons, I think we have little to fear," Styrax said boldly.

"But, friend Styrax, the glove and the horn are in reality harmless. They affect the mind of the foe, making him fearful, upsetting his judgment, weakening his purpose, but harming him not in the least. They are weapons of first choice. My sword is another matter; it is called Nothung; and is death to whom it smites, no matter what armor is worn."

The Wanderer picked up Nothung, raised it slightly, and brought it down upon a large stone near the fire. The moment he held it, the blade glowed from within, and as it hit the stone it cleaved through, leaving the stone in two pieces, the cut edges of which were as smooth as polished gems. "This is my weapon of last resort, the blade of necessity."

"How strange," Styrax mused, "that I lie here amid frightening tools of death preparing myself to kill when the very word sends shudders through the Elfin being. Oh, that Prosopia were sealed off from the rest of the world."

"It is as yet a world out of balance. Though it approached perfection in the ancient mists of time, it has since gone awry." The Wanderer's voice then grew stern, "Remember that we kill of necessity; we kill that which is destined to be killed. Unlike Man, we do not confuse our wills with necessity."

"But will a time of peace ever come again?" Styrax asked with great melancholy in his voice.

"Yes, my friend, it will come. Above all else, we must ever believe that peace will come again."

* * *

Before sunrise, the Wanderer and Styrax began their trek up the center of the pathless canyon, stopping only to drink from the small stream that coursed its length. At this high altitude, the air was crisp and thin, making the exertion of climbing even more difficult. They had gone almost halfway when the Wanderer signaled to Styrax to stop and listen. At once, Styrax's keen ears were aware of a grunting, spasmodic sound behind them. Then, in the distance, he espied two large beasts, larger than Man, shuffling clumsily along the stream and bending to sniff the ground.

"They have our scent," the Wanderer whispered. "Their sight is poor, and they have not seen us yet. But we had best move on quickly, for I see no stone walls as yet."

Though tired, they pressed on, ever watching behind them, and realizing that the original pair of Shags was soon four, then six, then more than a dozen. Though huge and seemingly awkward, the Shags moved rapidly and were closing the gap that separated them from the more and more exhausted Styrax and his friend. Frequently, Styrax looked ahead, searching the steep cliffs for stone walls, but he saw none. And soon, the Wanderer and Styrax found themselves moving into a box canyon from which there could be no escape.

Gasping for breath in the thin air, they found themselves backed into an ever-narrowing canyon formed by sheer granite walls so smooth and precipitous that they could find no way out and no place to hide. The Shags, numbering now at least fifteen, spread across the canyon's mouth, making escape impossible for the entrapped Wanderer and Styrax.

"These must be the stone walls Cleetus spoke of," Styrax gasped, "but I see no way to ascend them."

"Nor do I, my friend," said the Wanderer, throwing off his cloak. "We must fight and hope to escape the way we came."

The Shags moved forward gradually, knowing they had trapped their prey. Styrax raised his long blowgun and launched an amanita impregnated dart that struck the foremost Shag in the thigh.

He leaped backwards, wrenching the dart from his leg and bellowing in pain. Then, unaffected, he and the others continued to move forward. The poison would take effect but slowly from a thigh wound in so large a creature. Again and again, Styrax launched his darts with unerring skill, but still the Shags moved forward relentlessly. When they were within a hundred yards from the rocks upon which Styrax and the Wanderer stood, the largest Shag gave a deafening roar, a signal to charge. Like a whirlwind, they swept towards the hapless pair. The Wanderer, waiting till the last moment, brought the Horn of Fear to his lips and gave it a mighty blast that shook the very granite of the canyon walls. The Shags, stunned by the deafening sound, retreated in panic, but at a safer distance they regrouped. They approached again, only to be driven off by the fearsome noise of the Wanderer's golden horn.

"The Horn has done all it can," whispered the Wanderer. "They will not retreat the next time."

Forward they came, snarling and cautious. Styrax continued firing his poisoned darts which were beginning to take effect, though slowly. As the Shags came within striking distance, the Wanderer drew Nothung from its scabbard and held it above his head. The blade glowed brighter and brighter, casting brilliant light in all directions. The foremost Shag leaped forward trying to grasp the Wanderer, but in an instant Nothung swept forward and severed the Shag's arm from his body. Screaming in final terror, the Shag fell backwards and crashed to the ground. The other Shags quickly retreated to a safe distance.

"Look, Wanderer, the poison is taking effect," Styrax shouted.

One of the Shags had already collapsed, and

another was gasping for air. But Styrax's joy was short-lived, for as soon as one Shag succumbed to the amanita poison, two more came up the canyon to join the rest, oblivious to his dying kin.

Styrax and the Wanderer backed against the granite walls. Styrax had used all of his darts; the Horn of Fear had lost its power to frighten the foe; only Nothung stood between them and violent death. The Shags, now greater in number, left their dying companions and moved forward. The Wanderer stood in front of Styrax, grimness in his eyes, holding Nothung above his head. For a moment Styrax and the Wanderer looked deeply into each other's eyes. They were brothers to the end.

With a ghastly roar, the Shags charged. Nothung swept forward, again and again, smiting the Shags mightily, slaying one upon the other, until the Wanderer was surrounded by dead and dying Shags, but soon they came faster than the Wanderer could strike and the Wanderer was knocked from his feet. And just as the end was nigh, a great piercing screech filled the air. Cleetus and hundreds of his feathered kin descended from the sky, slashing and tearing Shag flesh with bloody talons. The screeching of the eagles and the roaring of the Shags filled the air, giving momentary respite to the fallen Styrax and the Wanderer. Quickly, the Wanderer was on his feet, Nothung biting into Shag flesh. But the Shags soon beat back the eagle swarm, for eagles were hardly a match for these great beasts. And even Nothung began to lose its sting as exhaustion took the strength from the Wanderer's mighty arm. One Shag had grabbed Styrax by the leg and was dragging him away when suddenly a huge rock crashed down upon the beast's head, killing him instantly. Styrax scrambled free, looking up just in time to dodge another great stone.

"Wanderer! Wanderer!" Styrax shouted with all his might. "Leap against the walls."

The Wanderer slashed his way free and backed against the canyon wall as more and more massive stones rained down upon the Shags, breaking and crushing them in an instant.

Amid the agonizing death cries of the Shags, Styrax and the Wanderer pressed against the granite and seemed to feel the stone wall giving way. They turned around to see a great fissure opening in the granite wall revealing a cavern within. Quickly, grabbing his cape, the Wanderer picked up Styrax and lunged into the dark, yawning cleft. And no sooner had they entered than the fissure sealed itself.

Chapter Seven

Thrett had little trouble following the crude map Vastar had given him, for the land of the Vergers and the fortress-city called Greydome were situated in front of the highest peak in the vicinity, Mount Turandor. He had traveled for three days across the grasslands when his exhausted horse gave out, too old and too weak to go further. He used the horse-meat to regain his strength, and he was now in sight of the mountains Vastar had indicated on the map. Thrett still pondered his last conversation with Vastar. He knew that he was being used by the Shaman, and he knew that if he returned with fresh horses and sturdy warriors, his own importance would be greatly diminished if he was not slain outrightly. Thrett had no love for the Beastums, a tribe he had the misfortune to be born into. He knew they were doomed—they all knew it—and they were too weak and exhausted to be salvaged. Better if they all die, he thought. But Vastar was not a Beastum. He claimed to be a Verger, the brother of Profundus the Guileful, the leader of that tribe. Vastar is shrewd, he mused; therefore his brother who drove Vastar off must be shrewder. Perhaps, I would be better off among the Vergers, if they would accept me, if Profundus can be deceived. Thrett was no fool, for he alone of the remaining Beastums had no real fear of Graspar, their brutal but doltish leader. But he feared Vastar and now he feared Profundus. How I loathe these wise men, he thought, who use their brains instead of their strength to control others. A Man can deal with physical strength by matching it, or by undermining it, or by flattering it. Graspar, though the leader, was easily controlled and guided. Thrett was sure of his ability to manipulate Graspar, but he felt no such certainty toward Vastar. He knows too much, Thrett mused; he knows of the past, of things a warrior should shun, of the inner workings of a person's mind. He is not to be trusted—no wise Man is to be trusted. But is Profundus any better? Probably not, he speculated, but Profundus has one disadvantage I could turn to my benefit: he does not know me as Vastar does and does not know that beneath my warrior's strength and vigor lies that same shrewdness that Vastar and Profundus think they monopolize.

As he entered into the foothills, he found himself surrounded by mounted and well-armed men clad in luxurious scarlet robes.

"Who are you?" they demanded. "What do you want?"

"I am Thrett, a warrior of the Beastum tribe. I have been sent by Vastar to seek the tribe of the Vergers."

"We are the Vergers," the scarlet warriors answered.

"I bring a message for Profundus the Guileful," Thrett said, holding up a sheet of folded paper.

The scarlet warriors looked down upon the bedraggled Thrett, shabbily clothed and without a mount. Had he not mentioned Vastar, a name of importance to the Vergers, and the brother and mortal enemy of their leader, the warriors would have slain Thrett on the spot, leaving his body to rot in the barren foothills.

Glaumus, the warrior's captain, demanded that Thrett give over his weapons. Then the men in scarlet robes led Thrett through long, twisting canyons and up a steep scarp to a vast, rocky promontory overlooking a swampy lake. Upon the promontory stood a massive, crudely-built castle of stone surrounded by seemingly endless thatched huts.

Profundus the Guileful was a little Man with a large head, too large for his diminutive body. He wore a loose gray robe that dragged upon the ground and on the robe were drawn strange symbols of magical significance. His eyes were small and deep-set; his voice was slightly gravelly; his movements were slow and deliberate. He dismissed Glaumus and the soldiers in scarlet and offered Thrett a seat by a fire burning in a crescent-shaped brazier.

"So, you have come from my brother, Vastar. May he roast in the pits of Hell. What message have you?" Profundus asked in a gentle and friendly voice.

Thrett gave Profundus the letter written in symbols not unlike those upon Profundus' robe. Slowly, he read the letter, smiling to himself.

"He writes of a great cache of gold across a river he calls the Rhus," Profundus said. "Do you know of this hoard?"

At that moment, Thrett decided to abandon Vastar. He spoke softly, "I know of no gold and care less." Then he lied, "I don't even know what it looks like."

"Ah, but that means little, for Vastar trusts no one. He asks for ten good mounted warriors so that he will be able to cross the river. Has he no men of his own?"

"He has no men at all. Graspar is our leader, but his tribe, the Beastums, are very close to extinction from starvation and the lack of children."

"You are a shrewd fellow. You have delivered Vastar's letter, but I'm sure that is not why you have come. I can see into your soul: you are not Vastar's flunky. You are your own Man. What is it you want? For the moment, let us forget Vastar and his gold. What is it that you want?"

Thrett said nothing for a moment. Then, instead of answering the question Profundus had asked, he posed a question of his own. "Are the Vergers—are *you*—content with the ravaged lands you now possess?"

"A question for a question. But you are not in a position to ask questions. You are here to answer. From what I can see, you are a tattered creature carrying a message from my hateful brother, a Man so vile and treacherous that I should like nothing better than news of his death, hopefully, a painful one. Your end is certain unless you tell me something to my profit, something that offers me significant gain. So, I give you one chance. What is it you want?"

Again Thrett paused, knowing the danger he was in. His answer was carefully calculated, "As I traveled through your land, I was forced to notice that it is poor, lacking in game, exhausted, not much better than the arid grasslands from whence I came. This is a blighted land, cursed by the hand of Man. If I stayed on the sere grasslands, I would surely die; if I stay here, I will probably die by your hand; but soon your tribe will also die as it is dying now."

"You are dense, my friend, for you seem incapable of answering a simple question. All that you say is, perhaps, true, but it does you no good. Whether the Vergers live or die is hardly your concern. What is it you have to offer? And what is the price?"

"Vastar has no gold. He wants your men to aid him in conquering a new land, a land he expects to rule. But he is a fool. He expects to conquer this new land with twenty or so men. His vision is small, for the land I speak of, untouched and abounding in game, can only be conquered by an army. I speak of a land so vast, so rich, a land untouched by Man, a land that would sustain a thousand armies."

"You have caught my interest, but you fail to answer my question. What is it you want?" Profundus demanded.

"I want to lead an army of strong and sturdy warriors; I want to conquer and subdue this new untouched land; and, above all else, I want power."

"Perhaps, you want too much. What is to stop me from killing you right now and then conquering this new land at my leisure. Surely, it can't be that difficult to find. Who inhabits it? What is their strength?"

"Finding the land is easy; conquering it is another matter. But I do not wish to rule. I know the land; I know the river crossings; I know the enemy. I am a great warrior—my strength is unflagging. I wish to be a warlord. You will be my king." Thrett spoke boldly, knowing that this might be his last gamble with life.

Profundus said nothing, though his mind was aflame. He stared into the fire. Thrett sat still and said nothing while he gazed at Profundus. Each Man was measuring the other, and each was sure he had the other's measure. He's right, thought Profundus; our land is tired, a land of the dying, a land of the dead. But can he be trusted? Has he the courage? Do I need him? And is he lying about the gold hoping, perhaps, to keep it for himself?

"Are you certain there is no gold?" Profundus asked.

"No, my Lord, I am certain of nothing. There may be gold in great abundance, for all I know. No one knows, for none have been able to cross the savage Rhus. Its current would sweep away your mightiest steed. Perhaps there is gold. But Vastar knows nothing of it." Thrett had elaborated on the gold, knowing, from Vastar, of Profundus' greedy weakness.

Profundus rose and slowly walked to an ornate cabinet on the stone wall behind him. He withdrew a large bottle and a small vial, and took them back to his seat. He sat a moment, then said, "You have gambled your life on this venture, I think. Now I will put you to the test. I ask you to join me in a glass of Verger wine."

He slowly poured the wine into two goblets. Then he opened the vial and carefully, put five drops from it into the goblet he offered Thrett. "You need not drink—then our business is concluded and you may return to Vastar. Or, you may choose to drink knowing that I have added a secret potion to your wine. It may be poison; it may not be poison. Will you drink with me? Will you join the ranks of the Scarlet Five Hundred?"

For just a moment Thrett paused, looking directly into Profundus' eyes. He knew Vastar was a master of poisons, and he assumed Profundus to be equally skilled. Then, quickly, he grasped the goblet and drained it.

Profundus watched Thrett carefully, finally saying with mounting excitement, "You have made your choice, and I have made mine. For many years

I have awaited for an answer to a riddle that has taunted me all my life. I trust few men—in that I am not unlike my brother. The Vergers, the Beastums, the Querques are all doomed by an evil visited upon them in the dark past. Then, from the sere grasslands, a stranger comes with balm for our wounds, with hope when we have already abandoned ourselves to despair. I rule tired men in a time-wracked land. My dominion is blighted, my people infertile. Perhaps, new land means new vigor, the resurgence of the once-mighty Vergers. And if there is gold, so much the better. You have brought us hope in the gathering darkness. But you—what am I to do with you?"

And as Profundus spoke, Thrett slowly felt more and more tired, and as he grew weaker, too weak to resist, he realized that the wine was poisoned and that he was dying. So this is how it ends, he thought in his dream-like state of mind. At least there was no pain. How grand it could have been! How glorious! As unconsciousness approached, his mind wandered, thinking, oh well, I tried, oh, how I tried—all or nothing, all or nothing. Nothing! And his consciousness ceased.

Chapter Eight

On entering the cavern and being sealed in by the closing of the stone fissure, Styrax and the Wanderer were amazed to see orderly arrays of stout battle axes, short swords and long spears lined against the brightly lit cavern walls beneath blazing torches. In functional rows were sturdy workbenches covered with weapons in varied states of manufacture, ax-heads, blades, hafts and strapping, and in the center of all this rose a huge stone smithy roaring with fire, the smoke of which blackened the lofty ceiling before escaping up a stone flue.

"Hello! Hello!" Styrax shouted as his voice echoed endlessly in the huge chamber. But other than echoes, no answer was to be heard.

The Wanderer picked up a partially finished spear from the workbench, speaking as he examined it in detail. "This is exceptionally fine work, comparable to the craftsmanship of the Nibelungen Dwarfs in the Pinus Mountains, but I have never known them to make this style of weapon. The designs are all symmetrical and made up of geometric figures. The Nibelungen designs are always floral in pattern. How keen are the blades. How sharp the points."

"Perhaps we have entered an armory in which Man makes his weapons," Styrax said with mounting fear.

"No. The craftsmanship is too fine, too precise and too skilled to be the work of men, and the weapons though finely made are much too small for the hands of Man."

"But where is everyone?" Styrax asked as he examined a nearby sword, feeling its keenness and a sense of power in holding so lethal a weapon.

Finding a winding staircase at the far end of the cavern, Styrax and the Wanderer carefully ascended the small stone steps which were lighted at reasonable intervals by torches imbedded in the walls. For a long time they climbed the stairway, step after step, rising ever higher and higher, until in the far distance there was a faint gleam of sunlight.

When they finally emerged, they realized that they were on top of the very walls that had trapped them in the canyon, and all along the top edge of the canyon walls were strange little men and women throwing massive stones down upon the now retreating, disorganized and greatly depleted Shags. And in the sky above, circling and screeing, as though in approval, flew Cleetus and his clan of eagles.

Both Styrax and the Wanderer stood in amazement as they watched the little people casting mighty stones, laughing and cursing loudly as they did so. Indeed, they were small, hardly more than two foot tall, but their heads were very large, almost a quarter of their height, and their skin was the color of bronze. And each and everyone wore a huge hat of straw that seemed more like an umbrella than a hat as it shaded each Dwarf entirely from the sun. Their small bodies were extremely compact and very heavily muscled which made the heaving of the large rocks a seemingly effortless task.

Suddenly, the stone-throwing ceased as a raucous brazen horn sounded from the passageway. The little people, as they turned around, were caught off guard to see such strange creatures as Styrax and the Wanderer staring at them. Slowly, but without fear, they came forward gathering in silence around the equally bewildered Styrax and the Wanderer.

The Wanderer was the first to speak. "Greetings, little people! I am the Wanderer, the servant of the Aged One, and this is my brother in all things, Styrax, King of the Prosopian Elves."

The little people stared for yet a moment but said nothing; then, with a rush, they all ran behind Styrax and rushed down the stairs, disappearing in the darkness. Then, as Styrax and the Wanderer looked at each other in surprise, a booming voice echoed up the stairway, "Enter in peace and friendship or enter not at all. King Jasper awaits you."

They descended the stairs slowly only to find themselves entering a completely different chamber, not nearly as large as the cavern they had first entered but one more richly appointed with benches along the side walls and a throne of gold at the far end. All the little people were seated on the benches, their large straw hats folded in front of them, and the King was upon his raised throne. The Wanderer, with Styrax behind him, walked straight for the throne, at the foot of which he knelt and bowed his head, and Styrax followed his example.

The King stood, looking down at his guests, and spoke in a voice so deep that the flames of the torches seemed to flicker. "I am Jasper, King of the Trolls, the finest warriors in the Dwarfenfold. I opened the walls of stone for your escape from the Shags at the behest of Cleetus, the guardian of our borders. Who are you? And what do you seek in Troll-land?"

"My name is Wanderer and I serve the Aged One who reigns supreme in the land of perpetual snow and ice. This is my boon companion, Styrax, King of the Prosopian Elves. We seek nothing in your land, my Lord, for we did not know of its existence, but we are enroute to the Hill of Light, the home of the Aged One."

"Bring seats for our guests and be quick about it, you clumsy oafs." And instantly upon the King's gruff words, two seats were carried forward. Styrax sat easily, but the Wanderer was too large for the chair offered him, so he sat cross-legged on the floor.

"We are much beholden unto you for saving our lives," said Styrax, "and much amazed at your magical powers in moving stone walls."

"Hah, you dunderhead, speak not to me of magic. The fissure opened by a mechanism of metal gears built by my workers, the finest metal craftsmen in the world. Now tell me why you are green, and why you wear no clothes or hat to protect you from the searing sun. A troll who goes out in daylight is a fool, and if he goes without a hat, he is an imbecile. You have no hat; you have no clothing. Perhaps your mind is weak."

"No, King Jasper, my mind is not weak," Styrax laughed as he spoke. "My people live in the sun. The sun gives us life directly through our skin—for that reason we can wear no clothing. To live as you live, in dark caverns, would be our death. We are green like plants, and like them, we thrive in sunlight."

Shifting his attention to the Wanderer, the King said, "And you, the tall one, are of the race of Man? Have you come to steal Troll gold to satisfy your endless greed? Like most men, do you lust after gold? You are certainly a strange pair, and I wonder if it is safe to allow you to leave the realm of the Trolls. I know of your Aged One, a cranky old fool by my reckoning but harmless and clever, and not like the rest of mankind. May they all be cursed and plagued forever."

"My Lord, we want nothing of the Trolls," said the amused Wanderer. "We seek only to continue our journey to the land of perpetual snow. We thank you, most humbly, for the timely saving of our lives, but our mission is of great import and cannot be delayed. Therefore, I humbly request that we be allowed to continue onward."

Then, from behind a curtain that covered the wall adjacent to the throne, a very stout and dumpy woman stepped forward wearing purple robes and a crown of radiant gold that shimmered in the torchlight. King Jasper instantly stood up, bowed, and offered her his throne. She sat down with hardly a look at King Jasper, smiled at the guests, and spoke softly in a warm voice, "Welcome, Wanderer. And welcome, King Styrax of Prosopia. I am Saphiria, Empress of all Trolls, Dwarfs, Kobolds, Nibelungen, Monacielli, Pitikos and others you know not of. I know of the Aged One, may his name be honored, and of the Elves, and I know of the great struggle yet to come. In Troll-land, you are welcome as honored guests and your journey will continue as soon as the requirements of hospitality have been met. We Trolls are not people of the daytime but people of the night. The sun is fatal to us, as it is life to you. Therefore, we will begin the festivities with nightfall, when we shall celebrate your visit to us and will speak further of your mission. My maidens will show you to your chambers where you may dress your wounds, rest and be refreshed. Until then, my friends and my people, all are dismissed."

The Empress, followed by King Jasper, quickly disappeared behind the curtain, and as quickly the rest of the Trolls disappeared into darkened corridors. Only four young Troll handmaidens remained, and they led Styrax and the Wanderer to the guest chambers.

* * *

Having bathed and dressed their numerous but minor wounds with an effective, earthy-smelling balm given them by the Trolls, Styrax and the Wanderer slept soundly until they were awoken by King Jasper's attendants.

"Arise, alien guests, for the banqueting hour has come upon us. The Empress Saphiria awaits you. The handmaidens will lead the way."

Through seemingly endless corridors, the handmaidens escorted their guests. At times, the darkened passageways seemed to ascend, then to descend, often seeming to turn back upon themselves.

Onyx, one of the handmaidens, explained, "Troll corridors are cleverly designed so that only Trolls can find their way. Many tunnels are dead ends; others have concealed chambers; and still others can be sealed at a moment's notice. In emergencies, entire tunnels disappear and new passages open at Troll command. It is thus that the Trolls have protected themselves against intrusion by Man and other creatures of the outside world." And as she spoke, the passageway before them quickly sealed itself as a huge mass of stone moved effortlessly across the opening. Then, by pressing her hand against an otherwise unremarkable section of the wall, Onyx forced a massive stone to slide open, revealing another corridor leading deeper into the mountain.

"Are there many passageways like this?" Styrax asked in amazement.

"Ho Ho, my green friend, here in Niflheim there are so many they cannot be numbered. By devious routes and seldom-traveled pathways, the Trolls and all their kin have undermined the upper world, which we call Midgard. When the Empress travels the many hundred miles to visit her vassals, the Nibelungen, in the Pinus Mountains, her highness need never to leave the corridors that undermine your world of sunshine and sky."

Then, through ever turning tunnels, they passed into large caverns filled with terraced gardens in which many varieties of mushrooms grew in great abundance.

"These are the Troll gardens that feed our hungry people." The handmaidens spread their arms proudly showing the work of their kin. For, truly, the mushroom gardens, hidden so deep within the earth, astounded the Wanderer and Styrax.

Finally, the corridor opened into a vast cavern brightly lit by hundreds of torches placed in the walls. Softly padded benches, all ornamented with intricate gold tracery, were everywhere, and a great number of Trolls were busy eating the many offerings placed upon a central banqueting table. Here were dishes filled with a great variety of mushrooms prepared in various ways: firstly, there were raw whole mushrooms of every shape and size, some in rich sauces, others not; next were mushrooms baked in stone ovens, smelling of the earth and rich spices and oils; and lastly, and most popular with the Trolls, were fried and braised mushrooms, brown and black, and skewered on batons of gold. Among the mushroom dishes were large bowls filled with roasted lizards, their stiff skins shining in the blaze of the torches, and ever larger bowls of charred bats floating in a pickled broth.

Styrax ate heartily of the mushrooms enjoying the new flavors, for the darkness of the Troll world had slowly drained his energy. But, naturally, he shunned the lizard and bat dishes not wanting even to see them or sit by them. The Wanderer ate everything with great zest, for he too had a great hunger. At the end of the cavern, Troll musicians played upon their brazen horns and drums music of a brash and staccato manner. In front of the musicians, a numerous group of Trolls danced in rhythmic stomping as they held hands in a large circle, shouting at certain marked beats, "Ho-La, Ho-La," in loud, deep voices. Laughter echoed and echoed again throughout the cavern, for this was a joyous occasion, a visit of their Empress and the intrusion of guests from the outer world, visitors the like of which few Trolls had ever seen before.

After eating their fill, Styrax and the Wanderer were led to a side chamber shielded from the laughter and noise in the larger cavern by heavy drapes covered with symmetrical geometric designs, and there they joined with Empress Saphiria and King Jasper.

"Greetings again, my friends. I hope you have found Troll-Land to your liking. I must ask your pardon for the abruptness with which I greeted you earlier," said the Empress. "If it were not for the Wanderer's awesome horn that seemed to shake our granite walls, and the timely warning from Cleetus, Warlord of the Eagle Clan and Lord of the Scarp, you both might now be food for the beastly Shags. We are people of the darkness, shunning the burning sun as toads shun snakes. Do you find all this so strange, King Styrax?"

"To be direct, Empress Saphiria, yes, very strange," Styrax replied. "For to live without the sun is inconceivable to the Elfin Brood. I only wish, now that we are friends, that you knew our land, Prosopia."

"Ah, but I do. I know of Prosopia; I know of King Styrax; and I know of Queen Canna. You are not strangers to us, though we are to you. The Nibelungen, you call them Dwarfs, of the Pinus Mountains are also my subjects, and they have been dealing with the Prosopian Elves of Mesquitana and other Elves for many a year. The Nibelungen hold the Elves in high regard, honoring them for their honesty, simplicity and directness. You see, these virtues the Trolls also honor. These are not the virtues we associate with our common foe, Man the destroyer."

"You spoke of other Elves, Empress. Are there others? We in Prosopia know of only two other self-aware creatures, the Pinus Dwarfs, or Nibelungen, as you say, and Man, and now since I have started on this journey, I know of the Shee and the Trolls. We have often speculated about other tribes of Elves in other lands, but we know of none."

"I know of one other kind of Elf, but there may be many more in lands beyond our ken, for we occupy but a small portion of this vast world. I speak of the Pine Elves who dwell in high mountains where great pine forests grow."

"What are they like? Are they like my people, like me?" Styrax asked with excitement in his voice.

King Jasper answered the questions. "They are like you, and they are unlike you. They have the virtues we have already noted. They are green and

adore the sun. But, unlike you, they are large creatures, much larger than our friend here, the Wanderer. They are solitary and do not live in villages
as do your people. They speak little and silently
guard the great forests. Instead of the blowgun,
the weapon of the Prosopian Elf, the Pine Elf uses
a mighty sling casting stones larger than my large
head. Beyond that, I can say no more, for the Pine
Elf seldom deals with others."

As they thus spoke, a Troll maiden brought in
a flagon of Troll wine made from a curious combination of mushrooms and cactus flowers. She
poured four goblets full before withdrawing.

"Drink carefully," King Jasper warned. "Troll
wine often opens worlds other than our own."

"The Wanderer and I are seeking the Aged One
to gain his sage thoughts concerning the encroachment of Man on our sacred lands," Styrax said as
he stood before King Jasper and Empress Saphiria.
"For reasons we Elves cannot fathom, Man seems
compelled to invade Prosopia and any other land
he sees, bringing death in his wake. My people,
the Elfin Brood, know little of war and violence,
but necessity is a hard master."

"Man is a curse, even unto himself," Jasper
shouted out. "Curse him! If I had my way, he would
be eradicated with joy. For he ever lusts after gold
and the power it gives him though he uses the
gold for naught."

"We, of the Dwarfenfold, worship gold as much
as the Elf worships the sun," Empress Saphiria
observed. "For we realize that the sun itself is the
father of all that lives, but as the sun is injurious
to our physical being, we worship indirectly the
metal that holds the essence of the sun, pure and
radiant gold. But, unlike Man, we use the gold to
make our weapons, our ornaments, and our practi-

cal things like bowls and pitchers, cup and dishes. But, unlike Man, Trolls seldom concern themselves with gold as a source of power over others."

The Wanderer, who until then had remained silent, abruptly asked, "Will you, the Trolls and the other dwarfs, join with the Elves of Prosopia in the mighty struggle that is to come against the unceasing encroachment of Man?"

King Jasper jumped up, holding his goblet before him, and said with great fire, "Aye, we will, for we are a brave and martial people when set upon, and we have long sought allies in the great conflict that Man foists upon us. Curse their gizzards! Happily, I drink to the downfall of the pestilential creature called Man."

Solemnly, they all stood and drank this fatal toast.

"We have made a stern compact, my friends. Many will die before the plague of Man has passed," Empress Saphiria said with sadness in her voice. "We only do that which we must do. Wanderer, I think that I shall accompany you to the realm of perpetual ice and snow, for surely I must speak with the Aged One before I allow my subjects to go to war. Many questions must be answered before I will rest easy."

The Wanderer, surprised by Empress Saphiria's plan to accompany them, said, "A word of caution, Empress. I was directed to bring only King Styrax to the Hill of Light."

"Wanderer, you serve your master as you see fit. But in my decision he has no say, for I go of my own free will, and as Empress of the Dwarfenfold, I need ask no one's permission."

"As you say, Empress, so shall it be," the Wanderer replied. "But another problem is that we must travel by day in lands of fog and bone-chilling cold.

I already have fears for the welfare of my boon companion, Styrax, who has never been beyond the warm lands of Prosopia. I fear the journey may be beyond your strength, your highness."

Empress Saphiria smiled and then spoke, "Surely, you must take me for a fool and a weakling. Never doubt the hardiness of a Dwarf, for we are as sturdy as the stone walls that surround us. I have no intention of trekking across your frozen wastelands. Have you not yet learned of our subterranean genius? We will travel to the Hill of Light beneath the land surface where temperatures never vary, where there are no storms and where there are no enemies. The passageways already exist, and we will carry adequate supplies of life-giving mushrooms to sustain you and King Styrax in the realm of darkness."

The Wanderer, after a moment's pause, agreed heartily, for his fears about Styrax's ability to withstand the rigors of a frigid world were no longer a problem nor had they now to fear Shags or Grendels or the ice creatures who haunted the snowy highlands.

"Then it is settled," said the Empress. "Enjoy the evening, eat boldly and drink deeply. Sleep through the day, and we shall depart at sunset tomorrow. In deference to your fears of my visiting the Aged One unannounced, I will dispense with my retinue and travel alone. A mighty trio we will make, the Wanderer, King Styrax and Empress Saphiria marching through the bowels of the earth."

Later that night, as the Wanderer and Styrax were preparing to sleep, Styrax observed, "The Troll wine is quite strong. Everywhere I look, strange colors flow toward me, as if the very air were alive and full of joy."

"So true, so true. And if I close my eyes, the colors become even more intense and vivid," the Wanderer answered sleepily.

Then later still, as they lay in darkness, Styrax asked, "Wanderer, are you asleep?"

"No, my friend, I am still enjoying the strange effects of the wine."

"Perhaps the wine has me confused," Styrax mused. "But just this moment, everything seems too complicated, too grand in scale, too removed from what I once thought was real. Not too many days ago, I thought my only serious problem was a few cruel men camped across the Rhus. Now, I suddenly find myself in strange lands, attacked by creatures I never dreamed of, befriended by other creatures the like of which I have never known. It is all so un-Elfish to be sitting in council planning for a war on a scale that transcends my limited capacities. Oh, how happy I would be if I were back in Prosopia lying contentedly by the Rhus with Canna snuggled in my arms. Wanderer, is that all gone? Is it gone forever?"

The Wanderer sighed deeply before speaking, "I cannot console you, Styrax, though I wish it were in my power to do so. Yesterday is a myth that beclouds our vision. Yes, the past is gone forever and ever and ever. Canna will still be there and so will Prosopia. Hopefully, we will return, and you will hold Canna in your arms. But it will not be the same again, ever. What is done and gone forever is your innocence, your ensiled view of the vast world around you. It is so much greater than we think, so much grander and so much more fearsome. Do not be overawed by the evil you discover. Remember that though there are Grendels, there are also Shee, and when you think of the beastly Shags, also remember Cleetus and Empress

Saphiria. Friendless, we left Prosopia, but in a short time we have found Fon-du-Fon, Jasper, Cleetus and the Empress. There can be no discord without harmony."

Chapter Nine

Thrett woke to someone violently shaking him.

"Wake up! Wake up! Are you dead? Wake up! Profundus awaits you," the messenger from Profundus shouted.

Thrett sat up slowly, stunned to realize he was still alive. He was further shocked to find himself clean-shaven and dressed in the same scarlet robes of the soldiers who had captured him when he had entered the domain of the Vergers. His mind was still fogged, and he struggled manfully to rid himself of these mists.

"What has happened? Where am I?" Thrett croaked.

The messenger replied amusedly, "Nothing has happened. You were drunk, dead drunk and you smelled bad. We cleaned you, dressed you and carried you to your quarters."

"My quarters?" Thrett rose awkwardly, still tipsy from the drug Profundus had given him. Looking around, he became aware of the richness of his surroundings, so unlike anything he had known as a Beastum. So, I have survived, he thought to himself. All or nothing! All or nothing! I have won the day. As he put on the scarlet boots that awaited him, he tried to get his mind clear. I

have won, he mused, but what have I won? I loathe
Profundus as much as I loathed Vastar, damned
wise men. But Profundus has an army; his men
are, as yet, strong. I must bide my time, and when
I no longer need Profundus, he can be easily dispatched, but, for the moment, he is necessary if
we are to cross the river, and we must cross the
river. Once again, I find myself a lackey to a wise
Man who leads with his tongue and his wits. Oh,
will a time ever come when the strength of a man's
arms will wash away these cursed wise men?

Profundus joined Thrett in the morning meal
which was sumptuous by Beastum standards.
Afterwards, Profundus led Thrett deep into the
center of Greydome where metalworkers plied their
skills amid smoke and fire.

"Here we make our weapons: keen swords,
mighty spears and crossbows of great accuracy.
This is the heart of our strength for few of the tribes
of Man or other creatures have weapons such as
these."

He passed a strong bladed sword to Thrett who
stood back and waved it threateningly through the
air.

"If you like it, it is yours," said Profundus. "Try
another. Test them all and find a blade to your
liking. Take a crossbow; learn to use it; learn to
master it."

Then Profundus led the still amazed Thrett into
a large hall with massive rafters. At one end of the
vast room stood a raised dais upon which stood a
full-sized statue of a scarlet warrior with his sword
drawn and raised above his head as if he were
about to strike.

"Ring the bell," Profundus shouted at a servant standing behind the statue. As the bell began
to toll, Profundus turned to Thrett, looked deeply

in his eyes, and said, "If the foundry is the heart of Greydome, then this temple is its soul."

"I see nothing but a statue and empty seats," Thrett said.

"They will soon be filled. The statue is of our legendary leader, a warrior of the first order," Profundus remarked with a sly look on his face. "What I say now to you must never go further, for herein lies the secret of my power and you had best know it as an unassailable power. Our famed ancestor, Castratus by name, is nothing more than a story I invented in order to build an army without equal in all the lands still doomed by men. Castratus' victories, conquests, adventures and mighty deeds are nothing more than products of my over-ripe imagination. His deathless state is my masterpiece. For men must have heroes to fire their soggy minds and to give themselves paragons on which to model their lives."

And as Profundus spoke, he led Thrett onto the dais. Slowly, the great hall began to fill with large men, all dressed in brilliant scarlet robes. Thrett noticed their massiveness, their huge shoulders and bulging arms, as they silently filled the hall. He also noticed that their faces all had the same expression—no expression at all. None of them spoke or even glanced at the others, they simply filed mechanically to their seats.

"From infancy, I have raised them, giving them the finest food and drink to build strong bodies. In their youth, I emasculated them. From childhood onward, they have daily practiced the martial arts until each and every one of them is a masterful warrior. In the land of the Vergers, they live well, having the best food, the finest weapons and horses, and the finest quarters. They have no fear of death, and, better yet, they have no fear of pain.

Their only goal in life is to attain glory in battle. And they have but one loyalty to Castratus and his high priest, me, Profundus the Guileful, a well-earned title, I think."

"How do you maintain control?" Thrett asked while the hall continued to fill.

"Sit there," Profundus said, pointing to a large chair next to the statue, "and you will see my power."

When the vast room was filled with five hundred scarlet-robed warriors, Profundus mounted the dais and stood directly in front of the statue of Castratus, directly beneath the statue's raised sword. Profundus raised his arms, and instantly the five hundred warriors stood, drew their swords and raised them to the same position as Castratus'.

"All hail Castratus," Profundus intoned three times.

"All hail Castratus," the five hundred answered three times.

"Give us eternal life, Castratus, that we may be heroes in the war-halls of eternity. Give us bread that we be strong. Give us courage that we may conquer. Give us cold hearts that we may not falter. Give us envy that we may despise our enemies. Be seated." Profundus lowered his arms, and the five hundred warriors sat.

Profundus stood before the warriors in silence. The sword held by the statue of Castratus just above Profundus' skull seemed to quiver, then to shake and then with a rush it descended toward the unguarded head of Profundus. And as swiftly as it fell, the sword stopped within an inch of Profundus's flesh. Then, slowly, it rose again to its original position.

"Verger warriors, men of scarlet," Profundus shouted, "last night I had a vision within a dream.

I lay in deep and frightening darkness when the thrice-mighty Castratus came to me in my chambers. He wore his scarlet armor, and his robe glowed the color of fresh blood. With his fearful sword drawn, he stood before me. Within his deep and fearful eyes I saw the war-halls of warriors slain in battle. He said unto me, 'Lord Profundus, this day I have had a wild and fearless warrior brought to you from the arid grasslands. He is a Man of great boldness, my very image in conflict. Too long have the warriors of Castratus stayed within the austere halls of Greydome; too long have their swords lain unused; too long has glory been absent from the arms of the Vergers. Rise up, my people. The time has come to go forth in conquest of new lands and new enemies. Rise up, my people. The wild warrior will lead the way. Rise up, my people. The wild one is with us, a warrior unto death.' With these words, Castratus has spoken."

The warriors instantly stood as one, shouting in mighty voices, "All hail Castratus! All hail Castratus! All hail the wild warrior!"

Profundus continued as his soldiers sat again, "You are to prepare your weapons, organize your servants, and steel your hearts. Within the week, we will go forth under the banner of Castratus and the Vergers. To victory or to death." Then, turning to Thrett, he motioned him to rise. "Here is your leader, the wild warrior Castratus has sent unto us. Here is Lord Thrett the destroyer."

The five hundred leaped to their feet, swords drawn, shouting, "All hail Lord Thrett! All hail Lord Thrett!"

Profundus stepped forward, standing next to Lord Thrett. He bowed his head and said, "Let us pray." Then in deep voices, all spoke in unison:

Hail Castratus, full of hate,

We are with thee.
Thy sword and thy armor grace thee,
For it is ever blessed to slay.
Hail Castratus, full of hate,
We are with thee.
Lead us in thy path,
To conquer or to die.
Hail Castratus, full of hate,
We are with thee.

Then, as the scarlet warriors left the martial hall, each and every one came forward and knelt for a moment before Profundus, Lord Thrett, and the statue of Castratus. In each warrior's mouth Profundus placed a small piece of seared rat meat as he said, "Take of my flesh that you may be strong and vicious." After which each warrior sipped from a chalice Profundus held as he said, "Take of my blood that you may have courage and show no mercy."

When the warriors had all gone, Profundus led Thrett back to his chambers, explaining as they went, "As the warriors are all eunuchs, they have little interest in life other than to conquer. They are the core of my army—fearless and thoughtless they must be led by a stern master. It is for this reason I chose not to poison you. The scarlet warriors are brave and relentless, but as they are emasculated, they seem without imagination and ambition; they are born to be led. You, on the other hand, seem destined to lead or to die and you know but one loyalty, to yourself. You are grasping, treacherous and have bold virtues I feel at peace with, for I too honor them. Remain useful to me, and you shall live well."

"Is there more to the army than the five hundred?" Thrett asked.

"To support the scarlet ones, I have 2,500 foot

soldiers, a pathetic lot, but necessary as servants and, more importantly, as breeding stock for the next generation of warriors."

"And how are the foot soldiers armed?"

"Most carry short spears, and the others are given crossbows but these weapons are issued only on the point of battle, for it would be foolish to allow the rabble to have arms. But, really, they are the feeblest of creatures, especially in battle when they flee in panic at the slightest opposition."

Thrett, who never saw more than fifty men under arms, and they but the rag-tag Beastums, was overawed at the strength and organization of the Verger army but mostly at his position as their leader. After a moment, he asked, "Are the foot soldiers good breeding stock? The Beastums have fewer and fewer children, and most of those they do have die in infancy."

"Aye, Lord Thrett, you have struck on the weakness that plagues all men. With each generation, over the centuries, we have fewer and fewer offspring and most of them are born deformed. I feed the foot soldiers well and minister to their needs, and, by pampering them, I can expect one reasonably fit child for every five mated pairs. Just enough to maintain my scarlet warriors, though when I cull out the weaklings and the thinkers, I am often forced to raid the peasantry for fat, healthy male children. But the peasants are vanishing slowly, not reproducing themselves adequately. Vergerland, as you have already said, and that boldly, is dying as is most of the race of men. I do not want to conquer new lands for pleasure, though there is great pleasure in conquest; I wish to conquer new lands in the hope that unravished fields and virgin wilderness will refructify our tired race, to return to the glories of the legendary past."

"I know little of the past," Thrett said firmly, "and I care little for the future, whether Man lives or dies. I wish to lead; I wish to conquer; I wish to bask in glory, even if for only a moment."

After a slight pause, Profundus said, "No doubt you will have your glory for whatever that is worth and hopefully for more than a moment. But tell me more of these new lands—what they are like and who inhabits them."

Thrett sat by the fire in Profundus' chamber as he spoke. "The lands are vast, having great plains full of game. From our side of the river, along the arid grasslands, I could see great herds of deer and antelope roaming free beyond the unending mesquite thickets and other dense growth that line the river and the lowlands. In the distance, great, towering mountains covered in timber rise, but what is beyond the mountains, I know not. The mesquite lowlands are inhabited by creatures called Yellfens, small, green beings shaped like men. I know little of them but they seem to be few in number, and seem to live in isolation from each other, for I espied no towns or villages. I do not think they are organized; I do not think they are war-like; and I do not think they present anything more than a momentary annoyance. The Beastums, who know no more of the Yellfens than I do, seem to think these little green creatures would serve as a new source of food, if there were enough of them. The river is the major problem; it has a fierce and unabating current and few crossings. I know of but one."

Profundus opened an aged, dust-covered book and showed Thrett an illustration depicting an Elf. "This is what you call Yellfen, a creature whose name is not Yellfen but Elf."

"Then you know of these little green people?" Thrett asked.

"I know but little and that little comes from rumor and peasant tales. The Elves are ancient creatures, the first born, older even than Man. They once held dominion everywhere there were forests, but as Man emerged and destroyed the great forests, the Elves vanished. Some say they now sleep through the ages, awaiting the annihilation of Man, their perpetual enemy. Others claim they are creatures of the sea to which they returned upon the coming of Man. And still others claim that they are nothing more than diminutive and crafty men. It is said they are wise and shrewd and capable of magic, but I hold no truck with magic or the fools who believe in it. The only magic I know of is a strong sword in the hands of a scarlet warrior. We must not underestimate them, though they seem hardly adequate rivals, or even a challenge to my army."

With that, Profundus led Thrett to a narrow window from which they could see an open courtyard below them. Wagons were being diligently loaded with provisions and arms; foot soldiers were preparing their heavy packs; and scarlet warriors were tending their massive horses.

Standing back from the window, Profundus looked directly into Thrett's eyes, saying, "Who knows what you have set afoot, Lord Thrett, but now there can no longer be any doubt, the war has started."

Chapter Ten

The tunneling of the Dwarfs was truly remarkable, astounding both Styrax and the Wanderer. Cleverly, the Dwarfs had built traps in the lengthy corridors, yawning bottomless pits that were unseen in the darkness, rock-falls that were triggered by the lightest footfall and nests of poisonous spiders that were released upon the unwelcome intruder. On occasion, the tunnels intersected huge natural caverns with resting places stocked with wood for fires and the making of torches. Despite the traps and snares, the pits and the spiders, all of which the Empress knew of, they made good time, for the corridors were smooth and dry and went straight to the destination. Here, within the tunnels, were no rocky canyons, no scarps, no dense underbrush and no foul weather and, more importantly, no Grendels, no Shags and no men. The dried mushrooms they carried were more than adequate as sustenance, and Styrax, though denied sunlight, had little trouble maintaining his strength. On the third day, Empress Saphiria led Styrax and the Wanderer into a hidden side passage that slowly rose toward the earth's surface and grew colder and colder as they ascended.

Finally, the Dwarf tunnel opened into a large

wind cave and the outer world. Styrax, whose shivering was beyond his control, stood in amazement and fear, gazing out upon a dazzlingly austere and frigid land of jagged rock formations shrouded in ice and snow. The sky was overcast, a dull, slate gray and nowhere was there a shrub or weed or tree or flower, though in the near distance, obscured in ice fog, something seemed to be glowing, though faintly.

"The glow that you see, Styrax, is the Aged One's dwelling where we will find warmth and welcome," the Wanderer said, knowing how difficult and painful the cold was to his sun-worshipping companion.

Empress Saphiria, gathering her great robes tightly around herself, said, "We must move on quickly. This bone-chilling cold is beyond my strength."

And from an ornate satchel she was carrying with her, the Empress withdrew a fleecy robe and gave it to Styrax. Quickly, he wrapped himself within its folds, trying desperately to generate some warmth.

Slowly, they made their way toward the dwelling of the Aged One, struggling over slippery ice and through deep drifts of snow, stumbling and falling frequently because of the unstable footing.

"Why does the Aged One choose to live here in this barren, inhospitable place?" Styrax asked with anger in his voice. "This is a lifeless, accursed land."

"For that very reason," the Wanderer replied, "because it is barren and frigid and lifeless, because here the Aged One finds peace from the prying and envious world."

"Who would envy this cruel land?" the Empress asked.

"None envy this world, but many covet what

he has done with it," was the Wanderer's answer.

As they drew closer and closer, the glow revealed itself to be a large hill made of multiple sheets of thick ice so interlocked as to create a vast irregular dome from within which the light radiated. As they approached the dome itself, two massive ice sheets slid in opposite directions leaving an opening just large enough for them to enter into a small room. The ice sheets closed after them and had no sooner closed than other ice sheets in the opposite wall opened. As they entered, their senses were stunned to see a tropical setting, as if they had suddenly entered into a jungle. The air was warm and moist, and everywhere plants grew in abundance—trees, shrubs, ferns, cacti and flowers. Styrax was filled with joy as he felt the warmth and his body felt the strong light that radiated downward from the towering icy walls that enclosed them. Quickly, he threw off the fleecy robe and returned it to the Empress. He was much beholden for the robe had protected him, but now that he was warm again, he was glad to cast it off, it seemed so unnatural to him to wear another creature's skin. The greenery was so dense that they could not see more than thirty feet in any direction, but they did notice small graveled paths leading into the undergrowth.

"I have heard of the magical powers of the Aged One," Saphiria whispered, as though she were afraid to break an enchanted spell, "and now I know of what is spoken."

"There is no magic here," the Wanderer said in reply.

"Where then is the Aged One's palace?" Saphiria asked.

"He has no palace, Empress," the Wanderer answered. "Only his garden which we are in now."

"He has no palace?" the Empress questioned, amazed. "The Aged One has no palace? How can that be? Is he not a great Man? No castle? That seems absurd. With his power, with his magic, he should have a castle without peer."

"He is content in his garden. He seeks no more," the Wanderer answered.

Beckoning the others, The Wanderer led them along a path that went deeper into the fantastic greenery. Styrax, his eyes wandering aimlessly, noticed that no two trees, no two bushes, no two flowers were alike, and that all the plants were well-advanced in their life cycle, that there were no young plants, no saplings, no new shoots rising from the rich earth. In the branches, colorful birds, unknown to Styrax, in brilliant red, greens and blues flew from tree to tree, and as the path turned he suddenly spied a small group of slender deer drinking from a flowing brook. The deer paid them no heed.

As they entered a small open glade by a waterlily-filled pond, a tall, glowingly beautiful woman with flaxen hair and in flowing white robes stepped toward them.

"Welcome to the Hill of Light, Empress Saphiria, monarch of the Dwarfenfold, and King Styrax of the Prosopian Elves. And a special welcome to my beloved."

And before Styrax knew what was happening, the beautiful woman ran forward into the waiting arms of the Wanderer. Both the Empress and Styrax stood by awkwardly as the embrace seemed to radiate musical warmth and long restrained love. For many moments, the lovers cleaved to each other, lost to their surroundings. Then the Wanderer turned and brought the woman to his companions, saying, "This is SHE, my beloved, the mate of my soul."

SHE bowed and offered her slender hand to both Saphiria and Styrax, and her smile went into their hearts. SHE led them to a simply-made table upon which were placed fruits and mushrooms unlike any either Saphiria or Styrax had ever seen before. SHE poured them wines that sparkled like diamonds. "Here you must rest and find joy, for I have no other care than to please you."

Styrax, thinking of Canna as he stared at SHE, muttered, "I hardly know what to say. I am bedazzled by this place, by your beauty, by everything here."

"You are my guest, King Styrax. You speak of my beauty, but you think of another. Canna is her name."

"But how did you know?" Styrax asked as though stunned.

The Wanderer laughed gently, then said, "Be careful, my friends, for SHE knows your feelings before you do. You need not speak; you need not gesture. Simply think of wanting something and SHE will give it to you. Think of a question and SHE will answer. Think of sadness, and SHE will cry."

Empress Saphiria, tasting the mushrooms, said, "What then am I thinking now, my Lady?"

Smiling happily, SHE answered, "The Empress Saphiria is wise, for she asks the only questions I cannot answer. You wish to know why the Aged One, my father, is not here to welcome you and whether he is aware that you have come without being asked or whether he knows you are here in the first place. I am sorry, Empress, I cannot answer questions dealing with my father, for though I can sense the thoughts of all other beings, I cannot penetrate the maze of my father's mind. He will see you when he chooses and if he chooses.

That is all I can say."

Styrax, enjoying the wines, was about to ask a question, but SHE saved him the effort, saying, "You wish to know how old my father is because he once met with your grandfather. Again as your question deals with the Aged One, I cannot answer directly. My father is very old, very, very old, and his age cannot be numbered in years as the lives of others are. My father is my father, my grandfather and my great grandfather. On that matter, I can say no more. Deeper explanation only he can give."

While SHE spoke, Empress Saphiria fell into a deep sleep, and shortly thereafter so did Styrax.

"I have given them a restful wine, my love," SHE whispered in the Wanderer's ear, "now they will sleep deeply for many hours, gaining the rest they need after so long a journey. Now we will be together. Does that not answer your question?"

Smiling, the Wanderer picked up SHE in his arms and carried her away.

* * *

Styrax was awoken from his blissful sleep by someone gently kicking his foot. As he opened his eyes, he saw the Aged One for the first time for who else could he be? The Aged One was aptly name: his body was almost doubled over; his hands were long and bony, and shook continually; his face was so deeply wrinkled that his eyes and mouth were hard to distinguish amid the many shriveled folds of flesh. He spoke in a strained, gasping whisper, as though each word he managed to utter was to be his last.

"Eh, eh, be quiet, eh, quiet, don't wake her, eh, eh." He gestured shakily toward the still sleeping figure of Empress Saphiria. "Eh, eh, I will deal with her later, eh, eh." And with gestures, the Aged One indicated that Styrax was to follow him, and he stumbled off uncertainly along a barely noticeable path into the dense undergrowth.

Styrax, confused and still not fully awake, followed the decrepit figure, fearing that the old Man would collapse at his next step. Slowly, they moved through denser and denser undergrowth until they reached a small clearing with a large table in the center upon which was a single sheet of paper and a single ebony pen.

"Eh, eh, young Styrax, eh, do not speak as yet, eh, eh. Later, in council, eh, eh, we will speak, eh, eh. Now you must, eh, eh, write down five questions, eh, eh, five questions that I will answer, eh, eh. Think deeply, eh, eh, for I will answer, eh, eh, no more than five, eh, eh."

"But I cannot write," Styrax blurted out.

"Eh, eh, no matter, no matter, eh, eh. Pick up the pen, eh, eh, and it will write, eh, eh, whatever you are thinking, eh, eh. Do not be afraid, eh, eh."

Styrax walked to the table and stood in front of the blank sheet of paper wondering what to do next.

"The pen, eh, eh, the pen."

As Styrax sat and picked up the pen, fumbling with it, the Aged One, all of a sudden, straightened up his decrepit body and stood towering over Styrax. Then with a swiftness that seemed impossible for so ancient a being, he leaped past the bewildered Elf and bounded into the undergrowth, disappearing instantly.

Styrax sat in awe shaking his head as if to wake himself, though he knew he was already wide awake. As he stood with the pen in hand, he felt a pulsing energy generating from the pen itself. Carefully, he bent over the table and placed the point of the pen on the paper, and in amazement he watched as the pen wrote:

1. Who Are You?
2. Who Is The Wanderer?
3. What Has Happened To Man?
4. Who Am I?
5. What Are The Stars?

Styrax dropped the pen and stepped back quickly. Surely, these were the questions he wished to ask, questions that haunted him, but they had not entered his mind as he stood with the pen in his hand. The pen had extracted the questions from him without his knowing it. Still wanting to ask detailed questions about the coming conflict, he stepped forward, picked up the pen again, pressed it to the paper, and nothing happened. He dragged the pen point across the paper, pressing down firmly, but it left no mark at all.

The Wanderer then appeared, saying, "Quickly, Styrax, follow me. The Aged One is waiting."

Styrax, still dumbfounded, followed his noble companion.

The council was held by a small, rippling stream, and the Aged One, SHE, the Wanderer, Empress Saphiria and Styrax sat on conveniently placed large stones on either side of the sparkling stream.

The Aged One, again bent over, was the first to speak. "So wicked men have finally found, eh, eh, the hidden realms of the Shee, the Dwarfs and the Elves, eh, eh. You are coming of age, my children, eh, eh. Reality is intruding, eh, eh, into your isolated lands, eh, eh. You must prepare, eh, eh."

"But how are we to fight the onslaught of men in hordes beyond our reckoning?" Empress Saphiria asked.

"Eh, eh, I cannot tell you what to do, eh, eh.

Only, what not to do, eh, eh. Do not meet Man on his terms, eh, eh. Your people, the Dwarfs, are known, eh, eh, for their feats of arms, eh, eh. But do not confront, eh, eh, the armies of men in the field, eh, eh. You must fight, eh, eh, as do the Shee, stealthily and mercilessly, eh, eh."

"Will we be victorious?" the Empress asked.

"Eh, eh, if I knew I would not tell you, eh, eh. If I said yes, eh, eh, you would become overconfident, eh, eh, reckless and daring, eh, eh. If I said no, eh, eh, you would become desperate, eh, eh, and vengeful, eh, eh. But, truly, eh, eh, I do not know, eh, eh."

"How long must this madness go on?" Styrax asked, not really expecting an answer.

"As long as there are men, eh, eh, the killing will go on, eh, eh. Man is without harmony, eh, eh, without constraint. His curse is in his nature, eh, eh."

"But you are a Man," Styrax protested.

"And the Wanderer is a Man," Empress Saphiria added, "but a true friend to the Elf and Dwarf."

The Aged One looked at the Wanderer and seemed to smile, though his wrinkled flesh made it impossible to be sure. "Aye, I am a Man, eh, eh. Aye, the Wanderer, eh, eh, is a Man. Use us, eh, eh, for we are your friends, eh, eh, but, remember, we are always men. Our path, eh, eh, is already chosen, eh, eh."

The Aged One sat back taking deep breaths while holding his hands against his chest. No one spoke until the Aged One continued, "But do not judge us, eh, eh, as you would other men, eh, eh. We have heard the knell, eh, eh, and abide with it, eh, eh. They hear it not, eh, eh, and struggle on for they know no better, eh, eh. Time grows short, eh, eh. My strength is waning, eh, eh."

"Have you no magic, no fantastical weapon, no arcane power to…"

The Aged One interrupted the Empress, seemingly annoyed and weary. He stood up shakily, "Enough, eh, eh, for I must tend to my garden, eh, eh. There is no magic, Empress, eh, eh. I sent for King Styrax, eh, eh, to answer his questions, eh, eh, but I did not send for you, eh, eh. Listen carefully, eh, eh, to my parting words, eh, eh. Organize, plan, think, eh, eh, use your minds, eh, eh; you have little else, eh, eh; fight valiantly, eh, eh. The council has ended, eh, eh."

The Aged One walked away, slowly and painfully.

As he departed, SHE brought five envelopes to Styrax, saying, "Here are the answers to your questions, King Styrax."

"But how can that be? I only put them on paper a moment or two before we met here."

"Have you not yet learned?" SHE asked softly. "He answers questions before they are asked. The letters I have just given you were written months ago. He must now return to his garden, for in that which he gives life, he finds life. Do not be angry, Empress Saphiria, if you think my father was abrupt. He seldom speaks, for his life is waning. He ever holds the Dwarfenfold in his heart knowing the Dwarf's valor and honesty. Now, you must go, for time is short, and the foe swarms toward war. Harmony be with you."

Part Two

The Letters

to you in understanding your enemy in the coming struggle. For Man, despite his fatal weaknesses, was capable of creating great and lasting beauty, much of which has already been revealed to you in the works I have given you, and much more will be revealed in times to come. All the books you have been given thus far have been stories, for Elfin lore and Elfin thinking are always expressed in story form. Though Man has found many varied methods to express his thought, none approach his story-telling ability for the expression of deep thought and the comprehension of the dilemma of time. For this reason I will answer your questions in story form.

Who am I? That in itself is unimportant for I no longer am a person but simply a tool you are forced to use. I am the Aged One, the eldest and wisest of my kind, the son and twin brother of my father, the grandson, son and twin brother of my grandfather. My age is beyond your reckoning and is of little matter. I am wise beyond your reckoning, knowing things which should not be known, for some knowledge is utterly worthless and causes pain without insight, and disrupts the governing harmonies. From this learning, you shall be absolved, and I will take it with me in the end. I continue to live on to complete my chosen task, my destiny, in which the Elfin Brood plays a major role. Heed well what I write, King Styrax, for your very existence and the continued existence of self-awareness depend upon it.

Many, many centuries ago, how many you need not know, in the time of man's ultimate ascendancy at the dawn of the second millennium, there was a Man called Goodman, renowned in the sciences. The sciences are the studies of Man through which he hoped to understand the physical world.

In this he failed, and failed ignominiously. For Man did not so much wish to understand nature as he wished to control it. Goodman had a wife and two children, but they were taken from him, and he was imprisoned. Once he escaped, he no longer dealt with his own kind, lest they imprison him again. Goodman was not a happy being, for he saw that the ways of Man had been corrupted by his power, or seeming power, over nature. Goodman saw the coming decline and ultimate extinction of Man and, sadly, realized that nothing could be done to alter this course, for Man had become the victim of the very sciences through which he hoped to escape death. Goodman's special field of study in the sciences was genetic engineering, a study that dealt in the manipulation of basic mechanical natural laws through which the nature of nature could be altered. Realizing the hopeless state of Man, he rebelled against his own people and became a thief. With each day, he stole more and more of the scientific instruments and equipment necessary to his skills. He also pilfered the great libraries of man's finest works of science, literature, art and music. You must realize that Goodman suffered terribly in having to steal, but as an outcast, he had no other choice. He also knew that the very books he stole were read less and less frequently—often not at all. For, truly, one of the great ironies of Man is his willful disregard for learning. The more free he became, the more time he had at his disposal, the less he read and the less he thought. He, thinking himself master of all he surveyed, could find no reason to continue thinking, to continue seeking for the essence of life. With infinite patience, Goodman moved the stolen items to this inhospitable land where, for many years, he built this vast and imposing structure, the Hill of Light, within which we now are. In effect, he carried all of man's learning, all of his intellectual achievements, and all of his expressions of beauty to the land of perpetual ice and snow. And there he worked for many hundreds of years even as his people entered the final and irrevocable pattern of decline. But he worked on in isolation, working against the relentlessness of time.

Goodman was a sagacious Man. He knew that the task he had assigned himself could not be accomplished within the span of a man's life; he had so much to do and so little time. Therefore, his first goal was to extend his own life span by special exercises and diets, by altering his environment and by chemically changing his own life processes. By careful experimentation, he developed a method by which he first doubled, then tripled his own already exceptional intelligence. This was the first milestone. But, though he had extended his life and increased his mental powers, he still grew old and feeble, and his chosen task was hardly yet begun. He needed a successor, someone to continue and expand the process he had begun. He searched the world over for a suitable heir, an honest and intelligent Man, but man's decay had already set in, and he could find no one ethically and intellectually fit for the demands of the work to be done. Finally, and this became the second milestone, he manipulated his own genetic structure and impregnated a woman he had taken in with his chemically altered seed. Within the allotted period, a son was born, but a son unlike any the world had ever known, for his son was a perfect duplicate of his father, looking exactly as the father had in his infancy and youth, and having inherited the father's extended life scale and the father's expanded intelligence. Goodman stood in awe of his creation, for there was no thought the father had that the son did not also have in the same instant. When the father discovered something new, the son was aware of it at the same time, even if he was hundreds of miles away. They had no need to speak to each other, for each knew the other's thoughts and each desired exactly the same things. It was thus that the father had created a son and identical twin brother at the same time. When Goodman finally died, his age was beyond a thousand years. He died peacefully and happily, knowing his work would continue exactly as he had planned, for it could be no other way, as in his death he lived on in his duplicate, his perpetuated being, his son.

Goodman's son eventually came to be called the Aged One by the occasional men who worked for him, and the name Goodman was intentionally forgotten. The son, without pause even for mourning, continued the father's chosen task, bringing it to its first fruition. The son lived longer than the father, and, as his end grew near, he did as his father had done and had a son engineered chemically to be exactly like his father, and, therefore, exactly like his grandfather. I am that son; I am that son, that father, and that grandfather, and I am over fifteen hundred years old. You ask who I am, King Styrax, and now you know. I am Goodman.

I have not spoken of my chosen task intentionally, for I hate repeating myself when there is so little time. The task will be clearly outlined when I answer another of your questions. I do not give you detailed knowledge of my achievements, for that form of knowledge, the sciences, which I have made my life by, is evil. My faint hope is that from

who called themselves the Coursers, a name derived from their exceptional ability with horses. The Coursers had no peers, for they were the swiftest of the swift and the boldest of the bold. Their leader or chieftain or King, for he held no title, was Profundus, often called the 'shrewd' or the 'guileful,' a Man of profound evil, who now leads the Scarlet Five Hundred and dominates Greydome and the land of the Vergers. Though he had many sons by many wives, the only one to survive his childhood was named Ravager and was trained from infancy onward to be a ruthless soldier and the leader of warriors. As a child, and as a Man, he surpassed all other children in feats of arms, showing implacable disdain to those he defeated and loathing for those who cried for mercy. Profundus, a Man of infinite ambition, had deep plans for his son, Ravager, but he reckoned not on his son's independence of spirit and devotion to his mother. It so happened that Profundus, weary of Ravager's mother, attempted to bring another, younger woman into his home. When the wife protested justly, he ordered his henchmen to slay her, and they did that very evening. Ravager, at that time, was campaigning in the south against the Vergers, a tribe weakened by the death of their king. When he returned victorious, Profundus told him his mother had died from the wasting disease. But, later, one of her handmaids told Ravager the truth. In a rage, he attacked his father, lusting for his blood. He threw Profundus to the ground, raised his sword, and was about to kill him when something deep within his warrior's mind cried out for negation of everything he had ever known. In the blindness of his rage, he sensed the horror of killing his own father. He trembled with his sword in hand: he wished to smite: he lusted for blood, for vengeance; yet, he struck not. Profundus, quick to realize his son's inner confusion, escaped and immediately fled to the south, never to see his son again.

Ravager, now King of the Coursers, led his warriors to a great succession of victories, driving his enemies to greater and greater fear and anger. He took a wife, and she bore him three children, a son and two daughters, of whom he was rightly proud, for most of his fellow men were overjoyed if they had at least one child—impotency still plagued Man. He took great pride in his offspring and spent many happy hours with them, for with healthy children he felt the future secure, the world seemed in order. Though still a dauntless warrior, he began to question the endless and often pointless killing his tribe indulged in happily. He began to long for a better land; he longed for peace; he longed for a more just world within which his children could find joy in something other than destruction.

But Ravager's past martial successes proved to be his downfall. The many tribes he had defeated now joined together in a vast array and marched upon the land of the Coursers. Undaunted, Ravager gathered his warriors together and led them against his mighty enemies. The battle was long and fierce, with each side gaining and losing the initiative, with each side losing hordes of men. Finally, from defeat, Ravager gained victory, for in a pitched battle, he feigned retreat, leading his foes deeper and deeper into a trap from which there was no escape. All day and all night, they fought on until Ravager's enemies were annihilated to a Man. His victory was so complete that he thought there were no longer enemies to fear. But as he and his remaining victorious warriors came within sight of their homes, they were stunned to see nothing but smoldering ruins and ash where once stood their proud dwellings, for while they had fought in the north, the Vergers from the south, under the leadership of Profundus who knew the Coursers were engaged in a distant battle, had attacked and destroyed their homes, their families and their village. Ravager's son died with his sword in hand; his wife and daughters were ravished, then slain.

To Ravager, it seemed as though night had fallen, never to cease. How empty his victories seemed; how joyless his life had become; how foolish it seemed to continue living. He left his village and wandered in the foothills, savagely attacking anything or anyone he met caring not whether he lived or died. At night he sat beneath the cold and indifferent stars, wretched, weary, defeated in his soul. His wife, his children, all gone, victims of the insanity of endless warfare. He stared at the stars, and they mocked him for his bloodlust. No longer did he want revenge; no longer did he want power over others, no longer did he wish to be among his own people. Deep within his being, he felt and welcomed the grasping tentacles of death. Slowly, ponderously, painfully, he became aware of the pointlessness of Man's existence, the futility of bloody struggles that led nowhere, except to even bloodier combats. His life was bereft of meaning, he thought, though, in actuality, he was thinking, for the first time, of life having meaning. He thought of killing himself, but even that seemed senseless. When he returned to his men, he was an altered being, and he failed to meet their demands for revenge, for blood to pay for blood. He simply went into his tent and ignored the pleas of his people. Without his leadership, the Coursers grew disorganized and suffered frequent losses in battle. In a short time, his once loyal warriors began to plot his overthrow and his death but only in secret, for they yet feared the might of his arm.

Finally, some of his own men turned on him while others remained loyal. These two factions attacked each other as Ravager stood aside, bitterly amused, hoping to see them all slain. As he was rushed upon by three warriors, he simply sat on the ground, covering his bare head with his arms, longing to feel the coldness of steel smashing into his skull.

At that moment, I interfered by throwing my cloak of invisibility over his wretched form. The warriors raged on, more angry and frustrated by his sudden disappearance. Eventually, the two factions destroyed each other, and the mighty tribe of Coursers, the swiftest warriors of the plains, vanished from the realm of the living to the deaths they had so laboriously earned.

You see, my friend Styrax, I had been watching Ravager for a long time. His troubled mind first attracted me, for I sensed the smothered remains of Man's goodness buried deep in his warrior's soul. I took him with me to the Hill of Light. He followed like a mindless brute, just tagging along, looking neither to the left nor to the right, speaking not at all, and eating only what I forced upon him. In my mind, I feared that I was too late, that his despair was final. For many days, I tried to teach the pulsing center of Ravager's being, but he simply sat there like a stone unaware of everything I said and did. In disgust, I thought of a potion that would give him peaceful death, for that was all he wanted. And that I would have done had I not noticed SHE staring intensely at the forlorn figure of Ravager. Finally, I gave him into the care of SHE, who senses all things.

Styrax, we have come halfway in the story of the Wanderer, a tale that must seem strange to your Elfin mind. But now I hesitate, I pause in wonderment, for what I must tell you now is stranger still, so strange as to bring into doubt even my understanding of nature. Now, we must go back to the time of man's ascendancy, to the time of Goodman.

My grandfather, Goodman, as he was known in those ancient years, traveled widely in acquiring, I should say stealing, the tools and instruments he would need to build the Hill of Light and to pursue his self-appointed task. In his perambulations, he found a sickly female infant, abandoned, no doubt, because of her physical infirmity, a disease that usually proved fatal. A Man of gentle nature who had no love of aloneness, he carried the child to the Hill of Light and tried with all his considerable skill to cure the child of her affliction. But he had little success, the illness being inborn. He found, after much tribulation, that though he could find no cure, he could arrest the advance of the disease by the use of a chemical he had derived from frogs, a chemical which allowed the child to live on in a suspended state of being not far removed from a coma. He found that if the child existed for a month in the coma-like state, she then was able to live normally for a week before her strength waned after which, she would be returned to the suspended state of living, a state my grandfather called half-life. And in this fashion, a long trance-like period followed by a short active period, he raised the young child as his own. In the artificial atmosphere and totally manipulated environment of the Hill of Light, the child thrived and proved a great boon to Goodman who often suffered from the loneliness of self-imposed isolation. But, though the child was now hale, her biological rhythms were inevitably altered. Alive, in our sense of the word, she was but one-fourth of the time; the rest was a death-like trance. She matured very slowly, reaching the flower of womanhood in her hundredth year. In her waking periods, she became my grandfather's assistant and part of his continuing experimentation, for she proved a woman of exceptional intelligence and loyalty. It was about the time of her coming of age that Goodman began to realize that the young woman had the unique ability to understand another's thought directly, from mind to mind. In fact, she often knew another's thoughts before he himself was aware of them. This talent seems to be the result of her long trances in which she stores up her psychic energy, for when she is in her waking state, her mind is active beyond that of normal beings. My grandfather, my father and I have the same ability, but ours springs from our intellects for in living so long, we have come to know how Man will behave. But she possessed the same skill from the moment she came to the Hill of Light.

As you have, no doubt, guessed by now, King Styrax, the infant grew into the woman we now call SHE, who, without aging, outlived my grandfather and my father, and, if you look at me now, SHE has the ability to outlive me also. But to return to Goodman and our story. When my grandfather realized that his very long life was coming to a close and when he conceived of creating a son exactly like himself, he created by scientific means an altered form of his own seed and planted it within SHE. For five years, SHE carried my father in her womb. After my father was born and grew to maturity, SHE became his assistant, and they both continued working on the task chosen by Goodman. When my father reached old age, he repeated his father's experiments, again implanting the altered seed within her body, and, again, after five years, a child was born. I am that child. SHE, in conventional terms, is my mother, and as I deal with her as my father and grandfather did, she is also my daughter, therefore, SHE is my mother and my daughter and lastly, my assistant in the great task. As a woman, she has served every function but that of a mate or wife, for we my grandfather, my father, and I are sexually impotent, a result of our altered natures. From infancy on, these many thousands of years, SHE has lived on within the Hill of Light, blissful, serene and loving, and, with her strange manner of living, it is unlikely SHE can live anywhere else but within the shelter of the Hill of Light.

Now to return to the Wanderer. As you recall, I brought the Wanderer, or Ravager as he was then known, here to the Hill of Light and gave him into the care of SHE. Gradually, during her waking periods, SHE returned him from the senselessness of despair. With gentle patience and womanly devotion, she taught Ravager the simplest forms of harmony in bird song, in flower coloration, and in the ebb and flow of simpler living things. As years passed, they studied the busy ant, the rapacious mantis, the ever-hungry locust. From these simple things and from her delicate but persevering devotion, Ravager slowly came back to life, struggling manfully to drive the evil of his past into oblivion, trying relentlessly to become a part of the new world SHE had penned to him. We ceased to call him Ravager, changing his name to Wanderer, a name fit for the role I had chosen for him. But to change from a Man of war to a Man of peace was not easy, for one cannot that easily erase the past. Yet, within the natures of all self-aware creatures lies a remedy that transcends the limits of knowledge, a remedy that seems to have a life of its own. For in the inescapable closeness between SHE and the Wanderer grew love. I stood in awe of their growing love, of their tenderness and of their passion. I stood in awe because I lacked the feelings and sensations inherent in sexual love. SHE was a woman thousands of years old, older than my father, and the Wanderer was barely thirty years of age. And as their love grew in intensity, he slowly put his past into the past, and his sense of harmony and balance in all things grew apace. Gradually, he came to know HRMNFTHSPHRS, the patterns that govern all life and are that life. In her love, a love that had lain asleep for hundreds upon hundreds of years, he found the balm to soothe the anguish of his past life and the stimulant to energize him in a new life.

And now we must concern ourselves with the Wanderer's duties, that which I brought him to the Hill of Light to accomplish. When I was young and capable of traveling throughout the land, I needed no assistance, but as decrepitude came upon me I needed someone to visit the lands and people I could no longer attend to. For I govern, in the strictest sense, all that exists within my realm, and in governing I must know that which I rule. The general sense of individual joy and suffering I gain through SHE's ability to sense all things. It was SHE who informed me of the torment of Ravager, of his immediate pain and of the deeper troubles of his mind, his questioning, his soul-searching. But I need to know specific things: how and what creatures eat; how they survive in hostile conditions; how carefully they husband their resources; how they share responsibilities; and, of most importance, how they deal with creatures different from themselves. From small particular things, great things can be known. Through the Wanderer, I have learned, and marveled at, Thuja's ability to speak with creatures other then Elves, of his friendship, the essence of harmony, with Ulmus the chaparral. Through the Wanderer, I know of Fon-du-Fon, the Shee, and their silken nets, of the Nibelungen and their golden horns, and of the Trolls and their hidden tunnels and caverns. Thus is the Wanderer appropriately named, for he roams the world over, seeing that I may see, hearing that I may hear. Rarely do I leave the Hill of Light, for the rigors of the outside world prove too stern for my aged frame. The Wanderer's task is to know of all the self-aware beings other than Man to aid them in their need, to teach them in their ignorance, and to guide them in their blindness of the larger world around them. He is an intermediary between the Hill of Light and the world it dominates. And lastly, his task is to watch the ever-continuing depredations of Man, such as the attack upon Prosopia by the Beastums. That I know so much of the Elves is largely due to the work of the Wanderer; that you are here now, reading my letters, is his work; that you, the Elves, are favored above others is partially due to his reports. When he leaves the Hill of Light to travel abroad, SHE lies down among the silken grasses, in half-life, awaiting the Wanderer's return, and awakening when he does.

The Wanderer is my assistant, my friend and my adopted son. Willingly, he shares my doom. For you, he is a companion beyond value, a steadfast friend, ally and guardian to the Elfin Brood.

Chapter Thirteen
What Has Happened To Man?

My Dear King Styrax,

Now, my friend, you bring me to the question I least like to answer, the question that brings me the greatest agony. For no matter how long I live, or how long my father and grandfather lived, I am still a Man. You have seen what Man has become, and if you judge him harshly, I fully understand your reasoning, for of all the self-aware creatures, Man is the most degraded. But in my ever-so-long memory and in my knowledge of the very short history of Man, I am occasionally aware of a being who at rare moments stepped beyond the pale of his limitations and soared among the stars.

For centuries, my grandfather, my father and I have tried to fathom the question of what went wrong with Man, of how this once noble creature came to his ignominious present state. With all our insight and with all our erudition, we have come to but one conclusion: Man was flawed from the beginning, from the moment of his acquisition of self-awareness, as though he was a creature born under an irrevocable curse. Born into a harmonious world, he brought cacophony and disharmony. Perhaps the first of the self-aware beings, despite the Elfin claim to be the first born, he was a creature of reason and emotion, but, in some fiendish way, his reason was ever subject to his emotions and his feelings, an initial imbalance. Herein was the fatal flaw. For all creatures who lack self-awareness are guided by impulse: to eat, to drink, to attack, to escape to live on for another moment. Though blessed with reason, Man acted on impulse using his mental powers simply to satisfy his impulsive needs. Some few men became reasonable, but they were far outnumbered by those who chose to understand little beyond immediate desires. Rarely did Man use his mind to understand the flow of life, the patterns of harmony that governed all living things, but instead he used his brain to manipulate and master all living things. But in his foolishness, in his refusal to be governed by his unique mental apparatus, he failed to realize that his short-term emotionalism, his insistence on living by his feelings, was the shortest path to self-destruction by destroying the very substance upon which life feeds. In short, he failed to comprehend that life is a unity in which all thrive harmoniously, in balance and in mutual reliance, or all suffer in fragmentary dissolution.

You, Styrax, being an Elf, will find it difficult to understand man's major failing largely because of your different natures. To you there can be no question of the proper balance between reason and feeling, a balance in which the mind and the emotions are one. Man's fundamental problem was born into him, being there in the beginning and being there in the end. In many ways, he seemed a being but partially made. In his most primitive stage, life was a constant struggle for sustenance, for the basic necessities of life. For short periods, food would be in abundance; then, for longer periods, food would be scarce. Man found himself chained to a wheel of necessity, the perpetual struggle to find food. The Elf can never know of this, for the Elf draws his sustenance directly from the sun, the origin of life. The Elf cannot grow hungry; the Elf cannot starve. The Elf never thinks of food as Man does; in fact, the Elf rarely thinks of food at all. That which Man must struggle for, the Elf has automatically. Man's reason taught him to hunt wisely, to farm with care, to preserve food for periods of want, but his constant fears, the seat of the emotions, made him want more and more and more, for he ever remembered the times of hunger and deprivation.

Man bred foolishly, for he mated as a matter of passion. Instead of having children to perpetuate his kind, he had children to enlarge himself, to guard against his fears of the uncertainty of life. Instead of having children for the sheer joy of participating in the eternal renewal of life, he had children to provide workers, soldiers, and companions. He bred not to create new life but to aggrandize himself to give himself greater power over the land. And, finally, he bred haphazardly, children being nothing more than an unfortunate result of his sexual pleasure. His numbers increased at the expense of other living things. More children meant the need for more food. Entire species of animals were slain to satisfy Man's insatiable appetite. Forests were leveled to create more farms; more farms led to more people; and more forests were hewed down. Man quickly dominated the world, annihilating any form of life that interfered with his dominant passion for more, more, more. He bred so quickly that everywhere the earth had to struggle beneath the ever-growing weight of Man. As the years flew past, Man grew shrewder and shrewder, but the shrewder he grew, the hungrier he grew. While some men gorged, millions starved. In his constant drive for more and more, he created great machines to do his work; he created vast cities to house his relentlessly increasing population; and he created greater and greater weapons to protect himself and his possessions. Gradually, he lost the ability to distinguish between himself and his possessions. And he continued to use his reason in a futile attempt to satisfy his passions, corrupting both the passions and his ability to think. He invented unbelievably complex religions to quell his fears: he was taught by his beliefs that the world was his to do with as he pleased, that the world was a thing totally subservient to his desires, that he, of all living things, was pre-eminent, that his life, and his life alone, had meaning. He created sciences that made it possible for Man to manipulate nature in petty ways to the detriment of all other life. He created blood-sport in which he took great pleasure, and gained great prestige, in killing other creatures not for food but for the sheer joy of killing. In few words, he raped and raped the land until it lost its richness and fertility, its capacity to bring forth life.

You may be shocked, Styrax, at man's rapacity and his seemingly brutal nature—his ignorance of what he was doing to himself. But the supreme irony is that Man always knew what he was doing. From the beginning, Man's wise men warned him of the dangers of uncontrolled population, inefficient use of resources and the emotional dominance of reason. Time and again, he was told by his seers that all life is linked together, that life depends upon life. His teachers attempted to stay man's greed and to harness his pride, but they were ignored, shamed, and, on occasion, killed. Man dreamed of Paradise, of establishing an Eden on the earth, but he did little more than dream. For at any given period in his history, Man was capable of building his Nirvana. All he needed to do was control himself but that he rarely did. Man never lacked for answers. His religion became his tool of justification, for that which he could not control, notably himself, he blamed upon his God or Gods, thus shielding himself from accepting responsibility for his actions. Unaware of the essential unity and immortality of life, he created in his religions a belief in his own personal immortality, consistent with his belief that the world and the very universe were created to satisfy his desires. And a common thread in all his many and varied religions was the tenet that each person's religion made each individual more or better than any other person, people, or their systems of worship.

Other kinds of creatures, by the thousands, were annihilated as Man covered more and more of the earth's surface. His machines multiplied with equal speed, all belching forth poisonous gasses and noxious waters. He created chemical poisons so deadly and lasting that he began to poison himself, for the poisons eventually migrated to his food, to his drink, to his body's substance and to his seed. He denuded the land of forests, and those that remained began to die from poisoned air and water. And, as the great forests disappeared, the air Man breathed began to change for the worse. His weapons became so ghastly and powerful that within an instant he could level vast cities, and his fears grew in relation to the power of his weapons. And as his fears grew more intense, his reason was more and more suppressed, leading to even more awesome weapons. His leaders proudly proclaimed that they could kill each of their enemies a thousand times over as if you could kill anything more than once.

Then, the great change began. The air was poisoned; the water was poisoned. His fertile fields began to wither; his animal food began to die; the sea produced fewer and fewer fish. And, in time, Man himself became more and more infertile. For the poisons he had foisted on the innocent world were now within his body. Not only did he have fewer and fewer children, but those that were born were frequently so deformed as to frighten the doctors and midwives, and had to be destroyed at once. The fuel that ran his machines was being used up, and as the machines stopped, his food supplies diminished, and hunger became rampant. His complex social structures, his governments, his religions, his day-to-day relationships with his fellow Man were ignored or cast away, and his life became little more than a minute-to-minute struggle for food, as it was in the beginning. The central authorities that governed the overpopulated earth began to collapse from within, for people lost all faith in their leaders and simply ignored them. All his mighty institutions, his hospitals, his schools, his governments, gradually disintegrated, no longer able to satisfy the more and more reckless needs of people. Disease, almost conquered in Man's prime, reasserted itself and wiped out vast sections of the population, and what disease did not accomplish, hunger did. Within a hundred years, his numbers were reduced to half of what they had been, and that was halved again in the next hundred years. Man's life was reduced to a tribal level of hunting and gathering, and even the tribes themselves were short-lived because Man's ever-increasing infertility gave no assurance of a next generation. The cycle had come a full turn. Man was madly rushing toward the primordial ooze from whence he came, and the earth is returning to its original and stable form.

Lastly, friend Styrax, I must tell you I know not that Man's destiny. Certainly, he is a creature greatly reduced in strength and intelligence. The fields, the forests, the streams, and oceans, all are gradually purifying themselves removing the taint of Man. Many of the creatures Man had almost annihilated have re-established their rightful place on earth. Again, the mighty bison roams the plains; again, the great cats thrive in the hills and mountains; again, the birds darken the sky. And man's impotency continues, seeming to indicate his eventual cessation as a living creature. The traces of once mighty Man, his ruins, are gradually being absorbed back into the living mass of the earth. But how long Man will occupy a place among the self-aware beings, I cannot say. If you were a Man instead of an Elf, you might ask why I, with so much power at my disposal, do not annihilate the remnants of mankind especially after I have drawn such an abysmal picture of my kind. We, my grandfather, my father and myself, have given this much serious thought, but we have decided not to intervene. There are but few fundamental laws governing life, at least as far as they are discernible, but one law that we could not ignore is the inherent prohibition upon killing one's own kind. This law never troubled Man much, for of all living things Man alone took pride in destroying his fellow Man. Perhaps that violation of natural law is the essential cause of man's decline. Thus, within the Hill of Light, not on the battlefield, I refuse to harm my own kind. The Wanderer lives under the same restriction, but as he must live within the pale of battle, he is free to choose, to make exceptions to natural law.

Now I will close my thoughts on this matter, Styrax. Recalling Man's troubled existence has darkened my mind. It is a woeful tale.

existed and co-existed with Man for thousands upon thousands of years, and it is equally interesting to note that in the long run, these creatures were hounded into non-existence by relentless Man. The Dwarfs are too busy to concern themselves with the past; the Shee are too silly to accept the existence of a past; but the Elves are very much concerned with their own origins and with their relationships with other living things.

In Elfin lore, three distinct ages of the world are recognized: the First Age is a period in which Elves, Dwarfs, Titans, Fairies and Man lived together on this earth, a time known only through misty legends; the Second Age is the age of Man, an age about to close, known primarily through the study of history; and the Third Age is the age in which we now live, a nascent age. Most Elves believe that during the latter part of the First Age, Man began to persecute the Elfin Brood so intensely and relentlessly that the Elves allowed their spirits to enter into the life cycle of the trees, in Prosopia the mesquite tree, thus ceasing to have corporeal form. As spirits within their chosen trees, the Elves lived on through the Second Age, the age of Man, ever waiting to resume bodily form. This tree period, the Elves call the Long Sleep. Then, as Man declined and the Third Age began, the Elves slowly resumed their original forms to become what they are at present. Though this is a popular belief among Elves, the more thoughtful Elves have never been satisfied with it, knowing that this belief is far too simple and far too self-serving. If I am not mistaken, and I rarely am, you, friend Styrax, are one of the doubters. What you know of the Elfin Brood can be traced back quite clearly to the time of your grandfather, but before there is only impenetrable darkness. It is now time to penetrate that darkness.

Styrax, my friend, I am sure that you have noticed that the works of Man I have related to you or the books of Man I have given to you deal primarily with man's literature, his art, or his history. What I have not given you, and will never give you, are the sciences of Man, his explorations into the structure of the universe, his feeble attempts at understanding the world in purely physical terms. This body of knowledge, these sciences, constitute a heritage of undisguised evil. I will speak further of this form of corruption when I answer the next and last question.

As I mentioned in a previous letter, Goodman's special field of study was genetic engineering. The object of this study was to find and then manipulate the essence of any given living creature. In each living thing are extremely small cells that determine what that given being will be, and each of these cells carries all the information necessary to the nature of that creature. Each cell in your body, Styrax, is Elfin, and from each cell another Styrax, an exact duplicate, can be made. It is thus that my grandfather created my father and thus my father created me. Man, at the peak of his knowledge, began, with little success, to manipulate these cells in an attempt to improve his own being and in an attempt to improve upon nature in general. Man for centuries changed the nature of living things through the mechanics of nature, at least as far as Man understood nature. By crossbreeding, he created mules, dogs of almost endless variety, plants that produced more food, and agents that lessened the diseases that tormented Man. Manipulating nature, according to the rules of nature, was, in itself, a good thing. But when Man went beyond these fundamental rules, when he began to alter nature itself, he stepped beyond his abilities, beyond the pale of reason.

Goodman was an extraordinary Man. His mental powers were extreme, even before he increased them in the Hill of Light, far beyond those of other men. In altering the very nature of nature, he had no peer. As he realized that Man was doomed, that his manner of living was leading to his own destruction, and that the course was inescapable and inevitable, and the destruction of everything surrounding him, Goodman retired from his people and created the Hill of Light, here in the frozen wastelands where Man has seldom come. Here, in isolation, he continued his experimentation, his quest for an escape from the deadly circle Man placed himself in. Remember that by this time Man had poisoned his food, his water, and his air. His infertility was already upon him. His societies had already begun to collapse. All order—social, moral, economical—was on the wane. His fuels were depleted. And his ability to learn began to diminish. Actually, Man's desire to learn diminished long before his ability to learn diminished. Another of Man's ironies, ghastly in its impact, Man's desire to learn began to ebb at the same time Man reached his highest level of what he thought to be advanced civilization. After one of his major wars that seemed to involve the entire globe, Man found temporary peace and a degree of harmony. Immediately, as ever, he produced too many children while creating truly free time for himself. He thought, rather foolishly, that the goal of life was to create leisure time, that is to work as little as possible. For the first time in his entire history, Man had created free time. His machines, his organizations and his exploitation of the earth had liberated him from the perpetual grind of tedious work. In a sense,

Man was finally free from the wheel of necessity, or so he thought. But, sadly, this was not to be. For most men had an absolute terror of being free, of being in charge of their own lives. No matter how much lip service was given the supposed virtue of freedom, most men shunned it as a plague, seeking, instead, more societal and governmental controls, and more and more insipid entertainment to fill the free time he found himself cursed by. His schools grew larger, but he learned less. Books became available to all, but fewer and fewer read. Learning became a mechanical function, called education, of his society, for it was reduced to the role of fitting people into the accepted scheme of order. Learning, which had always been the liberation of the mind, now became a system for deadening the creative mind and enslaving the mechanical brain. Man failed to realize, if he ever possessed the capability, that obsession with the mechanical world would inevitably lead to a world totally subject to mechanical law, a world in which Man became a machine among machines.

Thus it was that Goodman began to create life anew. By this I mean he began to create new forms of living things, beings that had never existed before, creatures that had no past and many that had no future. His progress was slow, and his tasks were many, but he persisted, knowing only that the task he had set himself was the only path by which self-aware beings could perpetuate themselves. One of his earliest failures, you have already encountered the foul-smelling beast called a Grendel. In simple terms, what Goodman did was to biologically fuse the essence of Man with the essence of the shark. He hoped to produce a self-aware creature capable of living in an aquatic environment, but all he actually produced was a being possessed of the shark's strength and predatory nature infused with Man's greed and rapacity. He tried again, but this time he abandoned the idea of living in water, for he felt that Man and the shark were too disparate in nature to make a successful cross. This time he chose a black bear, what you and your people call a scrubble bear, to fuse with the essential being of Man, for he felt that biologically and environmentally, the bear was closer to Man. Again, he failed, as you learned already, creating the nasty creature called the Shag.

Shortly after the creation of the Shag, Goodman passed on, leaving his task to my father who continued the work without pause. Having learned from earlier failures, my father reasoned that matching creatures of a similar nature was doomed to failure, for it gave rein to those traits that these creatures held in common. Thus, predatory Man and predatory shark created a creature of insatiable predation. Thus, greedy Man coupled with greedy bears created a being of almost unfathomable greed. A new approach was needed, a new insight into the cells he worked with. Gradually, over hundreds of years, my father began to catalog each independent characteristic of the living things with which he worked. Nature was far more subtle than my grandfather or father had been led to believe. Slowly, he isolated the fragment of being that constituted the drive and energy of the honey bee, a distillation of ambition in its purest form. Next, he isolated the essence of man's reasoning power. Finally, a degree of success was achieved, for from this combination came the creatures we now designate as Dwarfs or Trolls or Nibelungen. Hearken to what I have said, Styrax. Cast aside disbelief, and heed my words. My father created

the Dwarfs and the Empress Saphiria is a descend-
ant of that experimentation, though she knows it
not and, perhaps, will never know. That will be in
your hands, my dear Styrax. Now you may ask
why I call this achievement a 'degree of success'.
The Dwarfs are successful; they are intelligent and
peaceful; they are strong and joyful; they have persisted for many, many years. Why only 'a degree
of success'? Well, partial success implies partial
failure, and the failings of the Dwarfs outweigh
their successes. For what my father sought, he
found not in his latest achievement.

Now we must speak of Goodman's task, the
ideal he, my father and I have dedicated our lives
to. What is it we seek? What are we after? What
will satisfy us? First of all, we wish to perpetuate
self-awareness, knowledge, wisdom, whatever it
may be called. Nature, the world at large, will perpetuate itself. The world of worms and cats, ants
and coyotes, flowers and birds will continue, but
without self-awareness the continuity is unknown
and unknowing, directionless, beyond consideration, being without awareness of being. Goodman
knew that most creatures lived in a timeless universe, a world in which being is simply moment to
moment existence without time, without a past,
without a future, a world unaware of itself. He also
realized that self-awareness is nothing more than
knowledge of time, or knowledge suspended within
an arbitrary matrix which Man calls time. Thus,
the first requirement was to create an entity capable of reason, in fact, a being dominated by reason, by awareness of life in its entirety, and by joy
as the embodiment of that self-awareness. The
problem with the Dwarfs is not in their lack of
reason or their lack of joy, but in their lack of
awareness of the entirety of life itself, the oneness

of it all, the total harmonic interplay of all living things. The Dwarfs are dominated by their beeish nature. They work and work, ever smelting the metals of the earth, ever building weapons, brazen horns, intricate tunnels, but always limiting their view of life to the perspective of the Dwarf, as if the whole of creation, this volcano of life, existed solely for the welfare of the Dwarfs or Trolls or Nibelungen themselves.

My father worked on, happy with a degree of success but happier in the expectation of further achievement. Now he felt that the essence of the bee's drive was too potent, too all-encompassing. Now he realized that in his re-structuring of nature, he needed not only to fuse the qualities he sought, but to fuse them in terms of a hierarchy, in which the qualities were placed in a distinct order. If one fused ambition and reason haphazardly, the result was neither reason nor ambition but a disordered and pointless fusion of the desired traits. To be successful, Goodman needed to fuse reason in a dominant position over ambition, which was then controllable and subject to the more vital virtue. The failure with the Dwarfs was that the Dwarfs were happy in being Dwarfs rather than happy in just being. His next creation was based upon the essence of man's reason combined with the playful energy of the otter and the deliberate joy of the hummingbird. From Man, in this case a cell from SHE, came thought; from the otter, the restless zest for living; and from the hummingbird the persistence for survival. You have already guessed the result, have you not, my friend? Yes, my father created the Shee, the happy female tribe who saved you from the Grendels. My father was enchanted with what he thought to be successful. He had created a being of happiness,

an entity freed from the terrors of sexual reproduction and domination, a creature able to easily
control its birth rate, and a living thing of great
intelligence. But as the months passed, my father
realized his mistake, for no matter how hard he
tried to reason with the joyous Shee, the response
was inevitably that of laughter. He had created a
very happy but very irresponsible being again, a
creature unaware of the whole of life, a being in
whom reason was not the guiding force.

The final experiment began in my father's latter years when I was still a very young Man. We
reasoned that our lack of success with the Dwarfs
and with the Shee was closely related to the short-
ness of life span characterized by the beings we
had chosen—bees, otters, and hummingbirds were
creatures of days, weeks and a few years. If a
being lived for only a short period, it was unlikely
that it would have developed a point of view encom-
passing all life for in a short life little can be learned
at least in terms of totality, of all life as one life. If
a Man lives a hundred years and becomes wiser,
then a Man of a thousand years would be wiser
still. But men are short-lived and in their present
state their lives grow shorter and shorter. Therefore, we sought among the plants, especially those
plants whose life span made them ancient. If we
could cross man's reason with the longevity of the
bristle-cone pine, then we would have reason dis-
seminated over five thousand years, reason tempered at the forge of time. A good start but only
that. The new being had to contend with Man unless we could find an environment Man seldom
frequented. Then SHE, our mother and sister, suggested a being not subject to the constant demand
for sustenance, an entity not subject to perpetual
hunger. The problem was enormous, and decades

passed by slowly until I, serving my father as the Wanderer serves me, discovered a virgin land rarely visited by Man in the past and never visited by Man in the present. Here our new entity could prosper without interference from Man; here he could come to terms with the world of which he would eventually and hopefully become the custodian.

No doubt but you have already realized where my story is leading, for it leads to you, King Styrax, to the world of the Elfin Brood. From the mesquite, the most ancient of living things, I removed the kernel, the essence of long life, the plant's ability to draw energy, vigor, health and joy directly from the sun. From the Wanderer, I withdrew the reasoning essence of Man. Then with infinite care, I manipulated man's nature to a slight degree, slight but profound, for I shifted the essential being of Man from his emotions to his reasoning faculties. The object of my work, my dedication, my life was to produce a being governed in force by the reasoning mind, a mind so conceived that it would not shun the emotions but abide with and control them for the emotions are ever the impetus to life. Thus, my friend, I created the Elf, a being governed by his mind, a creature freed from the slavery of hunger, and a being capable of extremely long life, a life long enough to establish a sense of the oneness, the allness, of the force we call life.

The first Elves were placed in the land you now call Prosopia, the land of mesquite, for here the Elves could live and develop free from the encroachments of Man for, at that time, Man considered the Prosopian land to be a wasteland of impenetrable copses and infertile soil. It is only in recent times that Man, having exhausted his own lands, has shown interest in the land of the Elves. Only one major problem remained to give these new creatures, these Elves, an identity of their own. I could not have them believe that they were bio- logical offshoots of Man, for I wanted them to develop independently of Man. And, further yet, I wanted them to develop without the knowledge of man's existence. Therefore, I gave these brave new creatures an inheritance, I gave them the heritage of the Elfin Brood, those ancient beings who may or may not have lived in the First Age. And thus have the Elves lived and prospered until the in- trusion of Man, both the intrusion of Man as you have experienced it with the Beastums, and the intrusion of Man in the form of the Wanderer and myself, the Aged One.

You understand, Styrax, that all I have done was done under the premise that self-aware beings must persist, that reason is its own justifi- cation, that life without awareness of life is no life at all. For I, my father, and my grandfather wished to save all that was good in the creations of Man to perpetuate his creative works. I knew from the beginning, that is my grandfather, my father, and I knew that sooner or later whatever kind of beings we created would have to contend with Man, that sooner or later creatures of emotion and crea- tures of reason would confront one another. You might ask why I simply did not destroy Man in the first place, why I have left that onerous task to the Elves or the Shee or the Dwarfs. Herein lies the final dilemma, for throughout this lengthy dis- course I have stood apart from Man and tried to create something better than him, but, through- out these long centuries, I have ever been a Man and will die being a Man. Within me, the great battle still rages. My emotions cry out for the end of Man, for his extinction; my mind whispers for an end to killing, for an end to concepts like extinction. Within me, Man is already at war with the Elves. Within me Man has always been at war with the Elves. Therefore, I am helpless, for I cannot destroy part of myself without destroying all of myself.

Lastly, I must remind you that the destiny of self-awareness is in your hands and your hands alone. The decisions that you make must be Elfin, must spring from your own independent mind, and must not be tempered by any consideration to Man, particularly to Man in the form of the Wanderer, SHE, or myself. Ever remember that we are the race of Man and, perforce, must suffer the fate of Man. You must concern yourself with life in its totality. There can be no life without hummingbirds and nectar, without lizards and insects, without bears and honey. But there can be life without Man. Kill not the ant, my friend, for thy village rests upon his shoulders.

Chapter Fifteen
What Are The Stars?

My Dear King Styrax,

I have no answer for you. You ask a question even wizards feared to ask. You seek beyond your ken. You want to know the ultimate answer, the secret of life, the first premise. You ask the question I would have asked but I am a Man, not an Elf.

Now hear me, my green friend. Whatever is, is—that is the first and last premise. There is no ultimate answer. There is no secret. But, there are stars.

What are the stars? What would you have them be? What does your mind tell you at this very instant? When you and your beloved Canna look up at the sky on moonless nights, what do you think you see? Are not these remote points of light the crystallization of your own thought? For what you see is nothing more than what you want to see. I must now tell you not the truth but the truth as I would have it be. I want, but cannot prove, the stars to be endless suns, scattered everywhere across the sky, endless suns that nurture infinite worlds not unlike our own or, perhaps, very unlike our own. The stars are endlessness, perpetual mysteries, dimensions beyond our ken. They are HRMNFTHSPHRS, the harmony of the spheres, the music of life, life itself. A fire is a star for a moth.

What is it you wish to know, Styrax? What is it, to know? And what should we know? From Man's failings, you might learn what to know and, perhaps, what not to know. In the world of Man in his ascendancy, knowing generally took three indistinct but very different forms: religion, the arts and the sciences. Religion was knowledge through fear, the attempts of Man to impose a personal order on the universe. As death was man's final fear, all religions developed central themes which granted frightened Man some form of immortality, some form of escape from death and escape from the wheel of necessity. Through religion, Man aspired to rise above the natural world, and in so doing he assumed himself to be the master of nature and death. As if there were not enough terror in the natural world, the religions Man created infested the world with demons, devils, and angels, agents responsible for good and evil agents who by their nature relieved Man of responsibility for his immediate being. Man found himself existing in two worlds, the world that is and always will be, the natural, physical world, and the world beyond nature, the world as Man would have it be, the world of self-serving myth. And, foolishly, most men chose the latter believing, fiendishly, that the natural world served only to enhance the mythical world. A strange world, indeed, in which Man would cry out to God to ease the agony he himself had created. In simplest terms, the arts were concerned with embellishing, enriching and expanding life. Art is the enhancement of life, the celebration of it, the participation in it. The sciences, on the other hand, are the antithesis of life, the fragmentation of it. The sciences are man's fiendish attempts at controlling life, of making life a reflection of man's personality, of man's tragic assumption that he was life itself and, by extension, that the universe was his to do with as he pleased. The scientist was a Man who believed that if he took a clock completely apart, studied each part and reassembled the clock again, he then knew what time was when really he only knew what the clock was. The scientist was a Man who in his search for knowledge always moved in a direction diametrically opposed to the direction he wished to take.

But I must be careful, for you, not knowing of the sciences, will think that art is good and science is evil. Good men were scientists frequently, and bad men were occasionally artists, but that is neither here nor there, for we can only judge the arts and the sciences finally in terms of what they led to, not what they were. After all, what are the arts? A painting, a poem, a piece of music, a dance are attempts by Man to intensify his pleasure in life by enhancing what he saw, what he heard and what he felt. The arts capture the fleeting joys of living, making that which is personal, universal. The arts seek in color, in line, in tone, in pattern, in rhythm, in sense to establish and enrich the harmonies of life. A musician plays a lovely tune upon his pan-pipes, for it gives him joy. But the joy is limited unless he plays the melody to give joy to someone else. For is not the tune played by Man nothing more than the enrichment and embellishment of bird song, of laughing waters, of wind in the osiers? In essence, art is nothing more than the intensification of the natural world. Unfortunately, as Man grew more powerful and dominant, he allowed the arts to be corrupted by numbers rather than by quality. A painting became valuable because of the gold it could garner rather than for the joy it gave. Music was no longer the province of the music-maker, but the province of the Man who controlled the dissemination of the music, and that man's concerns were with his profits from the music rather than the music itself. Sadly, the artist was removed, step by step, from the very people for whom he had hoped to create. Over the years, the arts became a way to make money and to gain power instead of happiness. But, though the arts were corruptible, the quality of individual works of art persisted, for corrupt art feeds upon itself and is quickly forgotten. Real art, joyful art, cannot be harmful, cannot be evil, cannot corrupt, for it is based upon the eternal harmonies to which all self-aware creatures are attuned.

The sciences, really the study of measurement, were the products of many wise and good men who believed that their approach to knowing was an essential benefit to Man. Through these sciences many good things were accomplished: Man's health improved, Man's dependence upon fanciful religions waned and the world of hunger grew less painful. As the sciences grew, the arts began to weaken, for Man in general began to believe that the sciences were the key to richer lives, not enriched lives but richer lives. As the scientists continued to dissect the matter of existence, the world of Man became more and more concerned with the mechanics of what made the clock function. Slowly, Man put more and more faith in infinitely complex studies of the mechanical workings of the physical world. To a point, this faith had justification, for the sciences seemed to be improving the

lot of Man. But the seeming improvement led finally to disaster, for the scientists began to create
that which should never have been created, that
which had never existed in nature before, poisons
for which their was no antidote, no canceling agent;
weapons that were so destructive they had no
conceivable use and mechanical by-products that
corrupted the very water and air Man needed to
survive. Through his religion and science, Man felt
himself to be above, or apart from, nature. If his
poisons killed the beasts of the field, the fish in
the sea, and the bird in the sky, he worried little,
for these creatures existed at the whim and fancy
of Man, that is lesser beings who existed but to
serve Man. Little did he realize that poisons once
created can rarely be destroyed. The poisons were
misted in the air and on plants; rains carried the
poisons into the soil and the ground water, and,
finally, into the sea. Clouds became great carriers
of noxious substances that then rained down on
Man.

Yet, the essential problem of man's dependence upon the sciences was not in the things they
created nor the learning they stimulated. Rather,
the fatal problem was caused wholly by the method
of thinking common to the scientific community,
thinking that learning, experimentation, discovery
and achievement were the essential goals of life
regardless of consequences. Remember that the
scientists were the wisest of men though hardly
as wise as they saw themselves who found it almost easy to control the greater world of non-sci-
entists. Without knowing what they did, the scientists lost control of the very knowledge they had
created. Bellicose rulers used the notable achievements of the scientists to create weapons so lethal
that it is a wonder there was any life left on earth.

Merchants took the work of scientists and manufactured insect poisons that annihilated indiscriminately many, many species of insects, thus destroying the balance among insects, vegetation, birds and people; other merchants, under the guise of helping their fellow Man, made special chemicals which altered any Man's state of mind, drugs that deadened the brain while creating a false sense of joy. Both science and religion failed Man for essentially the same reason, it sought beyond Man for answers to the riddle of existence. Science sought to know Man and his world in purely physical terms, as if Man were compounded of clay and clay alone. Religion sought beneath Man by deluding him into believing he was other than mortal, a creature apart from nature. Certainly the world is physical, and all living things are part of it but life is essentially mental to those who are self-aware. The only meaning in life is what we perceive it to be, and truth is nothing more than self-awareness in accordance to the dictates of the physical world. Even the education of Man became corrupted as the sciences replaced the other forms of learning, especially the forms of learning that are presented in the form of a story, the only true process of learning. But behind it all was the premise that men of science had completely free hands in their continuing dissection of the substance of life. Without knowing it, the scientists began to believe that they and their method of thinking was the only valid method of thought, that they had surpassed natural law, that Man was ascendant in the universe and that they were the ultimate arbiters of life. They wished to know what the stars were, even as people starved upon their doorsteps. It was all very, very sad.

But I do not wish to linger on the failings of

Man, for Man is of the past, and his failings proceeded largely from his nature rather than his will. My concern now is with the Elves.

Seek wisdom, my dear Styrax, not knowledge. Beware of written words. Beware of the sanctification of learning, for it is little more than the sanctification of self and is ever self-serving. Beware of authority, for it comes from unreasoned fear. None of these things are evil in themselves but become evil when used to control the destinies of others. It is right that you should know how to survive with dignity. It is right that you should have knowledge of the world around you. But beyond these obvious needs, how much more do you want to know? How much do you need to know? And how does one know what to know?

And now I offer my advice and only my advice. You see, Styrax, I am a father who must advise his beloved son, but as a wise parent, I realize I must not govern or control or direct your thinking. You must remain free to choose as you will, as your inner being guides you. Seek to know that which contributes to the personal joy of yourself and those closely bound to your heart. Know that which makes your life fuller, more intense and meaningful. Seek to give joy, for in the giving of joy is the attainment of joy. Seek not the learning that brings power or wealth. Seek not to control others. Seek not the learning of numbers, the learning that deals with mass and quantity. But ever seek the learning that is qualitative, that distinguishes between good and evil.

* * *

One final thought, my son. All that I have said, all that you have seen, all that you now know is the future of the self-aware world. Though you are compounded of mesquite and Man, the latter is dominant by far and, truthfully, you are the heir of Man. Granted, you are more reasonable and less emotional than your forerunner. But beware of your own nature, for almost all corruption comes from within. The balance of reason and emotion is intricate, subtle and disarming. You differ from Man primarily in a slight shift of that balance which, hopefully, gives your reason more validity than Man's reason. Remember that you and all the Elves will be subject to all the temptations that haunted Man and will, ultimately, efface him. And remember, even if it causes pain, that you are product of man's reason, that you are the last hope of self-awareness in this universe.

I have said all that I am going to say. Go now, my creation, my son and my friend. May harmony continue to bless your life.

I am weary, and time grows short. Think carefully of what I have written. We shall meet again.

Part Three
The War Begins

Chapter Sixteen

For many miles, the grand army of Profundus the Guileful stretched across the barren and feature-less grasslands, resembling a great serpent as it slithered across a dry field. In the vanguard rode the scarlet five hundred, all mounted on noble steeds and fully armed with lance and sword, pre-senting a brave spectacle as they rode in precisely aligned ranks, chanting rhythmic and bold song that matched the pace of their horses. Behind the scarlet warriors rode Profundus in a richly ornamented wagon drawn by white chargers, and behind the wagon rode Lord Thrett on a huge chest-nut stallion. Next in line were the foot soldiers, armed with short swords and crossbows, but, unlike the scarlet five hundred, the foot soldiers were in slovenly disarray and were dressed in gar-ments barely better than rags. They spoke little and were covered with chalky dust raised by the scarlet warriors' steeds. Behind them came forty assorted crude wagons drawn by wretched-look-ing horses, wagons containing the necessary sup-plies and numerous machines of war, the most important of which were catapults. And lastly came the straggling horde of elderly servants, emaciated slaves, feeble women and sickly children, all struggling with tired horses or stumbling along on foot.

"How much farther to the Rhus?" Profundus asked, shouting from his wagon to Lord Thrett who was just then about to ride to the front of the army.

"We will be there tomorrow, my Lord," he answered, reining his stallion in close to the richly adorned and massive wagon.

"Then find a camp, for I wish to rest and plan before we come upon the Beastums. See to it."

As the sun moved deeper into the west, the army made camp and set out sentries, and, meanwhile, Lord Thrett was summoned to attend Profundus, whose wagon had been situated in the center of the scarlet five hundred on a small rise which gave Profundus a commanding view of his horde. Lord Thrett found his master seated beneath a large canopy suspended from one side of his wagon.

Profundus poured a glass of deep red wine and offered it to Thrett, gesturing for him to dismount and enter the shade the canopy afforded.

"So, Lord Thrett, the adventure begins. Not too many days ago, you were a ragged Beastum, without hope and without a patron. Now you have both. You have a noble future and all you need too is to obey."

"Aye, my Lord, I know my place," Lord Thrett answered with faint humility, for in his heart he loathed Profundus no less than Vastar. "You have but to command, and I will heed your call."

"Vastar expected you to return with twenty warriors. So shall it be," Profundus replied. "Take twenty men and enter his camp as if his plan were going as he would have it. Find out what has happened while you were gone. Then return here. Do you understand?"

"Of course, my Lord Profundus, as you wish.

But what will Vastar think when I leave so quickly?" Thrett spoke slowly, sipping the proffered wine cautiously, for he remembered all too vividly the last glass of wine Profundus had given him. He also sensed that Profundus' commands included more than had been said.

"I do not wish to meet with Vastar. I do not wish to see him, to talk to him, or to even acknowledge his existence. Do you understand?"

"I understand, my Lord."

"And remember, Lord Thrett, that I am in command; the scarlet five hundred are my warriors; and you are their leader only as long as I allow it. Do you understand?"

"I understand, my Lord."

Profundus looked squarely at Lord Thrett who was standing in front of his master clad in the scarlet splendor of a warlord. Profundus had found Thrett a useful and necessary companion at first, but now he realized that his new warlord was much more than he had expected. For too many years, Profundus had dealt solely with his castrated soldiery, men noted for loyalty, bravery and simplicity, but lacking in vigor, resourcefulness and intelligence. He found them useful but dull. Thrett was of another kind. He was shrewd and fearless, a Man undaunted by death and a Man whose loyalty was for sale. Profundus liked him and, therefore, trusted him not. And, yet, he liked him very much.

Profundus stood up and said, "You have your orders. Select twenty warriors and go. I await good news."

* * *

Cautiously, Lord Thrett led his twenty scarlet warriors into what had once been the camp of the

Beastums. All they found were the cold and gray remains of campfires and collapsed tents. The larger and more impressive tents of Graspar and Vastar were gone, as were the Beastums. Sending half his soldiery to scout the area, Lord Thrett dismounted and sat by the Rhus, almost in the same place where he had his last conversation with Vastar the Wise. How unalike these brothers are, Thrett thought, for Vastar, though treacherous, was not greedy or bloodthirsty, he simply did what had to be done. But Profundus was another matter, for in him Thrett sensed a Man who found ecstasy in pain and revelry in death. In Vastar, Thrett sensed a Man not unlike himself, a Man capable of any cruelty to achieve his goal, but a Man who found no joy in his cruelty. Profundus, on the other hand, was a Man who was not only capable of cruelty but found elation and deep joy in the acts of cruelty themselves, a Man whose governing pleasure was the infliction of pain. Slowly Thrett scanned the opposite bank of the Rhus, trying to espy some sign of life on the far shore. But he saw nothing but the dense, impenetrable mesquite crowded against the rushing waters of the Rhus. Somewhere in that undergrowth, Thrett sensed the eyes of the Elves staring at him. He pondered his foe but could sense little more than staring, curious eyes ever watching the opposite bank.

Within moments, he noticed three scarlet warriors returning with the wretched figure of an old Man stumbling before the warrior's horses, and as they came closer, he recognized the captive to be Will the Hostler, an aged but capable servant of Graspar.

As the captive was brought before Lord Thrett, he fell to his knees, bowing to the ground and pleading, "Do not kill me! Do not hurt me!"

"Stand up, Will," Thrett ordered, ever angered by the sight of a Man groveling. "Do you not know me, old Man? Where is everyone?"

Confusedly, Will struggled to his feet, looking questioningly at the scarlet warlord standing before him. He squinted his aged eyes and asked, "Is that you, Thrett? Is it really you? We gave you up for dead when you disappeared. We thought the Yellfen had killed you."

"I am now Lord Thrett, Warlord for Profundus, King of the Vergers. Remember, you old fool, to address me as Lord Thrett. Your life depends upon it."

Will quickly fell again to his knees, bowing as humbly as he was capable of. "Yes, Thrett, I mean Lord Thrett, I will do as you wish."

"Where is everyone?" Thrett demanded. "Where is Graspar? Where is Vastar? Where are the Beastums?"

"The Beastums are no more, Lord Thrett. They simply went away, those that did not starve."

"And Graspar? What of him?"

"I know not, my Lord. Six or seven days after Graspar, Strang, Grudge and Bastard left to find a crossing upstream, we were stunned to see the bloated bodies of Strang, Grudge and Bastard float past our camp. We dragged the corpse of Strang from the Rhus but found no wound or injury that could have caused his death. Someone, an old woman, I think, cried out that they had been killed by magic or sorcery for how else would three mighty warriors die without wounds?"

"What of Graspar?" Lord Thrett asked patiently, knowing that Will was not too strong of mind.

"I know nothing, my Lord. We all thought that they had captured him."

"They? They who?"

"The Yellfen, Lord Thrett, the Yellfen for it is said that they are all sorcerers and magicians, and can make the sky dark. Vastar told us that the Yellfen had enchanted the Rhus which caused our warriors to be sucked into the depths by great strangling river weeds, and when they were drowned, the weeds cast them free. That is why their bodies revealed no wounds."

"Must I always deal with fools?" Thrett asked angrily.

"But they had no wounds," Will insisted.

"Silence, you old ass," Thrett shouted. Then he continued in a calmer manner, "Graspar did not return, and you fools assumed that the Yellfen practiced their magic on him."

"No, my Lord, we knew nothing of the Yellfen and nothing of magic, but Vaster the Wise explained it all to us. In fact, he it was who advised the Beastums to leave, for if we did not, the sorcery would fall upon us. Vastar warned us that the Yellfen could make day into night, that they could make the mighty Rhus flow backwards, and that they could make the river leap over its banks, drowning all who opposed, or even pestered, the Yellfen. Within hours, my Lord, the Beastums had stripped the tents of Graspar, Grudge, Bastard and Strang, and then they abandoned the camp and headed for safer lands far to the south."

"But you stayed."

"Aye, Lord Thrett, I stayed to wait upon Graspar when he returned."

"The loyalty of a fool," Thrett said derisively. "And Vastar went with the other Beastums to the south?"

"No, my Lord, what Vastar did was stranger still."

Lord Thrett was disturbed, for of the Beastums he feared none but Vastar, and he knew that the talk of magic and sorcery was an intentional ruse on Vastar's part. But why? Why had Vastar frightened the Beastums away? "What strange things did Vastar do?"

"At first, Lord Thrett, he did nothing more than gather all of the remaining tent poles together, piling them by the river. Instead of ordering us to do it, he worked alone, chasing us away if we came too close. Each day, he spent hours lashing the poles together in the form of a raft, as if he were going to follow the other Beastums but by way of the Rhus. Each morning he would climb to the top of that high knoll and sit there for hours staring off into the east. Then, yesterday, he hurried back from the knoll and ordered me to follow the others. I refused, for Graspar is my master, not Vastar. And if Graspar returned and I was not here to tend his horse, he would have had me skinned. But Vastar grew angry and drew his sacred knife and attempted to slay me. But I ran off, and he failed to follow. Later, I watched him push the raft into the Rhus, but instead of floating downstream, he poled his way across the river as best he could. The last I saw of him, he was far downstream, where the current carried him, climbing up the opposite bank and struggling into the mesquite thickets."

"He crossed the river by himself?" Lord Thrett asked in amazement.

"Yes, my Lord."

"And you saw nothing else?"

Will paused, fearing what he was about to say but knowing he must say it. "Well, I did see something else, I think."

"Well, what was it?" Thrett demanded impatiently.

"After he crawled into the mesquite, I saw something green and fast rush through the thicket as if the wicked thorns were no longer there. Then I heard a strange cry, and the green shadow disappeared."

After Will finished speaking, Thrett paused a moment before giving his orders. "Take this fool away. Give him food and drink. Give him some decent clothing. He will be my servant, for he is talented with horses."

Thrett felt troubled, for he knew that Profundus wanted his brother Vastar killed. From what Will the Hostler had said, Vastar might very well be dead, a victim of the secretive Elves. But, Thrett mused, Vastar was no fool—not one to die easily. He realized that Vastar only crossed the river after he had discovered the army of Profundus about to descend upon the Beastums. Vastar had to realize that Thrett had betrayed him, for instead of twenty compliant warriors, he had seen a warlike host. Vastar knew that Profundus would settle for nothing else than his death. But was he dead? I think not, Thrett thought to himself. And deep in the recesses of his treacherous mind, Thrett feared, and grew angry with, the persistent and troublesome idea that Vastar had found some way to join the Elfin tribe.

* * *

Laughing deeply, Profundus managed to say, "So Vastar has escaped me again. My brother proves no end of woe."

Lord Thrett was astounded by the laughter of Profundus, for he had expected anger and worse. Yet here Profundus sat laughing foolishly at the failure of his plan.

"Excuse my laughter, Lord Thrett, for you have

no way of knowing my long and fruitless feud with Vastar, my brother in blood. How many years I have sought his death is almost beyond my reckoning, and yet I long for that death with an intensity that surprises even me. And he, for his part, equally longs for my annihilation. Yet, we both seem destined to be denied our greatest desire in life—the death of the other. I fear that the Elves will prove no match for Vastar if he lives. You see, my hatred is such that I care not how he dies, or when he dies; I seek only, as my ultimate joy, to see, and then rejoice over, his corpse even as he wishes to gloat over mine."

"I feared you would be angry, Lord Profundus," Thrett said with feigned meekness.

"I would have been angry, Lord Thrett, if I thought you were a match for Vastar. You are a warrior and no fit rival for a shaman. But long have I realized that so vile a creature as my brother, so vile and so shrewd, would find his death in no way but by my own hand. That is as it should be."

"Is it then your plan, my Lord, to attack the Elfin creatures at once? Shall we march north to the crossing and surge across the mighty Rhus?"

"That, perhaps, was my plan, but now I think I must reconsider. My original idea was based upon the supposition that we would attack as soon as Vastar was dead, but Vastar, I fear, is not dead. Even my mighty scarlet warriors would be no match for the deviously clever mind of Vastar. No, we must plan anew. The scale of the coming war has expanded. The enemy, Vastar and his green friends, will be prepared for us, and our mighty force is no longer mighty enough to win easily. For, Lord Thrett, this military lesson you must learn; never risk your essential strength, in this case the scarlet five hundred. Think what would happen if my scarlet warriors won the battle but were so seriously injured in the war to no longer be a strong force. Immediately, other soldiers, other warriors would rush in to destroy me and the weakened five hundred, and the victory would be theirs and we would be the vanquished and with the like of our allies, we would be vanquished and dead; that you may count on.

"Therefore, we risk our forces only when the risk is minimal, when victory assures the continued strength of the victors. Now we must seek allies, seek other armies to suffer the brunt of battle so that in victory the Vergers remain the strongest. I have already dispatched couriers to strong tribes that are likely to join our cause. Now we must wait for a grand conclave from which we will march with an army so vast, so irresistible, and so potent that we will erase Vastar and his green friends from the slate of life."

Chapter Seventeen

Styrax, the Wanderer and Empress Saphiria returned to the vast caverns of the Trolls shortly after the Aged One had given Styrax the written answers to his questions. On their way to Troll-Land through dark and damp tunnels, they spoke little. The Wanderer was saddened, as he always was, in leaving SHE, who never left the Hill of Light where, upon the departure of her lover, she slept trance-like until the Wanderer again returned. Empress Saphiria said little, for she was angered by the Aged One's brusqueness and disinterest in her visit. She was an Empress, after all, and felt quite miffed at being grandly ignored by an old fool no matter how much he knew. In fact, she also suffered because she felt that Styrax, a mere King of the naive Elves, had been honored when she was not, for envy had long been prevalent in the Dwarfenfold. Styrax, troubled by his visit to the Aged One, spoke not at all, for his mind was still pondering the weighty matters poured upon him in the letters. He longed to speak with the Wanderer, to question him about the information he had received and to assure himself of the Aged One's veracity, for at times he felt certain that the Aged One was daft. But with the Empress there, he dared not speak of the letters, of which Saphiria knew nothing. The Elfin King was troubled; he had been exposed to too much too soon; as yet, he could not grasp all that he had been asked to grasp.

Upon their return, King Jasper held a sumptuous feast in the grand cavern. When told by Empress Saphiria of the Aged One's cautious advice to organize, to plan, to think, King Jasper grew restless at first, then angry.

"I fear the Aged One has grown too old, too cautious, too fearful. He treats us as though we were children to be hidden under bushes whenever danger arises. I fear he overrates the power of men and underrates the might of the Trolls. We have fought with men before and will fight with them again. Always the Trolls have been triumphant."

"King Jasper seems to forget," the Wanderer said, "that the men the Trolls and the Elves have fought were but stragglers or renegades, not armies of seasoned warriors."

"But are we not seasoned warriors?" Jasper shouted as he paced restlessly around the banquet table pestering the many Trolls who were intent on eating. "The Trolls fear no one, and, though we are a peaceable fold, we bow to no one, especially Man."

"I do not doubt the valor of the Trolls, but your people, no matter how bold in battle, hardly have the numbers to face the legions of Man. With the Shee, the Elves, the Trolls and the Pinus Dwarfs, we will still be vastly outnumbered, out-armed and out-sized." The Wanderer spoke slowly, realizing the impulsiveness of King Jasper. "We must be cautious, and we must act in unison."

"Perhaps you are right when you speak for the Elfin Brood or the dainty Shee, but not for the Trolls," Jasper answered with spirit.

"Nonetheless," the Empress interposed, "you will do nothing on your own. As your Empress, I speak not only for the Trolls but for all the Dwarfenfold: for the Boggarts, the Wichtlein, the Nibelungen, the Monaciello and the Stillevolk. We will act in concert with our friends, the Elves and the Shee. And we will obey the commands of King Styrax and the Wanderer."

"It will be as the Empress wishes, naturally," King Jasper replied, bowing deeply, though he felt stung by the rebuke. "But my Troll warriors are a fitting match for anyone, Man or otherwise."

Styrax, who found the boasting of Jasper to be wearying, spoke next. "At present, we have no choice but to meet in grand conclave. The Elves, the Shee, the Dwarfs and whoever else will rally to our cause must sit in deep council, must establish a common plan and must act together, for the armies of Man that will descend upon us are like a great fire that burns all before it. If we are not prepared and organized, we will be swept away. Thus, I believe we must gather soon in my land of Prosopia, for it is there that Man has made his first inroads, and, I feel quite sure, it is there that the ultimate battle will be fought. The Dwarfs must remember that if Prosopia falls, the door is then open to the realm of the Pinus Dwarfs."

And as the hour grew late, and the debate grew tedious, all finally agreed to meet in grand conclave in Prosopia within two week's time. Meanwhile, Styrax, the Wanderer and Empress Saphiria would travel by the underground passages of the Dwarfs to the Pinus Mountains, from which Styrax would return home, the Wanderer would visit the Shee and the Empress would attend upon the Pinus Dwarfs known as the Nibelungen.

* * *

After three days of travel in the darkened tunnels, Styrax was overjoyed, almost ecstatic, to emerge into the sunlight. How rapturous it was to feel again the life-giving brilliance of the sun caressing his green skin that had grown pale in the days he had spent in Troll-land, the Hill of Light and the dark passages they traveled through. Instantly, he felt his old strength pulsing through his body, bringing back his energy and confidence even as it soothed away his fears and confusion.

As they emerged from the tunnel, they found themselves upon the crest of the mighty Pinus Mountains. To the west were endless forests of stout pine, fir, spruce and oak; to the east lay the entire valley of the Rhus. From this vantage point, Styrax, for the first time in his life, could see the entire realm of Prosopia and beyond to the arid grasslands almost hidden in the haze of distance. Here, the Empress bid them farewell, for her path led her along the cliff face to an especially steep and seemingly impassable escarpment riddled with vast wide caves.

"Farewell, my dear friends," the Empress said, "for now I must leave you to join my subjects, the Nibelungen, who live deep within the caves you see before you."

Styrax and the Wanderer watched as the dumpy figure of Empress Saphiria waddled with great skill over craggy rocks and into the depths of the first cave she entered. As the sun wested toward evening, Styrax and the Wanderer decided to camp where they were for the night, for in the morning they would part, the Wanderer heading north to meet with the Shee and Styrax heading east to return to his beloved Canna.

As the dark prevailed, Styrax and the Wanderer built a fire and settled down for their first night under the stars, a sight they had not seen for many a day.

"Do you know of the letters the Aged One gave me?" Styrax asked.

"I know of them, and I know of their contents. The Aged One allowed me to read them before he met with you."

"Forgive me, my friend," Styrax spoke hesitatingly, "but I have been told so much in so short of a time, so much that seems to contradict all that I had thought before, that I can but question and question and question. I am in awe of the Aged One, for he seems truly wise. But I am not certain that I can accept everything he has written as the truth. So much of it seems the spawn of madness."

"Nor should you, Styrax. I have many doubts of my own. When I was young and still a warrior amid the Coursers, my father Profundus, may his name be torn from the book of life, spoke to me of a world very different from that of the Aged One. I then believed Profundus. Now I believe the Aged One. The former gave meaning to death; the latter gave meaning to life. All I now know has come from the Aged One, and all that he has taught me has proven true. True but fantastic so much so that at first I questioned his sanity and then my own."

"Then you do not know that what he says is true," Styrax said with intensity.

"Yes, I do not know, for I have been with the Aged One but a short time. That which he writes of happened deep in the misty past."

"I feel as though I had been told that the sun is not the sun and the sky is not the sky," Styrax said bitterly. "I have always been proud of my Elfishness—Canna often chides me for being too narrowly Elfish. But now, an old Man proclaims that I am the heir of Man, his descendent, and his mortal enemy. If what the Aged One has written is true, then I am like a son who must slay his father."

"But a father who intends to slay his children, for Man knows naught of the Elfin heritage." The Wanderer spoke with care, understanding his companion's torment. "You forget, Styrax, that I am in the same position, perhaps even worse, for Man is only remotely related to the Elfin Brood, but the leader of our common enemy is my father, may his name be blighted."

Styrax sat quietly staring up at the stars. It can't be true, he thought to himself. The Aged One must be mad from centuries of isolation. Finally, he spoke, "I cannot make a decision. At one moment, the Aged One seems a seer, his wisdom beyond doubt, and the next moment he seems a fantastical figure living in a world where dreams and reality are hopelessly jumbled. I must seek further, for now I am an Elf suspended between two very different worlds."

* * *

The following morning the two friends parted with the Wanderer following the steep ridge line northward and Styrax descending into a deep, heavily treed canyon which finally opened onto the mesquite covered flood plains of Prosopia.

Bounding from boulder to boulder, Styrax happily descended the steep and rugged walls of the canyon. He reveled in the sunlight, his excitement mounting as he leaped from stone to stone, knowing that soon he would be among his beloved mesquites and ever nearer his beloved Canna. For the moment, he had thrust the Aged One and the letters from his mind. When he reached the bottom of the canyon through which a lovely stream flowed, he paused to drink of the sparkling waters.

As he sat resting by the stream, he began to sense the presence of another living creature lurking nearby. Cautiously, as he looked about with his sharp Elfin eyes, he placed a dart, lightly dipped in poison so as to stun, into his blowgun. He was sure he could hear heaving breathing in the undergrowth. Then, as he rose, a huge beast, seemingly catlike, sprang from deep cover and was upon Styrax long before he had a chance to raise his weapon. His body was dashed backward, his head striking a boulder as he crashed to the ground. Instantly, the beast picked the unconscious Styrax up in his large jaws and bounded off effortlessly through the dense growth along the stream.

* * *

Styrax regained his consciousness hours later. He found himself lying next to a huge fire built within a clearing ringed by towering pines. His head throbbed painfully, but after feeling the injured area, he realized that the skin was not broken. As he sat up and looked across the fire, he found himself staring directly into the eyes of a giant, a creature green like himself but easily standing twelve foot tall. Lying at the giant's feet was the beast that had attacked him, and Styrax recognized a mordant, the giant puma of the Pinus Mountains, a creature the Elves had heard of in song and legend.

"Are you well, little creature?" The giant's voice boomed.

"Where am I? How did I get here?" Styrax spoke slowly, for his brain had yet to clear.

"You are here in my mountains. My friend, Sandar, brought you to me. He was amazed to find a green Dwarf so far from his cave."

Standing slowly, Styrax shook himself, saying, "I am not a Dwarf. I am Styrax, King of the Prosopian Elves."

"Your mind has been rattled by your fall, little Dwarf." And as he spoke, the giant rose and walked over to Styrax. With his great chin pressed against his chest, the green giant looked down at the tiny figure of Styrax, who, with his head bent back severely was looking straight up into the eyes of his captor. "Ho, ho, ho! I am an Elf. How can someone as tiny as you are think that he is an Elf. Say it no more, little Dwarf, lest you insult and anger me."

Certainly, Styrax had no wish to offend this green giant, but he could not help but notice that though the giant was at least four times larger than himself, he was very like Styrax in feature and form. He also recalled King Jasper's mention of the huge Pinus Elves.

"What is your name?" Styrax asked boldly.

"I am Rhamnus the Elf."

"And who is your king?" Styrax asked.

"I have no king," Rhamnus answered gruffly. "There is no king in the Pinus Mountains. Each of us is master in his own domain."

"Then there are others like you?"

"Of course, there are. Are you sure that blow on the head has not upset your thinking?" The giant asked in a not unfriendly tone.

"Where is your village?"

"Village? What is a village?" And as he spoke, Rhamnus sat cross-legged in front of Styrax.

Relieved at no longer straining his neck looking upward, Styrax spoke, "A village is a place where creatures live together, near each other in a permanent group."

"How disgusting! You mean that they actually live within sight of each other?"

"Of course. They live close enough to touch each other."

Rhamnus scratched his huge head, for he had noticed how much alike he and this little creature were. "I can think of nothing more repulsive than having to see others all the time. But to touch each other! How vile. Why would anyone wish to touch someone else? Can't they keep their hands to themselves?"

Not knowing how to explain himself, Styrax simply answered, "Well, they live close together. That is the way many creatures live."

Rhamnus continued scratching his head in amazement, finally asking, "But how can you be free and joyful and harmonious when constantly crammed together like worms beneath a rock?"

Gradually, as the pain in his head subsided, Styrax and Rhamnus talked more freely, finding pleasure in each other. To answer Styrax's questions about the lives of Pinus Elves, Rhamnus explained that Pinus Elves live in complete solitude, each being responsible for protecting the section of pine forest he or she had selected as a home. He told how during mating season, every twenty years, a male would select a female or a female would select a male, and they would mate and then part. If the female Elf bore a child, the rearing of the child would be shared by both parents so that the child would learn his pinelore, the child spending half a year with each parent. Finding Styrax confused by the solitary nature of the Pinus Elves, Rhamnus continued by explaining that though each Pinus Elf lived alone, he occasionally met others of his kind and frequently met with the Nibelungen who used the forest to gather dead wood for the great fires so important to the lives of Dwarfs. When asked if he had any friends, Rhamnus stroked the sleeping mordant, Sandar, for the great cat was his only companion and his only friend.

"And what do you know of Man?" Styrax asked.

"Who?"

"Man. The ancient creature who lives beyond the Rhus in the sere grasslands."

"Is this creature a Dwarf?" Rhamnus asked confusedly.

Then Styrax explained, as best he could, the history of Man and his present fatal relationship with the Prosopian Elves, the Shee and the Dwarfs. He then described Man in detail.

"Oh, ho! You mean the sickly pale creature," Rhamnus interrupted, "who stands fully twice your size and carries weapons with which he tries to fell my kin, the mighty pines."

"That sounds like the creature I call Man," Styrax answered.

"He is a foul creature who takes his ax to my ancestors. Yes, yes, I know of him, though few have come this way in the last hundred years. Sandar and his friends eat these creatures, or I kill them, then feed them to Sandar."

"Then Man is your enemy as he is mine?"

"Anyone who fells trees is my enemy, be he Man or Dwarf, though as I have said already, the Dwarfs collect only dead wood that lies upon the ground."

Styrax sat silently for a moment, staring directly at his huge companion. When he finally spoke, he did so with care. "Then, Rhamnus, I must say what I said earlier. I am an Elf, a Prosopian Elf from the great plains that cover the land from the foot of these mountains to the banks of the mighty

Rhus. We are mesquite Elves who guard our trees as energetically as you guard the pines for the mesquite contains the souls of our parents and their parents before them. Is that not the way of the Pinus Elves?"

"Yes, Styrax, that is exactly the way of my kind," Rhamnus said, pausing as he spoke. "Yes, I see now that you are as I am, but ever so much smaller. Yes, I grant you that you are an Elf like me for only Elves enter into the being of their trees. But, little Styrax, do you realize what we have discovered? The Elfin Tribe is already larger than I ever suspected now that I know of Prosopian Elves. But are there more Elves? If I am a Pinus Elf and you are a Mesquite Elf, then are there not Oak Elves? And Fir Elves? And Sycamore Elves? Yet among these trees I have lived for many a century, and you are the first being I have met who also claims to be of the Elfin Brood."

"Until I met you, Rhamnus, I thought all Elves were from Prosopia and were like me."

Thus they spoke, deep into the night and thus they became friends, an experience of great pith for Rhamnus, who until this very night had never entertained the notion of friendship with another self-aware being. Styrax told of all his adventures with Man, with the Wanderer, with the Shee, with Empress Saphiria and her Trolls, and with the Aged One. He spoke of the great war that was to come, of the grand conclave to be convened in a short time. For Styrax, still over-awed by the gigantic Rhamnus, was hoping to enlist him as an ally against the depredation of Man.

"Will you join us in grand conclave, Rhamnus?" Styrax asked as he finished his lengthy tales to which Rhamnus gave intense attention.

"No, that I can never do. Can you imagine me

trying to stumble through your twisted and spiny mesquite? No, Styrax, though I now have the joy of your friendship, a joy I have never experienced before, I cannot leave my sacred responsibility. For now I see the virtue of what you call 'living together'. You may leave your land, and other Elves will assume your duties, but I live alone, as it should be, and can never leave my sacred groves. Nor do I wish to enter into your world of massive strife. This, though, I promise you for after all, we are both Elves and that is a bond not to be taken lightly. In defeat, or in victory, you and your kindred, all the Elves of Prosopia, will find safety within the precincts of the soaring pines, and here you need fear no one, especially this Man creature. This shall be, through all the ages, your haven."

Styrax felt tears forming as he answered, "You are an Elf, Rhamnus, and you are my kin. That I now see. When the evil has gone, I will come again to share your fire amid the pines. But now I must sleep, for with the faint light of morn, I must return to my land and my people. You know, as I know, there can be no retreat from our blessed mesquite, for there we must conquer or die."

Sadly Rhamnus answered, "This is as it should be. In the morn, I shall send Sandar with you to protect you as far as your own thicketed land. From the crest, I will watch my friend Styrax return to his home and often, thereafter, I will watch to see your campfires that I may think again of the first being I have called friend."

the cluster of Beastums by the shore. He heard their fearful cries, and, more importantly, he heard the voice of their remaining leader explaining that the warriors had been killed by Yellfen magic, for the bodies seemed to be without wounds. Shortly thereafter, he watched as the terrified Beastums gathered their ragged belongings and headed south along the Rhus. Thuja thought to follow, but just as he was about to leave, he noticed the leader, now alone, return to the banks of the Rhus to re-examine the bodies of the dead warriors. Strange, Thuja thought, he has told the others of death by Yellfen magic, but he seeks the real cause of death. Thuja watched as the leader of the Beastums discovered the tiny wound of an Elfin dart in the shoulder of one of the dead men. The leader milked at the wound and tasted what he found. He knows about poisons, Thuja realized, and he now knows how they died. But why has he sent the others away? Thuja continued to observe the Beastum's leader as he examined each body. When he was done, he pushed each body back into the current, watching as they drifted downstream.

Each day, Thuja watched the leader as he gathered wooden tent poles and lashed them together to form a raft. And finally, he watched as the leader rushed to the river, launched his raft and began polling for the opposite shore of the Rhus. Thuja, who thought the raft was to be used to follow the other Beastums downstream, was astonished to see this long, gaunt leader of the Beastums polling frantically toward Thuja's side of the river. Carefully, he followed the raft until the leader jumped ashore on sacred Elfin soil. Pushing the raft back into the current, the leader started to struggle his way into the mesquite which was especially dense along the river edge. Thuja raised his blowgun and inserted a dart that had been lightly dipped in poison, for Thuja did not wish to kill, just to stun, so that this Man creature would be a prisoner to await the return of Styrax. Carefully, he aimed and shot, and the dart, flying true, struck the leader in the back of the thigh. He quickly pulled the dart free, and as quickly he drew the point across his tongue, spitting out what he tasted. He showed no sign of fear as he shouted out, "I have come as a friend of the Yellfen. Do not kill me! I come as a friend."

Thuja quietly watched as the leader struggled in the deep thicket, growing weaker and weaker until he fell backwards slipping into unconsciousness.

* * *

Later that day, Thuja and five other Elves struggled to carry the stricken leader to a large, deep pit just outside the village. Gently, they lowered the unconscious body down into the pit that had such steep sides, escape would be impossible. Thuja stood guard until sunset, ever watching the strange being, not certain that he would live. That night he told Hebe and Canna of his adventure, and they all went to the pit to see the captive Man. Canna and Hebe stared in amazement, for they had never seen a Man this closely, except the Wanderer.

"Oh my, but he is large and very ugly. His face is covered with hair," Hebe said in disgust. For Elves have no facial or body hair, and, traditionally, the Elfin Brood associated hairiness with the Dwarfs, deeming it their worst feature.

"Is he dead?" Canna asked.

"I don't think so," Thuja replied. "I barely dipped the dart into my poison pouch. If you look closely, you can see that he breathes, ever so slightly. I thought of killing him, but then I thought Styrax might wish to speak to him and I want to know what he is up to."

"You did as you should," Canna said, easing Thuja's mind, for in the absence of Styrax, Canna was the ruler of Prosopia.

"His face is all wrinkled, and his hands are bony," Hebe observed. "If you look closely, he even has hair coming out of his nose and all around his ears. He is uglier than a horny toad. Are they all this ugly?"

Thuja laughed at Hebe's repulsion, saying, "The Wanderer is a Man, and you think him quite dashing. I think much of the ugliness you see is really old age, for this creature is much, much older than those Styrax and I confronted. For Man does not join his ancestors as we do. Man lives on to wither and shrivel, like the creature in the pit."

"You mean they die by decaying, by allowing themselves to rot. Do they not seek unity and peace when they are ready to die? The more I see and hear of Man, the more frightening he becomes. Take me away, Thuja, for this creature sickens me."

* * *

The following morning, Canna and Thuja returned to the pit to find the captive alive and awake. As they peered into the pit, the captive, seeing them, spoke, "Greetings, green creatures. I assume you are the Yellfen. Am I right in that?"

Canna answered, "I know not what a Yellfen is. We are Prosopian Elves. My name is Canna."

Speaking in a friendly and submissive manner, the captive answered, "My name is Vastar, of the Beastum tribe. I would speak to your king, or someone in authority."

Thuja leaned forward, staring down at Vastar. "You are speaking with Canna, our Queen. Her mate, our King Styrax the Fleet, will be with us soon. It was I, Thuja, the right hand of Styrax, who captured you."

"You are the Queen?" Vastar asked in astonishment as he stared at the slender, unclothed form of Canna.

"Is that hard to believe?" Canna asked gently.

"Forgive me, Queen Canna, for the rulers of men are usually aged men dressed in pompous robes. You are so small and delicate and wear no clothing at all." Vastar spoke with care, knowing his position. "Are all the Elves as tiny as you are?"

"If we are so delicate, why are you in the pit?" Thuja asked sternly.

"A good rejoinder, Thuja. I spoke from curiosity, not malice."

"Tell us why you have come. And do not lie. Thuja's next dart will be dipped deeper into his poison pouch," Canna said.

"Then hear me, Queen Canna, for I come as a friend who can be of service to you and your tribe. I know you hate the race of Man and it is right that you should. But my tribe, the Beastums, is no more. Those that have gone downstream will soon starve, for they are already near death."

"We care little for Man, in that you are right," Canna spoke with authority. "But Elves do not hate—it is not in our nature. If Man is our enemy, it is because he would have it so. I had thought of having you dispatched, but first I will listen to your thoughts and arguments, and will see if you offer anything of benefit to us. What is it you can do for us?"

Vastar, ever shrewd, spoke humbly but forcefully. "True, you have no reason to trust me, and my execution would be, perhaps, no more than I deserve. But, on my behalf, I must say that Vastar the Wise knows many things that would be of use to the Elves of Prosopia, so much so that my assistance might tilt the balance in the Elves' favor. I am no fool. Mark that well. I am alone, and I wish to live and it matters not if I live with Man or with Elves. Man has little regard for my knowledge, for he lives by the strength of his arms. The Elves seem wise; they will not shun wisdom, even if it comes from one as despised as I am."

"We do not despise you, Vastar, but we do not trust you," Canna said firmly.

Thuja, sitting on the edge of the pit with his blowgun handy, said to Vastar, "You speak well, old Man, but so far you have offered us little but talk. You disparage Man but you are a Man. You compliment us now, but a week ago you sought our deaths. I have little trust in you and think, perhaps, that the Elfin cause would best be served by your instant death—one less enemy to kill. But in this, I am ruled by my Queen."

Canna, taking her cue from Thuja, spoke slowly and coldly, "Give us a token of your faith, Vastar, or die."

Vastar, looking directly into Canna's narrowed eyes, spoke quickly, "I wish you no harm. My fortunes have led me to your camp. I wish only to live and in order to do this I must serve. Listen carefully, Queen Canna, and then judge my worth."

"Go on," Canna ordered.

"This very day, a new enemy of the Elves will appear. Watch carefully, for they are mighty warriors, strong, organized and well-armed. They will be dressed in scarlet and will be led by Profundus the Guileful, my brother in blood and my mortal enemy. His army is vast and merciless, and his goal is the conquest of all the lands you call Prosopia and all the lands further west beyond yonder mountains. I alone understand Profundus and his method of waging war, and I alone can give you the victory you must have."

Canna rose and signaled to Thuja that the interview was over. "You will stay where you are, Vastar. Your life is of little value to us. But, perhaps, your information might be of some use."

As Canna and Thuja walked back to their village, Canna said, "Watch him carefully, Thuja, and watch the river to see if his words are true. If so, he may be of use to us. That will be for Styrax to decide. Meanwhile, feed him and see to his needs. I do wish Styrax would come home."

Later that day, Thuja witnessed the arrival of Lord Thrett and the twenty scarlet warriors. They are stout men, well armed with fresh mounts, he recognized, but they are hardly a vast army. Later, he watched, as the scarlet warriors rode back the way they had come.

Chapter Nineteen

During the windless afternoon, Canna became aware of a subtle rustling in the mesquite thickets, as if the trees and bushes were whispering to each other. She ran to the large mesquite tree that hovered over the home she and Styrax had built many years before. Reaching up, she grasped a branch in each hand avoiding the cruel spines and pulled the fragile leaflets tightly against her ears, closing her eyes as she stood motionlessly. Her excitement was growing.

Thuja and Hebe, having brought food to Vastar, had just returned to the village when they spied Canna holding the branches against her head.

"Is something wrong?" Thuja asked as he ran up to Canna.

"No. Nothing is wrong," Canna said smiling. "They whisper glad tidings."

Canna let go of the branches and rushed to Hebe, embracing her excitedly, tears staining the softness of her cheeks.

"Styrax is coming home, the trees sigh in joy, and I must be gone."

With that, Canna ran off to the west so swiftly that Thuja and Hebe stood dumbfounded but happy, for all of Prosopia rejoiced when its king returned.

* * *

Styrax stroked the muscled neck of Sandar the mordant and bid him to return to Rhamnus, for now that he had come upon the outer edges of Prosopia, he no longer needed the protection of the great cat. Quickly Sandar bounded into the undercover and disappeared into the steep hills leading back up to the crest of the Pinus Mountains.

How good it felt to be in the sun and to be home again, Styrax mused, as he touched and caressed the mesquite bushes nearest to him. Happily he watched as the mesquite began to rustle from bush to bush to bush, spreading in all directions like the ripples on a pond. Quickening his pace, Styrax trotted toward his village, his Elfin heart beating in expectation. After an hour of running, he sat in the shade of a shallow arroyo beneath what the Elves believed to be the most ancient of mesquite trees, for it was a giant among mesquites covering the entire arroyo for the space of a hundred yards. As he sat back regaining his breath, he began to sense another being approaching, and on the gentle desert breeze came the aura of his beloved. Within a moment, Canna came running up the wash, her lovely hair trailing in the wind. They rushed toward one another until their bodies came together, kissing and embracing beneath the benign sun.

As Styrax caressed his beloved, he noticed that the tips of her lovely tresses had turned to a glowing red, as if her hair was beginning to glow with flame. Proudly, she stood back, saying softly, "Our time has come, my love; I feel new life coursing through me."

Styrax drew Canna towards him. For long moments, they stared deeply into each other's eyes, feeling the intensity of the moment and knowing that their love would now lead to fruition. Gently, Styrax lifted Canna in his arms, carrying her into the timeless shade of the most ancient of mesquites, and here amid their ancestor of ancestors, they made love.

For Elves do not breed as men do, in careless rages of passion. To an Elf, the physical nature of love was but a preparation for the carefully awaited period of fertility which seldom came before the hundredth year and rarely more than six times in a female Elf's life. The ripe moment for conception was upon them and was signaled when the female's hair became richly red at the tips, making her ever more beautiful in the eyes of her beloved. And Canna's time had come, the time she had longed for since her childhood days when she first came to know and love Styrax, a time when they were still children. Canna would carry her child for two years, and its birth would cause great rejoicing throughout Prosopia, for their first born would be the next king or queen.

That afternoon, the Elves of Prosopia were startled when they noticed that throughout their sacred land, the mesquites suddenly began to writhe and twist about violently even though the breezes were gentle. And for a moment, they thought the sun had paused in its passage above the azure sky, paused and then moved on.

* * *

The following morning, Thuja told Styrax of all that had happened while Styrax was still at the Hill of Light. Styrax was confused by the news of the capture of Vastar. He had hoped to be able to dismiss the subject of Man from his mind, at least for a few days, but now he had to face the

Beastum's shaman. Hebe and Canna were assigned the task of calling all the Elders to council as soon as possible. Thuja was to bring Vastar to the house of Styrax.

As Vastar was lead by Thuja to his meeting with King Styrax, he attempted to kneel before the person of the King.

"Don't do that," Styrax ordered. "We have no need for ritual in Prosopia. You are a Man. Stand as a Man should."

Vastar quickly stood up, making only the slightest of bows.

"I have little time," said Styrax, "for dallying with my sworn enemy. Thuja was, perhaps, foolish in not slaying you as you entered our sacred land. If you wish to live, then you must answer all my questions quickly and directly, and if I am pleased with your answers, you might be allowed to live. If not, you will meet your destiny in a pit of scorpions. Do you understand?"

Vastar nodded his agreement but said nothing. Styrax had tried to sound severe, had tried to sound Man-like in his bravado, though he was somewhat embarrassed by trying to be what he was not. For though Styrax and Canna made threats upon Vastar's life, neither of them was capable of the frightening threats each had made. Styrax had learned to kill in battle, for he had no other choice, but to kill a helpless prisoner, no matter what his crimes were, was beyond Elfin powers. Yet, he realized he must act sternly, even cruelly, for Man understood no other language.

"First of all, why should I bother to spare you?" Styrax asked abruptly.

"Simply because I am a Man," Vastar answered. "Because I think like your enemies, because I know how they think, and, finally, because the leader of your enemies is my brother, Profundus the Guileful, may his name be cursed."

"You would strike your own brother?"

"Yea, I would strike him. I would gouge out his eyes and have him torn apart by mighty steeds. He and I have sworn death upon the other and death it will be.

"You may wonder," Vastar continued, "why this enmity is so deep, King Styrax. From our youth onward, we have striven for power and riches, the only reason for Man to live. From childhood on, Profundus has loathed me as a rival, as an enemy, and as a contender to the throne. He has slain my wife and children, and my retinue, and would have slain me instantly had I not escaped in time."

Styrax found Vastar's story both gruesome and wearying, for in the telling Vastar did little more than confirm Styrax's already profound disdain for Man. Immediately, Styrax was disturbed by Vastar's motive, his seething hatred for his brother, for Styrax instinctively knew hatred to be a treacherous guide. How strange, he thought, that Man's motives were always based on passion instead of reason, and if Man used reason, it was but to serve his emotions.

"Tell me more of Profundus," Styrax said, "and tell me of his armies."

"He is very powerful and thinks himself very wise. His greatest strength lies in his hatred for his own kind, his fellow men. His only desire is for power, for ascendancy and for wealth, for they are all one to him."

"Has he no family?" Styrax asked, knowing that Vastar was unaware of the Wanderer's existence.

"He has had many wives, all of whom he has cast out or slain. He had only one child, a son, but none have seen him for many years and most assume that he is long since dead. His army is large but not well trained, except for the Scarlet Five Hundred, his essential force. These warriors are sexless, being neutered in infancy, and have but one goal in life, to be victorious in warfare. His scarlet warriors are masters of the crossbow, the lance, and the sword, and their steeds are fearless in battle. To defeat Profundus, you must overthrow the Scarlet Five Hundred—the rest of his army, nay, the bulk of his army is nothing more than a rabble."

Styrax pondered the words of Vastar. He believed the words he heard because he could find no reason for Vastar to lie. He was Styrax's prisoner whose only hope for continued life seemed to depend upon how useful he could make himself to the Elves.

"Will Profundus come alone? Or will he have allies?" Styrax asked.

"I think he will seek allies, for with the demise of the Beastums, he will realize that the Elves are a more formidable enemy than he first expected. Also, Profundus will not commit the Scarlet Five Hundred to battle unless he is certain of victory. Generally in battle, he commits his other forces or his allies' forces with great sacrifice of life, holding back the scarlet warriors until he knows that they will sweep to victory. In this fashion, he rarely gambles, rarely loses many of his best warriors and leads the Scarlet Five Hundred to continue to believe in their own invincibility. If he seeks allies, they are likely to be the few remaining tribes of men still living in this part of the world: the Querques, led by Yen the Cruel; the Shams, controlled by Lusta the Bitch; and the Gluttas, ruled by Gasher the Bold. They alone are foolish enough to follow the devious plans of Profundus."

Thuja whispered in Styrax's ear, "Perhaps, that is why I saw only a few of the scarlet warriors. They came ahead as scouts and now have retired to await the coming of the rest of their army and those of their allies."

Styrax nodded, for he had had the same thought.

"How will Profundus cross the river?"

Vastar paused a moment before he answered, "A question I cannot answer with anything more than a wise guess. One of the Beastums, a savage warrior called Thrett, has joined the ranks of the enemy, and he will, no doubt, tell them of the crossing to the north. As Profundus' army and the armies of his allies will be vast and heavily equipped, my only guess is that he will attempt to build a bridge of some sort at that place, for his many loaded wagons cannot cross the rushing Rhus."

Thuja interrupted, "What do you mean by 'heavily equipped'?"

"Mainly his battle catapults, a form of weapon well suited for war with your people."

"Catapults?" Styrax asked. "What are they?"

"You really know little of the ways of men. How strange, for your foes are equally ignorant in that they know little of the ways of the Elves. The catapult is a huge machine for throwing great stones, easily the size and weight of your largest Elf, that can crush the most formidable walls. The catapults can also be used to throw fire in great balls of burning pitch. It is a frightening weapon."

"Is there no defense against these catapults?" Styrax asked.

"None. But their range is short. I suggest you move your people and their dwellings back three hundred yards from the river then you will be beyond their range. The only damage will be to the mesquite thickets."

Both Styrax and Thuja were appalled to think of damage to the sacred plants of Prosopia, but they also realized the wisdom of Vastar's recommendation.

Vastar continued, "And the catapults give you a distinct advantage in that these massive machines of war are ponderous and difficult to move and will reduce your enemy's mobility. With catapults, he must move slowly."

Silence reigned for many moments as Styrax pondered the problem of the catapults. Finally, King Styrax spoke, "We will speak again, Vastar, for I have many questions. Meanwhile, you are free to do as you please. The Elfin Brood has no use for captives. You may cross the Rhus and rejoin your tribe. You may cross the river and join your brother, Profundus. Or, you may stay here among the Elfin Brood. Whatever you do, we will learn from your actions."

When Vastar was gone, Styrax told Thuja to warn all the Elves whose homes were near the Rhus to be prepared on command to move away from the river.

Chapter Twenty

Styrax had chosen an open field, enclosed by mesquite, well back from the river for the Grand Conclave with the Shee, the Trolls, the Nibelungen and any others who would join in the struggle against Man. Canna and Hebe had signaled by smoke-fire all the Elders of Prosopia, and already they had begun to arrive and congregate.

As this was to be a grand occasion and as others besides the Elves were to be present, Styrax decided that all the Elders were to wear their ceremonial robes, something very rare indeed for the Elfin Brood. As the Elves must be exposed to the sun, the wearing of any garment at all was unusual and the wearing of formal robes almost unheard of. But, the gravity of the meeting, the inclusion of creatures other than Elves and the need to impress his chosen allies made the ceremonial robes a necessity. And Styrax insisted on the wearing of these robes to allow his allies to feel at ease, especially the Dwarfs who were bewildered by Elfin nakedness. The robes themselves were simple and cape-like, being woven of osier canes ornamented with colorful stones, mostly turquoise and carnelian.

That moonless evening beneath a star-filled

sky, Styrax addressed the Council of Elders and explained to them his trip to the Aged One, his meeting with Fon-du-Fon and the Shee and his adventures with Empress Saphiria, King Jasper and the Trolls.

He spoke also of Profundus and the Scarlet Five Hundred, the catapults, and Vastar who many of the Elders had spoken to that very day. He also informed them of the grand conclave scheduled to begin within the week when all those opposed to Man would meet as one people.

The first Elder to speak was Acanthopanax. "Though my time has come to begin my second life, I have decided to postpone my departure until the end has become clearer. I am weary and ready for peace, but Man has denied me that. Therefore, I will stay among the Elfin Brood until I am certain of our freedom or of our death. Styrax has done well, and his burden is heavy, enough to crush most others. We have long lived in seclusion wholly within the bounds of Prosopia. This must now end. The Elf must once again have commerce with the rest of the world. Man must be defeated so that harmony may once again rustle through the fields and be borne on the wind. I say that we must do as we must do."

Lupinus, the Elder of Mesquitana, the Elfin village at the foot of the Pinus Mountains, and an uncle to Styrax, spoke next. "We are a small people with feeble weapons; our foes are huge with mighty engines of war. The enemy is trained to kill and, in fact, takes great pleasure in the act of killing; we are untrained and loathe the very thought of injuring another living thing. They are trained to act in concert; we are by nature doomed to act individually. Yet, Acanthopanax and Styrax, my nephew, speak of war, speak of killing, speak of death. Is this reasonable? Is this Elfin?"

Thuja, who stood behind Styrax and who seldom spoke at councils, stepped forward boldly. "Rest assured, Lupinus, that killing, though against our natures, is not as difficult as you make it seem. I, who had never destroyed another living thing, have been forced to kill our enemy, Man, and found it no more difficult than killing a snake that threatens a child. If we are to live, they must die."

Callistemon followed, "I do not wish to debate the ease with which we can kill others, nor do I wish to speak of battle tactics. Have we spoken with this creature Profundus? No! Have we attempted to reason with Man? No! Have we considered the plethora of horrors we are about to set loose? No! Too quickly, we have decided upon war, the madness that has been Man's ultimate curse. Are we being entrapped in a snare not of our own making? Granted that Thuja and King Styrax have faced and killed the enemy, but have they faced these catapults or have they faced trained armies? The answer is no. Perhaps King Styrax can speak to this matter."

Styrax whispered something to Thuja who immediately trotted away from the council. For many moments, the council talked within itself. Then Thuja returned with Vastar.

Speaking aloud for all to hear, Styrax said to Vastar, "Vastar, I will give you an opportunity to demonstrate your usefulness to our cause. How are we, the Elfin Brood, armed solely with our blowguns, to withstand the awesome might of Man's war machines? And will it benefit our cause to attempt reasoning with Profundus the Guileful?"

Vastar, standing to the side, spoke humbly,

realizing how inappropriate it was for him to be addressing the Elfin Council of Elders. "You must use that with which you have been endowed by nature. These engines of war are deadly, but they are also cumbersome, difficult to operate, and extremely slow to move. The Elf is agile, fast and unburdened by heavy weapons. You must attack quickly, strike accurately and disappear as quickly as you came. Man is in his most dangerous state when he is organized. Disrupt his organization, and you will have an edge. I do not suggest that you parley with Profundus or any of his allies. First of all, he will assume that your desire for a meeting is a sign of weakness and fear. Secondly, his treachery is such that he will, most likely, slay any agents you allow to cross the river. And thirdly, your enemy will then know who and what you are. Man is still cursed by his superstitious nature and his fear of the unknown. Play on these fears. Let Man struggle against the mesquite while the Elves remain secretive, unseen and unknown. By mentioning Elfin magic, I struck fear in the hearts of the Beastums and now they are no more."

Sambucus, an Elder from the north of Prosopia, asked, "Why should we place stock in this Vastar creature's words? He is one of them."

Styrax answered, "You speak as I once spoke of the Wanderer. He is also a Man, but I have come to trust him as I would Canna, my Queen. Now, Vastar is hardly to be mentioned in the same breath as the Wanderer, except that they are both men. Listen to Vastar, perhaps he speaks the truth; perhaps he lies. But what he has just said is true, and we will gain by it. Vastar has come among us to preserve his own life; that I can understand, and if he can be of use to us, then we must use him."

"Fear not, Elves of Prosopia," Vastar said, "for I mean you no harm. Already, I have come to honor your Elfin ways, though I have been among you but a few days. You are gentle and guided by reason—strange virtues in the eyes of Man."

"But do we have the strength to oppose Man? Are our numbers sufficient? Are our weapons adequate?" Styrax asked.

Vastar paused a moment, then spoke, "I do not know. But numbers rarely determine anything. Your enemy is equipped to fight in organized and open warfare—that is all he knows. He wishes you to put an army in the field to face his army, for this form of warfare allows Man to use his frightful weapons. But these same weapons are generally useless when the opposition fights from cover, attacks when least expected and retires when challenged openly. I fear that Elfin strength will prove inadequate against Man if the Elves choose to fight as Man does. Your best defense is the mesquite thickets. Use them wisely."

The arguments lasted well into the night, but at the conclusion of the council all agreed to support the actions of King Styrax, simply because there was no other action to take. And, finally, all supported the King because he was the King, a burden few of them envied. In the Elfin world, a king had no more significance than a heron or a lizard. Though he was born King, Styrax was just another Elf until the time of extremity. Then his birthright became an awesome burden and his power became absolute.

* * *

Later, as Thuja and Hebe, and Styrax and Canna sat by the Rhus, Canna observed, "I have taken a liking to Vastar. He seems a harmless old

Man, lonely and haunted by his past."

"Harmless?" Styrax echoed. "But only under present conditions. His power is not in his arms but in his mind. He is a manipulator of others, having them do his will. Whenever he speaks, I am on guard. As long as we keep him isolated, without others to use, yes, then he is harmless."

"Then, after we have found out what we need to know, should we not send him back to his kind?" Thuja asked.

"Is that just?" Styrax replied. "He has helped us thus far, for we play upon his fears and hatreds. He will help us again. Would it be right to send him back knowing that Profundus seeks his death?"

"No. That would be wrong," Hebe answered. "He is old and, perhaps, Elfin ways may change him and make him aware of the harmonies Man seems senseless to. I know he is ugly, but that is no crime."

Canna, ever wise, took Styrax's right hand in hers and said, "You seek more from Vastar than his aid in the coming war. Am I not right?"

Styrax squeezed Canna's tiny hand and said, "Yes, you are right. Many things the Aged One has told me have caused me great pain. I want to believe him for he is wise; yet much that he has said seems beyond my ken, seems too fantastical to be believed. When the moment is right, I must ask Vastar about the Aged One. I must know more."

"Can you speak of it, my love?" Canna asked softly.

"Not yet. From you, I can hide nothing, but until I know more, it would be foolish to share my inner confusion, my torment. I know things now that I wish I had never known. I must know more."

"Surely, you can speak among your friends,"

Thuja innocently offered.

"No, Thuja, I cannot speak among friends or enemies, for that which I wish to speak of is so muddled in my mind that I cannot give it voice, I cannot find words to express the terrors that haunt my soul. I must know more."

As the hours passed, they lay beneath the night sky playing an ancient Elfin game in which the ever-changing stars created pictures in one person's mind and the others tried to guess what was imagined. And soon they slept as the Rhus rushed by.

Chapter Twenty-One

On the day preceding the grand conclave, Empress Saphiria, bedecked in her royal robes of varied shades of blue, the favorite color of Dwarfs, waddled quickly into Styrax's village. Warmly was she met, with all due respect for an Empress and her Nibelungen guard of twenty soldiers. The Nibelungen were shorter and stockier than the Trolls and generally of a darker complexion. Like most Dwarfs, they were severe in appearance, heavily bearded and reserved in manner at least until they were convinced of the intentions of their hosts, and as the Elves were by nature outgoing and genuinely friendly, the Nibelungen soon found themselves relaxed and happy with new-found friends. The Nibelungen soldiers proudly wore their golden armor, gleaming radiantly in the intense sunlight, both as an indication of their wealth in gold and as a demonstration of each Dwarf's skill at metal-working. They all carried but one weapon, a huge, two handed battle-ax. The stoutest and the strongest of the Nibelungen was King Sard who wore a large silver and gold crown embellished with intricately carved turquoise stones, and the handle of his ax was fashioned in delicate traceries of polished gold.

As soon as the formal introductions had been made, King Styrax led the Nibelungen contingent deep into the shade of a mesquite bower, knowing that the beloved sun of the Elves was a sore burden to the Dwarfs who rarely ventured outside the shelter of their elaborate caverns.

"It gives me great pleasure," Queen Canna said to the Empress Saphiria, "that you have come a day early, for I have long wanted to meet with the Nibelungen. All I know of your people is that they make beautiful brazen horns upon which we make Elfin music, the most satisfying of our enchantments. Tonight, we will talk and listen to Elfin song."

The Empress, happy with her reception and pleased with Queen Canna, was somewhat confounded when she was introduced to Vastar, for until that moment she had never set eyes upon a Man other than the Wanderer and the Aged One. Her coolness was obvious, and Vastar soon moved away, knowing the discomfort he was causing.

"Good Heavens," the Empress burst out, "he's so wrinkled and thin, his arms and legs are little more than spindles, and his eyes are so deeply sunken within his haggard face. He seems hardly a foe to reckon with. I do not trust him nor should you."

"He is our willing captive, Empress," Styrax answered. "He has given us valuable information about our enemy and the weapons we must inevitably face, and he seems to seek nothing more than a chance to continue living in peace. But, as you say, I trust him not."

That evening, the Elves made a grand feast of Elfin food: roasted grasshoppers and cicadas, mushrooms of every sort baked, boiled, and fresh, smothered in tangy sauces and bedded on savory

mesquite pods. The Nibelungen joined in by roast-
ing lizards and baking bats, foods they brought
with them realizing that Elfin food was, perhaps,
not to their taste, and they carefully avoided Elfin
liquors having been warned by Hebe and Thuja
that all Elfin wines contain thornapple and
amanita, poisons to creatures other than Elves.
And while they ate, the Elfin musicians performed
on their musical instruments, giving the brazen
horns of the Nibelungen special prominence. King
Sard was especially pleased, for though the Dwarfs
made the brazen horns, they lacked the talent of
the Elves, using the horns for little more than
hunting and battle calls. He was also charmed by
the wooden flutes the Elves fashioned from tamarisk and scrub oak limbs, and before the night
was over, the Elves had given each Dwarf a wooden
flute upon which the Dwarfs made screeching
noises and other grating sounds well into the early
morning hours, causing some slight annoyance
in the camp.

Long after the feast had concluded, Styrax and
Canna, Thuja and Hebe, and Saphiria and Sard
sat by a fire next to the river. The Empress and
King Sard drank Troll wine which they had brought
with them, a present from King Jasper, while the
Elves drank Fool's Delight. As they rested, content within themselves, listening to the harsh whispers of the Rhus beneath the star-filled sky, Hebe
softly sang an ancient Elfin song:

Ever the river flows, night and day,
Ever the wind blows.
Ever my beloved would stay.
Ever my beloved goes.
And the owl sings the night is long.
Softly the river flows, morn and eve,
Softly my beloved sighs.

Softly the breezes weave
Softly singing amid the trees.
And the owl sings the night is long.
Sadly the river flows, day and night,
Sadly my song is sung.
Sadly we ever seek the light,
Sadly we cease to be young.
And the owl sings the night is long.

Empress Saphiria with tears running down her plump cheeks took Hebe's tiny hand and said, "How beautifully you sing, my child. You have moved my callous heart and given me great joy. When these troubles have passed, when Man is gone, when peace again reigns, you must come to Niflheim to teach Dwarf maidens the art of song."

"More than song, dear Empress," Styrax offered, "we must share more than song though that would be an excellent beginning. For ages, our peoples have lived side by side but have not joined in closer union. The age of isolation is no more, no longer are we ensiled. We must learn to live together, to live in active harmony or not live at all."

"Perhaps the curse of Man," King Sard replied, "is no curse at all. Perhaps Man will leave us a blessing in that he forces the union of the remaining self-aware creatures."

"Hold on, my friends. We are not rid of Man as yet," Thuja said. "Music, friendliness, happiness — I am for all of that, but first we must face an enemy whose power we can only guess and hardly imagine. How many soldiers have the Nibelungen? Are they fierce in battle? Are not these the questions we should be answering?"

"Friend Thuja," the Empress answered, "these questions can only be answered in the field of battle, while this night is for revelry and friendship. But, fear not. The Nibelungen will field one thousand soldiers, as brave as any in the Dwarfenfold."

"Nor should you forget the ancient saying of the Nibelungen," King Sard said. "Beware the Nibelungen ax-Man, for he fells his enemy as a woodsman fells trees."

The adage brought laughter to all, for all were feeling the powers of the liquors they had drunk.

Suddenly, a voice spoke from the darkness beyond the fire. "Greetings my friends Styrax, lovely Canna, doughty Thuja, sweet Hebe, Empress Saphiria and a new friend. I am the Wanderer."

And into the light he strode. Styrax immediately grasped his hand with great warmth. Thuja grasped the other hand and introduced the Wanderer to King Sard.

"My heart rejoices at the sight of the famous Nibelungen ax-men. Our cause grows ever more strong. Let the foe beware," the Wanderer said as he shook King Sard's strong hand.

"Has all gone well?" Styrax asked.

"All has gone as planned."

"But where are the Shee? I thought you were to bring them with you," Styrax questioned.

The Wanderer smiled broadly, then burst into loud laughter.

Surprised, Styrax asked, "What makes you laugh so?"

Still laughing, the Wanderer replied, "Dear Styrax, your memory is short. The Shee are here. They are upon us."

Then from all the trees surrounding the fire, the happy girlish laughter of the Shee could be heard. All those around the fire stood in amazement and confusion, and even as they stood, the small and lithe bodies of the Shee jumped lightly into the light of the fire.

"He-he-he, the Shee are here, he-he-he." And

quickly about twenty Shee stepped from the depths of the darkness, their tiny silvery forms reflecting the firelight and their large green eyes sparkling with even more brightness.

Before anyone could speak, Fon-du-Fon, ancestral queen of the Shee, had introduced herself to each of the company, ever laughing and ever in motion. "I have come, he-he-he, to your mighty war council, he-he-he, to speak of vile and nasty things, he-he-he."

King Styrax and Empress Saphiria cordially offered to share their wines and viands, but the Shee gracefully declined, for they never drank liquid in any form, eating only fermented berries which had much the same impact as Troll wine or Fool's Delight. Each of the Shee wore nothing more than a light diaphanous cape thrown loosely over her shoulders, and all of the party realized that what Styrax had said was true—all the Shee were female.

King Sard, though happy to find new friends and allies, was somewhat dismayed, for the Shee were so delicate looking and were so petite that he assumed them to be worthless in warfare.

The Wanderer, seeing the doubtful look in King Sard's eyes, quickly said, "And my friends, the Shee, are warriors of great renown ever foremost in battle."

"Surely, you jest," King Sard said expectedly.

"Do I jest, Queen Fon-du-Fon?" the Wanderer asked as he looked toward the Queen of the Shee.

"Perhaps, King Sard would like to test our mettle, he-he-he," Queen Fon-du-Fon responded. "Perhaps one of his mighty ax-men, he-he-he, would attack one of my maidens."

King Sard, a bit embarrassed, answered, "My soldiers are not used to playing games."

Fon-du-Fon bounded over to the smallest of the Shee and led her over to where King Sard stood. "This is Zebrina, the smallest of the Shee. Have your boldest warrior attack her, he-he-he, and not as in game; let him attack her as if she were a mortal foe, he-he-he, as if she were the evilest of men. Let him be as savage and ruthless as he can."

"I fear for your maiden, Queen Fon-du-Fon. My ax-men are feared by all." King Sard was in deadly earnest. "But if you insist, then I will order Shale, my right hand, to do as you wish."

Without pause, little Zebrina leaped backward and waited for Shale to charge her. She stood half-crouched, her feet set apart with her hands held loosely in front of her middle. Shale, confused by his tiny opponent, paused a moment, hoping to be excused from this embarrassment, but seeing that King Sard was not going to intervene, he slowly raised his ax in both hands and rushed half-heartedly upon the form of Zebrina. He swung the ax with frightening quickness, but it slashed little more than air as Zebrina simply leaped beyond the ax's range. Again, Shale sprang forward, this time handling his ax with greater care. He feigned a blow; Zebrina leaped aside; again he made a movement as if he were about to strike; and Zebrina bounded to one side. And as she landed, the ax descended in fatal precision, as if to cleave the tiny Shee into pieces. Hebe and Canna jumped up in terror as the ax fell, for they were certain Zebrina was doomed. But just as the ax's keen edge was about to taste Shee flesh, Zebrina leaped straight up in the air at least three feet above Shale's coursing blade, and in mid-air, Zebrina whipped her gossamer net from behind her and cast it over the flailing figure of Shale. Violently, he tried to escape, but the more he tried, the tighter the meshes of the net wrapped around him until he was helpless and had fallen to the ground. Zebrina straddled the helpless Shale with her dagger raised.

"He-he-he, enough Zebrina, you have won, he-he-he, and it would not do to slay our friends, he-he-he. Has anyone anymore doubts, he-he-he, concerning Shee prowess, he-he-he?"

Zebrina carefully undid her net from the stammering Shale, gently caressing his hair as she hummed a pleasant melody.

"You must not be fooled by the seeming fragility of the Shee," the Wanderer said. "Had Shale been a Man or a Shag, Zebrina would have dispatched him with her dagger before any of us could have moved, no less rendered assistance."

King Sard stood with a severe look on his face. "I offer my deepest apologies for doubting the Shee."

"He-he-he, we are the Shee of ancient days. Our survival, he-he-he, has been at the expense of others who, he-he-he, were foolish enough to doubt our strength. Now King Sard knows the Shee, he-he-he, and now we will be not only friends but fellow warriors."

"But as you have seen," the Wanderer spoke, "the Shee, like the Elves, are warriors of the night who fight best from cover and ambuscade, for they wear no armor which would deny them their essential strength, their speed. On the other hand, the Dwarf is a warrior for the open battlefield wherein he meets his foe face to face and shield to shield."

"And how does Man fight?" Empress Saphiria demanded.

"Man prefers the open battlefield much like the Dwarfs, for in the open field his physical strength is unfettered and his gruesome war machines are most potent. The Aged One's advice not to meet Man on his terms is a specific warning against open warfare."

"But that is the only warfare we know," King Sard interrupted.

"Aye, King Sard, and therein we have a problem, for the Dwarfenfold must restrain itself until man's strength has begun to wane. We must fight defensively."

Then King Sard and Queen Fon-du-Fon embraced as laughter gradually replaced the tension of moments before.

And in that dark night, the Elves, the Shee and the Nibelungen formed a friendship deeper than eternity.

Chapter Twenty-Two

King Jasper arrived with his guard of twenty sturdy and heavily-armed Trolls on the following morning. After lengthy introductions and refreshments, King Jasper sat beneath a shady tree and told the entire company a very strange tale.

The Trolls, having traveled for long days and nights, decided to rest near an opening of their endless tunnels. The opening was on the east side of the Rhus and south of the great ruins, the realm of the Querques, Styrax and the Wanderer had skirted the day before they encountered the Grendels and the Shee, enroute to the Hill of Light. As the Trolls looked out over the sere grasslands, they were surprised to see a small contingent of Man-warriors, numbering fewer than a dozen, four of whom were carrying a small cage. Standing within the cage was a small being unlike any creature the Trolls had ever seen or heard of. As the small, disordered group of men passed the cave mouth, King Jasper, ever bold, stepped into the sunlight, banged his shield with his sword, and shouted, "I am King Jasper, monarch of the ancient tribe of Trolls, the mortal enemies of Man. Your appearance has angered me. Will you do battle as warriors? Or will you flee as cowards?"

The leader of the men laughed uproariously at Jasper's solitary and diminutive form, shouting back, "Go away, little creature. We have no time for dalliance."

King Jasper, ever ready for combat, walked forward revealing his heavily-armed Troll warriors to the enemy. "The challenge has been cast."

Seeing more than a solitary Troll, the men set down their cage and unsheathed their long swords. Without so much as a moment's pause, they charged wildly toward the cave where King Jasper and his Trolls waited. Fiercely, they rushed forward, screaming madly, but without any military order or discipline, so easily they expected to sweep the small Trolls away. But Jasper's soldiers were tested warriors and immediately formed a compact line of shields directly facing the charging men. The skirmish was short, for the disorganized men rushed foolishly upon a wall of extended spears deftly handled from a line so compact and unyielding that the men could not advance beyond the fatal spear points. Again and again, the men surged forward trying to break the shield row, but as they seethed forward, the long spears of the Trolls bit deeply. Seven men were slain, and the others quickly fled.

Two Trolls released the creature from the cage and brought him to their king. He was very small, smaller than the Shee, and very aged; his face a mass of wrinkled care. From his forehead, two small horns protruded, and his fingers were webbed like those of a duck. His coloring was dark brown, like moistened soil, and his small, deeply sunken eyes were black. He stood before King Jasper with his head lowered, as if he were expecting death.

"I am King Jasper of the mighty Trolls, who

fear no living thing. Have no fear, little creature, for Man is our only foe. Who or what are you?"

Slowly, the creature raised his head looking King Jasper boldly in the eyes. "I am Gaius Fortunas Duergar, Lord of the marshes, the last of the once mighty Duergars, a tribe destroyed by Man."

"And in what land did your tribe reside?" Jasper asked as he studied the Duergar's webbed fingers.

"Our homeland was in the bosques south of the land of the Querques, for we were people most content in watery lands, finding our foods in marshy lakes and rivers. We were wooed from the safety of the marshes by Lusta the Bitch, Queen of the Shams, who promised our people a pact of amity, but once we were on solid land, the Shams attacked and killed all of my tribe."

"Where were these men taking you?" King Jasper asked.

"I know not. My captors were the accursed Querques who are on their way to a meeting with many other tribes. Their main force has already passed but hours ago, and it was an army of great strength led by Yen the Cruel."

"And why were you not slain with the rest of your kind?" Jasper demanded.

"Among my people, I was honored as the greatest of historians, for I alone know of the ancient days. The Querques allowed me to live so that I might entertain them with tales and legends they know little of. In fact, they know nothing of the past and care less. I have survived these many years by telling a different tale each night as the Querques gathered by their fires. And as I recited, night after night, I longed for my doom and the doom of my captors."

Styrax was not surprised to hear of the

Querques moving south, toward Prosopia, for Vastar had warned him of the possibility of Profundus seeking allies.

And as King Jasper finished his astounding story, two of his Troll warriors brought Gaius Fortunas Duergar forward where he kneeled before Styrax and Canna.

"Please stand, Gaius Fortunas Duergar, for we dislike ritual in the land of Prosopia," Canna said gently. "Here you are welcome. You must excuse our ignorance, for we know nothing of your tribe."

"My people were annihilated many years ago, my Lady. I am the last of the Duergars."

"Then you must live among us," Empress Saphiria said, "amongst us as a free being and friend, for we, the Nibelungen, the Trolls, the Shee and the Elves are engaged in final combat with the loathsome creature called Man."

Gaius Fortunas Duergar paused, then stepped forward with his hands upon his hips. He carefully looked around, and then spoke slowly, as if reciting, in a deep and throaty voice, "I know of your suffering and of the war to come; I know of Elves and Dwarfs and Shee, of the Aged One and of the Wanderer; and I know of beginnings and endings of the first, second and third ages. I am Gaius Fortunas Duergar, the master of lore."

"Then you are thrice welcome, Gaius Fortunas Duergar," Styrax answered. "We are this day to assemble in mighty conclave to prepare for the onslaught of Profundus the Guileful, the leader of men and their armies. There is much that I would speak of with you when our present business is finished."

* * *

The grand conclave was held that day beneath the most ancient of the mesquite trees, the very tree beneath which Styrax and Canna had recently made love. King Styrax and Queen Canna, Thuja and Hebe, and all the Elders were the first to arrive, all dressed uncomfortably in their ceremonial robes. Next came the Wanderer who sat beside his boon companion Styrax. Then came the Trolls, garbed in martial splendor, their armor glinting in the sunlight. They marched in precision and sat to the right of Styrax and the Wanderer. Shortly thereafter came the Nibelungen, resplendent in golden armor, and they sat to the left of Styrax and the Wanderer. Empress Saphiria entered by herself and sat between Styrax and the Wanderer, thus avoiding the problem of favoritism had she entered with either the Trolls or the Nibelungen Dwarfs being foolishly jealous of each other. The atmosphere was solemn until the Trolls and the Nibelungen were settled. Then the Shee came forward like quicksilver, laughing and darting here and there, thoroughly confusing everyone, especially the more sedate and stern Nibelungen and Trolls, who, though they knew of the Shee prowess, could not seriously accept the Shee as fellow warriors. Queen Fon-du-Fon was the last to arrive, announcing boldly, "The Shee are here, he-he-he. Let the silliness begin, he-he-he."

After all were settled, and the confusion had subsided Styrax rose to speak, and all grew silent.

"I have chosen this sacred site, for we sit beneath the most ancient mesquite tree in Prosopia. It is here that all Elfin questions of matter are settled. It is here that we first declared the Elfin land. And it is here that we will die, if we must.

"Today, we, the Elves, we, the Nibelungen and Trolls, we, the Shee, and we, the Wanderer, meet in solemn conclave. Today, our ancient tribes abandon our isolation and join together forever to establish and maintain those eternal harmonies that Man disrupts. No longer can any of us live alone, for all must flow together or flow not at all.

"There can be little doubt that the enemy is gathering mighty forces and that the great assault will come soon and will come at the northern crossing, the only place the enemy's armies can ford. As I see it, we must concentrate our forces both north and south of the ford, and I suggest that King Jasper, and the Trolls, and King Sard and the Nibelungen encamp to the north while the Shee and the Elves encamp to the south where the undergrowth is most intense. Our plans cannot be made more particular in that we fight a defensive war, awaiting the actions of our foe to determine how we will upset his plans. Our weapons are weak in comparison to theirs; our numbers are no match for theirs. We must be of stout heart; we must be fast; and we must be wise."

As Styrax sat down, King Jasper jumped to his feet, obviously displeased with the cautious words and passive manner of King Styrax.

"I agree that we must act in unison, for that is wise. I agree that we must abandon our isolation, for that is wise. I agree that the attack will come at the northern crossing, for there are no others. But, I disagree, I heartily disagree with the strategy offered by my friend, the noble Styrax, for his plans are foolish. I am not familiar with the martial affairs of the Shee or the Elves, for neither tribe wears armor or carries the ax, the lance, or the sword, our chosen weapons. The Trolls know but one manner of warfare, as ancient as the Trolls themselves. We meet our enemies face to face, shield to shield, warrior to warrior and troop against troop. We do not doubt our strength nor our weapons, for are we not masters of the forge?

Are not our spears balanced? Are not our swords the keenest edged? Is not our discipline in combat the finest known? Is not a single Troll the match for five of man's finest warriors? I say we cross the river—the tunnel is already in place to the north. I say we meet Man in the field. I say we meet him and defeat him that we crush him with our valor."

King Jasper's speech was greeted with a deafening din as the Nibelungen and the Trolls pounded their swords and axes upon their shields to show support of Jasper's bold advice. The Elves remained silent. And the Shee, flitting about, only laughed.

The Wanderer rose to speak. "King Jasper speaks bravely. His spirit is that of his abiding heritage. But he forgets the advice of the Aged One not to fight Man on his terms. No doubt the Trolls and the Nibelungen will fight with great prowess and honor, and Man will suffer extensive losses. But his armies are vast; ours are small. His weapons are awesome; ours are adequate at best. We dare not cross the river in force until we have reduced both his power and his numbers."

Empress Saphiria next spoke. "The warriors of the Dwarfenfold have no peers but as Man's forces are so great, I fear we must agree with King Styrax and the Wanderer."

King Jasper quickly interrupted. "Though my allegiance is ever to the Empress, I still disagree. You reduce my soldiers to ineffectiveness, for we know not how to hide in bushes, how to skulk in shadows and how to spring from ambuscade. A sword must be met with a sword, a lance with a lance."

King Sard, heeding his Empress, then spoke against King Jasper, for in truth Sard and Jasper did not see eye to eye and were ever feuding, as was the way within the Dwarfenfold. King Sard said, "King Jasper and the Trolls, valiant though they be, are being foolish in that they..."

King Jasper jumped up, his face reddening. "Does Sard call me a fool? For if he does, I will..."

Empress Saphiria broke in, and her booming voice stilled both Jasper and Sard. Both Kings fell to their knees as she spoke, "Silence! Both of you, be silent! I speak for the Dwarfenfold alone. Have you both forgotten your places? Troll swords compared to catapults are like dust before the wind. No one doubts the bravery of the Trolls, or of King Jasper. We only fear that in the heat of our debate, we will allow courage to supplant wisdom and impetuosity to replace reason. The Aged One has spoken. Do not fight Man on his terms."

As the conclave continued, Jasper and Sard kept on quarreling, often loudly, and Empress Saphiria continued to silence them. King Styrax argued for purely defensive warfare, countering every move that Profundus and the tribes of men made. The Shee, oblivious to reason, laughed and bounded about the encampment, further angering King Jasper. And finally, it was decided that within two weeks all the armies of the Shee, the Trolls, the Nibelungen and the Elves would gather at the northern ford, there to take up the positions King Styrax had originally suggested. But as the solemn meeting drew to a close, it was perceived by all that harmony of command had not been achieved. King Sard remained close-mouthed as he fumed against King Jasper; and Jasper, though held in check by the Empress, seethed with rage against Styrax and, especially, against the Shee, who he considered little more than pesky children. The Shee paid little heed to anything, for the Shee are ever the Shee.

Chapter Twenty-Three

Lord Thrett stood behind Profundus the Guileful who was seated on his elaborate throne situated on a dais erected to welcome his allies. In two widely separated but precise ranks, the scarlet warriors stretched from the impromptu platform far out into the grasslands, creating a long corridor for the expected armies. The remainder of Profundus' army was encamped far to the right on a prominence that stood out above the rolling hills of dry grass.

The first army of his confederates had just appeared in the distance and now rode slowly into Profundus' camp, marching between the ranks of the Scarlet Five Hundred. Dressed in multicolored and ragged garments loosely thrown over their armor, the soldiery of the Shams approached the dais cautiously, each soldier suspiciously watching the scarlet warriors on either side, for the Shams had little affection for Profundus and his men who for many years they had fought viciously over the same infertile ground. Leading the Shams was Lusta the Bitch, a woman of enormous size and strength, whose sword arm was easily the match for the strongest of men. She wore purple robes that flowed loosely from her shoulders to cover her steed's flanks, and on her handsome head, she wore a massive crown made from a circlet of fashioned gold into which twelve jeweled daggers had been fastened. It was said among the Shams, and quietly, that each dagger represented a warlord Lusta had slain either in open battle or in her bed, for Lusta had an insatiable appetite for strong men.

As she rode toward Profundus, he turned and whispered to Lord Thrett, "This is Lusta the Bitch, a warrior without peer, with a desire for power and wealth that rivals my own. She loathes me, for we are long-standing enemies, but her strength makes her a useful ally at least until we conquer the Elfin lands. Then I will do away with her. Treat her carefully, and be aware of her allurements, for beneath that armor rages a beautiful body and an insatiable lust. She has slain many honored warriors who have failed her on the field of battle or, worse yet, failed her in her bed."

As Lusta boldly drew her horse up to the platform, Profundus rose with a smile, spreading his arms and shouting for all to hear, "Welcome, Queen Lusta! Welcome, the mighty Shams! As my guests you have come, and as my guests you shall be treated. Though in the past we have fought many times over worthless lands, we will now fight side by side, shoulder to shoulder, over rich unspoiled territory, the like of which you have never known. Look you, upon that hill where my army is encamped. Join them as friends, as allies in our great cause, for they await you and have prepared much revelry and a noble feast. Queen Lusta, while our warriors carouse, come and sit by my side."

Slowly the Shams dispersed, making for the promised feast. Lusta dismounted and sat on the right of Profundus.

"This is Lord Thrett, my captain in arms; he has joined us and knows the foe. He is of the tribe of Beastums, that are no more," Profundus said.

Lord Thrett bowed deeply, for he was much taken with Lusta's beauty which he found amazing and challenging in so strong and massive a woman.

"May fate lead us to victory," Lord Thrett offered.

"Fate will lead us nowhere," Lusta replied in a deep and warm voice. "Victory depends upon strength, upon boldness and courage. Fate has little to do with affairs of war."

Then, as Lusta sat, the great army of the Gluttas began to enter the field before the dais. In serried ranks, they moved forward in careless order, for though the Gluttas were noted for their ferocity, they were also noted for their lack of internal discipline. In battle, they were savage and unruly, winning not by cunning or bravery but by sheer force of numbers. Leading the Gluttas was Gasher the Bold, a warrior king of vast size, easily weighing 400 pounds, and though he seemed fat and awkward, Gasher was of great strength and surprising speed. His outward demeanor was cheerful, and he was given to wild laughter and cruel sport, his favorite being to watch captives torn apart by wild horses. He rode in an open wagon loaded with spears, axes, lances and swords, all thrown carelessly into the bed of the wagon, for these were the weapons of enemies Gasher had slain, weapons which he used at random and with great dexterity.

As Gasher approached, Lusta whispered to Profundus and Thrett, "So you have chosen Gasher as an ally. His army is large, but he cannot be trusted. You know that. His obesity grows even more loathsome."

"But he has the strongest army of all the tribes, and he will carry the brunt of battle while you and I are busy selecting the spoils." Profundus laughed after he had whispered back to Lusta.

"Welcome, King Gasher," Profundus shouted. "Welcome to the fierce Gluttas. Foes we have been but that can no longer be. New lands, new riches await us, my friends, and our time of struggle will soon come to a close in our victory over the Elfin Brood. Join us now as allies. My army is preparing a mighty feast for all of you. King Gasher, come and sit by me and Queen Lusta, an enemy once but now a friend and formidable ally."

Gasher intentionally chose to sit on the opposite side of Profundus, as far away from Lusta as possible, for the Shams and the Gluttas had great enmity between them.

They had all no sooner sat than the army of the Querques appeared, marching in double-time and shouting their battle cries. Though dressed raggedly, their armor was burnished and their weapons were keen. Though they carried both sword and spear, the Querques were noted for their mastery of the long bow, often felling their foes before they could come within a hundred yards of the Querques. Their leader was Yen the Cruel, a tall but thin warrior famed far and wide for his diabolical vengeance upon his enemies. For the Querques took no prisoners and ate of the flesh of those they had slain, believing that when the enemy was eaten, his strength became the Querque's strength.

After the armies had all joined in the great feast, Profundus, Lusta, Gasher, Yen and Thrett remained upon the dais where servants brought them food and drink.

Yen was the first to speak. "One of my captains

has had a skirmish that seems to indicate that we have an additional foe. About a dozen of my men had been assigned to the task of bringing the Duergar here to entertain us with his tales of the past, but they were challenged by a troop of Trolls, those devils who live in the great northern gorges. My men attacked boldly but were soundly beaten by these little creatures who carried the Duergar with them. I consider it a damnable loss as the Duergar had no rival in story-telling. Our nights will be dull without him. Naturally, I executed myself those fools who escaped the Trolls. Oh, the shame of being defeated by inferior creatures but half our size."

Profundus was disturbed, and that deeply, by these tidings, for he well knew of the Troll's skill in battle and at weapon making. "Are you certain the Trolls were coming this way to join the Elfin Brood?"

"Why else would they be that far south and in daylight, when we all know the Trolls rarely leave their own land and seldom venture out in daylight," Yen answered. "But, fear not, I will have my revenge."

"This is bad news for the Trolls are implacable enemies," Profundus replied.

"Does Profundus and his mighty Scarlet Five Hundred fear the Trolls?" Lusta asked teasingly. "For brave as they are, how many warriors can they field? At most, perhaps, five hundred. I think they can make but little difference to armies as vast as ours. They might even prove a pleasant diversion for our soldiery. Let the Elves gather as many friends as they can; they cannot stop our onslaught; and when it is over, we will have rid ourselves not only of the pesky Elves but the nasty Trolls as well. Or, better yet, we might enslave them so that their skills in weapon-making will not be lost."

"Forget the Trolls. They are of little matter," Gasher burst out. "What is your plan, Profundus? For you are not called the Guileful without reason."

"Ho-ho! But I have many plans each dependent upon the other. Yen's news of the Trolls does not bother me in and of itself; after all, another five hundred to slay is no major difficulty. But if that damned Empress Saphiria of the Dwarfenfold is involved, she can muster all the tribes of Dwarfs who number in the thousands and who are all skilled in the making of the finest and deadliest weapons. The Dwarfs are dedicated warriors, disciplined to perfection. With this in mind, I have just devised a special scheme that will be dear to your treacherous hearts. When we are ready, when our armies are in place, we will invite, under a guarantee of safety, the Elfin and Dwarfish leaders to a council to discuss the prospects of peace. How I hate that word. After we have parleyed and after we have discovered their weaknesses, we will slay them, thus removing their leaders at the very moment we attack for, though I know little of the Elves, I do know that the Dwarfs are helpless without their captains."

The others quickly praised Profundus, for all of them took great pleasure in any form of treachery, especially as the plan afforded them the opportunity to meet their foes before the battle began. For in Profundus, as in Lusta, Gasher, Yen and Thrett, burned the insatiable desire to see and speak to the Elves and the Dwarfs, creatures with whom they had never met directly and therefore, knew not what to expect.

"What weapons do the Elves use?" Yen asked Thrett.

"I do not know. I know they are small, very fast and green in coloring, but little else can I offer. The Beastums, before they fled, recovered three warriors that the Elves had killed, but no wounds were on their bodies, that is according to the Beastums."

"Do the Elves practice magic?" Lusta asked lightly.

"Magic! Magic!" Profundus broke out in anger. "There is no magic. There never has been and never will be anything that is magic. The fools probably drowned crossing the river. Graspar always was an idiot."

"Ah, the Rhus," said Lusta; "the mighty Rhus. Perhaps we will need magic to get across ourselves."

Still annoyed, Profundus answered bluntly, "Magic will serve us not at all. We will need a bridge."

"A bridge? Where? How?" shouted Gasher.

"Lord Thrett knows of a shallow crossing, and in my army are master bridge-builders. How else do you expect to move our heavy weapons, especially my catapults and wagons, across the surging river?"

"But a bridge will take too much time," Yen the Cruel said. "Is there no other way across?"

"No, unfortunately," Thrett answered. "And if we try to cross without a bridge, we will be easy targets, struggling in the turbulent Rhus, for whatever weapons the Elves possess."

"And Dwarf spears are deadly," Lusta offered, "for I have lost many a battle with nasty Trolls. It is unfortunate that Lord Thrett knows so little of our enemies, for though I have heard of the Elfin Brood, I have no idea what to expect."

And as Lusta finished, she smiled and nodded

THE ELFIN BROOD 247

toward Thrett, unbeknownst to the others.

"But we have other matters with which to concern ourselves," Profundus said. "First of all, I will have supreme command. Is that accepted?"

"As long as you have the upper hand in the struggle and the rewards are in the offing, I have no objection to your command," Lusta answered. "But if you fail or if you delay for..."

"I do not fail," Profundus interrupted.

Both Yen and Gasher accepted the terms of command, knowing that Profundus' leadership promised rich rewards.

"Then, I agree," Lusta said, "but I will reserve the right to abandon you if your plans go awry. I know you, Profundus, and will not fight your battles for you. We must all contribute or the Shams will return to the grasslands that your son, Ravager, once ruled."

"Speak not of my son," Profundus demanded, rising in anger, "for his death or his disappearance still haunts me."

The council continued for many more hours, during which Lord Thrett found it difficult to keep his eyes from Queen Lusta. But though he frequently stared at her, she seemed to avoid his attention. The din from the feasting armies was deafening, for Profundus had been particularly lavish with food and drink, and the soldiery caroused the night away. Finally, when all had retired to their individual tents, a messenger visited Thrett with a summons from Queen Lusta.

When Lord Thrett entered Queen Lusta's tent, he found her alone and dressed in a silken robe. Though very large, Lusta was perfectly proportioned and aggressively attractive. Thrett stood just within the tent, his mind enraptured by the Warrior-Queen.

"You stare at me with hunger in your eyes, Lord Thrett," Lusta said.

"I have never known a woman-warrior," Lord Thrett stammered.

"A woman is a woman, warrior or not. If you wish to bed me down, then have at it. I also lust for you."

She rose and gently lifted Thrett in her powerful arms, kissing him on the lips, alarming him, but her strength was such that his faint resistance proved futile. Held tightly in her arms, Thrett was quickly carried to her bed.

Chapter Twenty-Four

King Jasper had returned to Troll-land to marshal his forces, then to return. Empress Saphiria and King Sard had returned to Niflheim to prepare the Nibelungen army for war, then to return. And the laughing Shee simply disappeared, advising Styrax that when the hostilities started, when they were needed, the Shee would be there.

As the evening sun set in golden splendor, King Styrax and the Wanderer sat by the Rhus as Vastar approached with Gaius Fortunas Duergar. Vastar stood on the fringe of their campsite, frequently staring at the Wanderer, while the Duergar sat cross-legged opposite Styrax.

"Gaius Fortunas Duergar, last of the Duergars, I want you to tell us all you know of the Elfin Brood, especially our history," Styrax said, "and, please, Vastar, come and join our discussion as you may be able to add to what the Duergar has to say."

Vastar moved closer to the fire but still hung back, staring intensely at the Wanderer.

"Come forward, Vastar. You have naught to fear here among the Elves," the Wanderer commanded.

Vastar moved forward slightly,

"You seem frightened of me," the Wanderer said to Vastar. "Do you not know me, old Man?"

"My Lord Wanderer," Vastar answered sheepishly, "my mind is, perhaps, aging, and my thoughts are not as clear as they once were, but, somehow, your visage haunts me, as if you were someone I knew many years ago."

The Wanderer paused. He studied Vastar and knew him well, but wondered whether to enlighten the old Man. For when he was young, his Uncle Vastar had been both kind and gentle until his wife and children were slain. Then the horrible feud between brothers, his father, Profundus, and his Uncle, Vastar, erupted, and Vastar fled for his life. From that day to the present, the Wanderer had not seen his Uncle. At last, the Wanderer spoke, "You do not know me, for many years have passed, and I have become a new and different Man. I care not for my past and will not speak of it. But this I will say once, and only once, to lessen your confusion. Look hard, Vastar. Do you not know me now, Uncle? I am Ravager, your nephew, the only son of the accursed Profundus, your vile and evil brother, and my father."

"Is it really you, Ravager?" Vastar blurted out in astonishment. "I seemed to recognize you, but you have become so different, so unlike my..."

"We will speak no more of it," the Wanderer interrupted. "I do not wish to revive the shame of my past life. Silence now. You know who I am. Content yourself. Ravager is dead."

Vastar moved closer, sitting beside the Duergar.

"Now, Gaius Fortunas Duergar, speak of the Elfin past, for we Elves know little other than the present age."

The Duergar rose and stood facing King Styrax and the Wanderer. Before he spoke, he spread his legs, twisting his ankles to and fro, as if to plant himself in the sands of Prosopia. He placed his hands upon his hips, and, though a very small being, he seemed to swell up as he prepared to speak. "In the First Age, when the world, Gaia, for whom I am named, was young, there were many, many tribes of self-aware beings, the least important of which was Man. Gaia was populated with the Firbolg, the Tuatha De Denann, the Shee, the Leshiye, the Nibelungen, the Dryads, the Gwyllion, the Trolls, the Salvenelli, the Duergars, the Elves, the Skogsra, the Liosalfar, the Tylwyth Teg, the Kobolds, the Stillevolk, the Pitikos, the Domoviye, the Massarioli, the Napfhans, the Duendes, the Monaciello, and the Boggarts, Powries, and Dunters, and many more whose names have been lost beyond recall in the dense fog of the unknown and unknowing past. Each and every tribe lived within a designated area, each independent and unconcerned with the others, each in a domain appropriate to the nature of its being, and all the creation of the timeless Ymir, the fuser of ice and rock from whence all living creatures derive. Ever blessed were these realms, for therein abided eternal harmony. Many were the heroes and villains of that age: Vainamoinen the Steadfast; Soemundur the Wise; Gwydion the maker of illusions; Math the Ancient; Volga Vseshavich master of form; Merlin the Enchanter; Arawn, Taliesin, Manannan Mac Lir, Lemminkainen, Afagddu, Louhi, Baba Yaga, Hecate, Arianrod, Ceridwen and Nyx. All self-aware beings, with the exception of Man, met but once a year on Samain Eve to consecrate the Arthame and to read from the Grimoires. For this was a time without time, when days and years went without name or number, a time of bliss.

"The knell of this long age, and none know how long, came slowly, imperceptibly, and from a creature no one had reason to fear. For though all beings suffered from the error of pride, Man alone suffered from the error of greed. Man became the friend of the Duergars, the Stillevolk and the Dryads, and from each he garnered their unique thoughts and individual customs. Man grew stronger and stronger, gradually driving all other self-aware creatures toward the western seas, until Man stood alone where others had once stood.

"The Second Age is the age of Man, a period of great evil and disharmony. For though Man had been victorious over other creatures, he lacked the ability to live with his own kind. For that which he took from the Elves, the Shee, or the Tuatha De Denann did not satisfy him, he wanted more thus Man began to fall upon Man in perpetual slaughter. The history of Man is little more than a succession of wars and conquests ever fed by man's inconceivable and idiotic inability to control his reproduction, for whatever Man is, he over breeds, destroying both himself and the land upon which he tries to live. Man breeds like fungus, filling all possible space until the sheer density of his kind consumes the very essentials of life."

"The Duergar speaks well," Styrax said, "but we are little interested in the affairs of Man, for his story is wearying and ever the same. But what became of the other self-aware beings?"

"All creatures, other than Man, dispersed, losing contact with the other beings and, often, with their own kind. Many ancient tribes have ceased to exist, gone from the book of life. The Elves, ever shy, found deeper and deeper forests within which to hide. The Shee just disappeared, as they always do, and the many tribes of Dwarfs and the Duergars remained to fight Man on his terms. For centuries, the struggle raged on, and though the Dwarfs and the Duergars fought with great valor,

Man eventually drove us deep into the bowels of Gaia to create Niflheim, the land of the lower regions, the subterranean world. The Dwarfs found Niflheim to their liking, but the Duergars longed for the green surface of the earth, and that was our downfall, wherein all the Duergars, except for me, were slain by Man-swords."

"But what of the Elves?" Styrax asked.

"Of the Elves, I can only speak of that which I have heard from others, for the Duergars and the Elves were separated from each other by Man at the end of the First Age. As Elves are intimately associated with trees, each tribe of Elves attached itself to a different kind of tree. The Elves withdrew from Man-dominated lands and fled to the great forests. But even there, Man pursued them, relentless as death itself, until the Elves, by a mystic power common only to Elves, fused their beings with the trees sacred to them. As trees the Elves lived on, though many were destroyed as Man began to hew down the forests. Then with the dawn of the Third Age and with the collapse of Man, the Elves, once again, took their proper form."

"What else do you know of the Elfin Brood?" Styrax asked.

"Naught else, my Lord, that can be called history," the Duergar answered. "But there is a legend forgotten by all except myself. In the darkest mists of time, it is said that the Elves were the first-born of self-aware creatures and that they were compounded from the music of the celestial spheres. And it has been said through the ages that the Elves will return the troubled earth to its ancient harmony."

"And is that all you know of the Elves?"

"Yes, King Styrax, that is all I know," the Duergar answered as he sat down again.

"And you, Vastar, what do you know of the Elves?" the Wanderer asked his uncle.

"I, my Lord, I know nothing, really, for until I came across the Rhus I knew only that little green creatures lived here and were called Yellfens."

Styrax was displeased, for the Duergar had told him nothing he had not heard before, and most of what the Duergar related seemed too mythical to be worthy of belief. Styrax knew Vastar had little knowledge of the Elves, for he well remembered the surprise and confusion on Graspar's and the other Beastums' faces when he confronted them at the northern crossing. Styrax realized that Man knew little of the Elves, but the Elves knew a great deal about Man. That has to be an advantage, Styrax thought.

The Wanderer said little, for he knew the torment of Styrax, he knew of the Aged One's letters, and he knew that Styrax was having great difficulty in believing what the Aged One had revealed to him.

"What do you know of the Aged One?" Styrax asked Gaius Fortunas Duergar.

"The Wizard of the North? I know he is very wise and has great power, for Man lives in terror of him. He is no friend of Man, but then he seems to be friendly to no one. The Querques explained to me that the Aged One was responsible for creating the great, ugly Shags who live in the forests surrounding the land of perpetual ice and snow. He is thought to be quite Man, a wizard demented by his own excessive wisdom, for he knows that which was never meant to be known. He has stepped beyond the mirror and has seen the horror of knowledge."

For a moment, all were silent, deep in their own thoughts.

"Perhaps I can offer something about the Aged One," Vastar said, breaking the silence.

"Tell us what you know," Styrax directed.

"I really don't know much, for as the Duergar says, my people have great fear of the Aged One, whom they often call 'Goodman'. He is thought to have great power over nature, making it do his will. How else can he survive in the frozen and lifeless lands he calls his own? Many years ago, before Lord Wanderer, my nephew, was born, Profundus, may he be ever accursed, led his warriors to the north, hoping to gain knowledge of the source of Goodman's power, but his soldiery was slain in awesome avalanches or in bitter, unrelenting cold. At the time, I was my brother's ally, and he told me that the avalanches and the intense cold were not natural and were caused by the clever machinations of the Aged One. But other stories I have heard of Goodman have made me believe that he is insane. It has been said that he claims to be thousands of years old, that he lives in a warm forest amid the ice and snow, that he creates monster's to plague Man, and that he plans to destroy all the world when he dies so that none might live after him. It is also said that he flies like a bird, that he suddenly appears anywhere he wishes, and that he can darken the sun and halt the moon in its career. Until now, I had thought that he was a figment of Man's devious imagination, an attempt to re-create the Gods Man once fiercely believed in, powers beyond and above Man's powers. But you speak of him as if he were real."

"He is real. And he has great power," Styrax said, but he said no more and only the Wanderer knew why.

With that, King Styrax dismissed the Duergar and Vastar, and when he was alone with his friend, the Wanderer, Styrax said, "Come with me, Wanderer, and I will show you the single thing that makes me doubt the teachings of the Aged One."

As they walked through the mesquite thickets, the Wanderer doubling over to avoid the mesquite spines, Styrax continued, "If the Elves are the creations of the Aged One, then I must assume we are not the ancient people who were born in the First Age and who lived through the Second Age, the dark age of Man, by fusing our beings with the mesquites in Prosopia, but that we are creatures only of the present, of the here and now, complete unto ourselves and without a past, like children without parents."

"I follow your thought," the Wanderer replied.

Then Styrax paused by a particularly large and well-formed mesquite tree. He placed both of his hands upon the mesquite's stoutest boles and said, "Wanderer, my dear friend, I am now holding within my grasp the tree I have always believed to be the resting place of my grandfather, and beyond it, over there, is the mesquite that contains my father in his second life. Do you understand me?"

"Yes, Styrax, I understand."

"But, this cannot be, if the Aged One is right, for we should live and die as other creatures do. Do you agree?"

"I think I do, my friend. But you must remember that I have accepted the Aged One's teachings as a matter of faith, for my understanding of things beyond the immediate realm of Man is wanting."

"Then watch!" Styrax said with great intensity as he bent his head downward and his hands began to shake from the firmness of his grasp upon the tree trunks. "Watch! And behold the Elfin miracle."

Styrax closed his eyes, and his hands squeezed

tighter yet as he cried out, "Grandfather! Grandfather! Can you hear me? I am greatly troubled. I have been to the Aged One, and I can no longer see clearly. Grandfather, it is I, Styrax. Can you hear me?"

As Styrax spoke, the Wanderer stepped back, feeling that he was intruding in something never intended for Man's eyes. And as he watched, he was stunned to see the large tree begin to sway softly though no breeze was felt, and he noticed the long, extended mesquite limbs tended to close toward Styrax, as though in an intended embrace. He looked beyond Styrax to the other mesquite tree that Styrax had identified with his father, and it too was swaying slightly, though no other mesquite moved at all. A cold sense of fear moved up the Wanderer's spine.

Styrax moved away from the mesquite and sat exhausted on the ground. Wearily, he spoke, "Only you have seen what all Elves see throughout their lives. This is no religion, no belief in the unknown, no folk legend devised to unite Elves. This is real. You have seen it though you know not what was said to me."

"What was said?" the Wanderer asked, bewildered by what he had seen.

"The words my hands felt were 'I am your grandfather, my son, and the Aged One is good'. That is all that was said, for the transmission of words seems to exhaust the energies of the tree, the energies of my Grandfather. I know it is painful for the mesquite to respond in Elfin terms, and I only trouble my Grandfather when I am deeply disturbed. You may ask why I do not speak with my father in his tree, for the Father is closer than the Grandfather. But, you see, I did speak to my father first, many years ago, and he had great difficulty in answering, though he finally seemed to say, 'Speak to your Grandfather, my Son, I do not yet have my strength'."

The Wanderer, sitting next to Styrax, took his hand, saying, "Styrax, I know your pain, and it is now mine. I have seen your Elfin miracle. I know not what to say. Believe the Aged One. Believe your Grandfather and your Father. And if they seem in contradiction, then believe them both. For one can believe in love and hate, life and death, though they contradict each other."

"Yes, I will try. But I am the King of my people, and I must know who and what I am. Am I a descendent of Man? Am I an Elf, pure and simple? Or am I the bastard spawn of separate camps, killing my kind whichever way I turn?"

"You are Styrax, King of Prosopia. You are leading your tribe against an evil foe who is set on destroying Elfdom. What you are or what you were has little meaning now, for your only concern is what you will be. I know your agony, my friend, and I know of no way to lessen the pain. What more can I say?"

Slowly, they walked back to the river, and for a long while they both lay on the grassy bank watching the ever-restless Rhus rush by.

Chapter Twenty-Five

The following morning, Empress Saphiria and King Sard returned from Niflheim with a retinue of thirty Nibelungen, armed not with sword, spear and ax but with pick and shovel. The Empress quickly found Styrax and the Wanderer working on crude maps of Prosopia and the surrounding areas, maps that were to be used in organizing and stationing the Elfin, Shee, Troll, and Nibelungen warriors.

The Empress waddled quickly to the nearest shaded seat in front of the simple home of Styrax and Canna. "Oh, my heavens," she sighed, "these long walks in the sun shall be the death of me."

"We are happy to see you both so soon again," Styrax said.

"Well, my friends, I am happy to be seated in the shade, but I never will understand the Elfin love of the sun." The Empress paused to wipe her moist brow, then continued. "We had barely gotten to Niflheim when King Sard came up with a fine idea, so important that I insisted we return to the Rhus immediately."

"What is it, King Sard?" the Wanderer asked.

King Sard stepped forward, looking toward Empress Saphiria to see if she intended him to speak. The Empress, breathing heavily, waved her hand exhaustedly in signal for him to proceed.

"Well, my thought is this: we are separated from our enemies by the swift Rhus: they on their side, we on ours. Sooner or later, we know that they will cross, and, as you have suggested, they will probably cross to the north in a broader and shallower portion of the river. Am I right so far?"

, "Thus far, we are in complete accord," Styrax replied.

"But, if this is so, we are placed at a distinct disadvantage. For they can move toward us, but we cannot move toward them. And, perhaps more important yet, is the fact that they can cross the river whenever they want to, thus giving them a great edge in determining when to attack. An ancient Nibelungen adage has it that above all one should never allow his foe to select the time of battle, for this then becomes an obstacle not easily surmounted."

"I agree thus far," Styrax said softly.

"I agree also," the Wanderer offered, "but what choice have we as they already posses the advantage?"

"None, as things stand now, for Man will have very little trouble in crossing the Rhus where it is shallow. Man is large and strong, the waters of the Rhus hardly reaching his waist. But we Dwarfs and the Elves and the Shee are small creatures, and where Man would cross, we would be swept away. It that not so?"

"That is so," the Empress replied with annoyance, "but do get on with it. You always drag out your thoughts and drive everyone to distraction."

"The point is that we must have a way to cross the Rhus, singly or in force, in order to neutralize man's present, fearsome advantage. I suggest that you allow my master diggers to build a tunnel beneath the Rhus, thus giving us the ability to attack them when we choose, and if we choose, and also the ability to spy upon our foe so that we may comprehend his plans and then subvert them. This, then, is my thought, and with me I have brought the finest diggers in all the Dwarfenfold."

Both King Styrax and the Wanderer were happily stunned by the brilliance of King Sard's idea, for both had already realized the dangers in leaving all initiative to Profundus and the plague of men.

"Tunneling beneath the Rhus is not difficult? Can it be done?" the Wanderer asked.

King Sard smiled as he spoke, "Can it be done! Why there is nothing simpler for master miners. You need only show us a safe and secretive site for the tunnel, and within two days it will be ready."

"Empress Saphiria! King Sard! You have devised a marvelous plan," Styrax stammered in delight. "You bring joy to my troubled mind, for now we will be less helpless, less dependent upon a purely defensive role. And I know of the perfect place for the tunnel to the south, just beyond that hill."

Styrax pointed to the south where a long, hilly ridge line descended steeply into the Rhus. "Just beyond that hill, the Rhus rushes over rock shelving, and on either side of the river are deep thickets of shrubbery which will completely mask the tunnel openings."

"Excellent, King Styrax, excellent. Our enemies are concentrating on the north, for only there can they find a crossing adequate to their needs. They pay but token heed to the south. Lead on, King Styrax, for the sooner we dig, the sooner we will be done digging."

Immediately, Styrax and the Wanderer led King

Sard and his thirty diggers to the site proposed. Empress Saphiria remained where she was, lest the sun further addle her stout senses. Queen Canna sat with the Empress, and they passed a quiet afternoon beneath the speckled shade of the mesquite.

Though Styrax and the Wanderer offered to help, the Dwarfs politely refused any assistance, fearing, perhaps wisely, that unskilled diggers would only slow down the master-diggers. After a brief survey, the work began and Styrax marveled at the Nibelungen industry.

The Nibelungen first formed themselves into working pairs, each pair composed of a pickman and a shoveller. The fifteen pairs formed a single line with the first pair starting the digging. The lead Dwarf picked mightily into the rocky soil as his partner, the shoveller, removed the soil that was loosened. Gradually, the hole grew larger and larger as the first pair of Dwarfs disappeared from sight and the next pair entered the growing tunnel entrance. The first pair dug in a forward manner, shoveling the rocky soil backwards where the second pair enlarged the sides of the tunnel and continued to shovel backwards. Slowly, pair after pair of the Nibelungen entered the tunnel as more and more soil was passed backwards, leaving the final pair the task of spreading the disgorged earth beneath the shrubbery so that no trace of the tunnel entrance could be seen. As they worked, the Dwarfs accompanied their digging movements with a guttural chant composed of natural grunting noises as their picks and shovels moved in essential unison.

Later that afternoon, two scarlet warriors rode down the bank of the opposite shore as pickets. As they approached the site of the tunneling, the last pair of Dwarfs, who also served as lookouts, ordered their companions to be silent, and the digging ceased. The scarlet warriors, not particularly observant and bored by their seemingly thankless task, rode slowly by, and, once in the distance, the digging resumed.

Meanwhile, King Styrax and the Wanderer had returned to their map-making as Empress Saphiria napped loudly in the shade.

As they pored over their maps, Thuja and Hebe came running into the clearing with Ulmus running after them. As they sat beside Styrax, Ulmus jumped up and sat on Thuja's right shoulder.

"Ulmus has told me that the enemy is on the move to the north," Thuja said as he caught his breath. "In fact, Ulmus said, 'Many, many, many men and many things,' by which he must mean the wagons or the catapults."

"They are moving to the northern crossing," Styrax answered. "But what I do not understand is how they expect to move the wagons and the catapults across the Rhus. Their warriors surely can ford the river, but the wagons and the massive catapults would be swept away."

"Yes, that has been bothering me also," the Wanderer joined in. "Profundus, my father that was, does not move until he has a plan. What is he devising?"

"Perhaps he plans to use great rafts," Hebe offered.

"I thought of that," the Wanderer replied, "but large rafts are difficult to control in swift water and would be very vulnerable to our spears and darts. No, I do not think they will use rafts."

"Surely, they are not digging a tunnel as the Nibelungen are doing," Styrax mused. And then realizing that Thuja and Hebe had just arrived,

Styrax explained to them the project in which the Nibelungen were then engaged.

The Wanderer pondered Styrax's thought for a moment, then he spoke, "No, they have not the Dwarf's skill. A tunnel would be beyond their abilities."

"Then what is left?" Thuja burst out. "After all, their mighty engines of war are quite useless on their side of the Rhus."

The Wanderer stood up suddenly, "A bridge! A bridge! They are going to build a bridge. It can be no other way. Profundus has craftsmen who specialize in bridge and road building, for without them his catapults would be worthless. What Ulmus has seen is not the northward movement of the warriors but the movement of the bridge-builders and their equipment. I no longer have any doubt: Profundus plans to build a bridge at the northern crossing."

Styrax was taken aback. "Are you so sure? A bridge would take time, and the workers could be exposed to our darts."

"Not so, my friend, for with archers and the catapults, the enemy can drive the Elves back from the river, thus securing time for the bridge-builders." The Wanderer sat down again before he continued. "They will build a bridge. And it presents new problems, for if they succeed and can move their armies and heavy war machines across the river, we will be driven back, deeper and deeper into the hills away from the Rhus."

"Then we must stop the bridge or stop them at the bridge," Thuja said bravely.

"And building a bridge will take months," the Wanderer answered. "That will give us more time to prepare."

"Thuja, stout heart, I have a task for you and

Hebe," Styrax said, "for we must watch their progress carefully and impede it whenever we can. I want you and Hebe to follow the contingents of men that are moving northward, and the moment they start upon the bridge you must inform me. Let Ulmus attend you, for few things escape his hungry eyes."

"I will watch them carefully and I will harass them if I can," Thuja said happily, for he was ever a creature of action.

* * *

Thuja and Hebe had already gone north when two days later King Sard reappeared in the clearing where Styrax and Canna were blending dart poison from amanita pulp and crushed thornapple. Canna had discovered that by adding fine ashes from the fire, the poison became more effective, more potent and more rapid in taking effect. Styrax was very pleased, for he remembered how slowly Graspar and the Grendels died.

King Sard was all smiles beneath his bushy beard. "The tunnel is done, King Styrax. Come, the diggers are ready and eager for your inspection."

Styrax called the Wanderer from the river where he was thinking of the problems the enemy faced in building a bridge across the Rhus. Quickly, King Sard led them to the tunnel site.

They were amazed as they approached, for the Dwarfs had so cleverly hidden the disgorged earth and stone that all looked as it always had. The entrance was shrewdly hidden by dense shrubs as was the exit on the opposite side of the Rhus. Twice, since the completion of the tunnel, the scarlet warriors had passed by on picket duty, and both times they had passed the opening on their side of the river without even pausing. Carefully, Styrax and the Wanderer descended into the tunnel. Slowly, they walked along, marveling at the smoothness of the walls and the evenness of the walkway. The tunnel itself was narrow, allowing but one person of Dwarf size to pass at a time. The Wanderer was frequently forced to crawl along where Styrax walked easily. As they progressed, they saw light ahead and moved more rapidly, for neither Styrax nor the Wanderer felt comfortable in the damp and narrow passageway. Very cautiously, they emerged on the far side of the Rhus.

How strange, Styrax thought, *that I have lived my entire life on only one side of the Rhus*, for this was the very first time he had ever been on the far shore. They stayed within the thicket that hid the opening, peering out from the dense cover. In the distance, to the south, they saw two scarlet warriors moving along the river in their direction. Quickly, they descended back into the tunnel emerging on the Prosopian side where they sat in cover until the scarlet warriors had passed by, again passing the tunnel opening without the slightest suspicion.

King Sard then showed Styrax and the Wanderer a huge lever made of stout tamarisk which was partially imbedded in the tunnel wall. "This is our safety device," Sard said proudly. "For if three sturdy Dwarfs force it sideways, the entire tunnel will collapse. In this way, we protect ourselves if Man happens to discover our work."

"Excellent, King Sard," the Wanderer replied, "you men dig with the skill of moles."

"Well done! Well done!" King Styrax shouted for all to hear. "I will have two eagle-eyed Elves stand guard on the tunnel, both day and night."

They returned to camp to find the Empress

awake and anxious to return to Niflheim, for the bright sunlight was just too much for her.

Styrax shook the hands of all the diggers and praised King Sard loudly and frequently as he stood near the Empress, knowing how proud she would be on hearing her people spoken of so highly and knowing how happy King Sard would be when his praises were sung before his Empress. Styrax informed the Empress and Sard of the movements of the enemy, and of their belief that Profundus would attempt to build a mighty bridge to cross the Rhus. The Empress and King Sard left shortly thereafter to prepare the Nibelungen warriors and then to march northward to join their allies at the crossing.

Chapter Twenty-Six

As the evening darkened, Profundus, Yen, Gasher, Lusta and Thrett met in solemn council. After much heated and prolonged discussion, all had come to accept Profundus' plan for building a large and sturdy bridge at the northern crossing. Yen and Gasher thought little of the bridge concept, but as they found no alternative for crossing the turbulent Rhus, they grudgingly acquiesced. Lusta, though no strong advocate for the bridge, quickly sided with Profundus because the bridge placed the entire burden upon Profundus, and if the plan failed Lusta believed that she would then be able to dominate the combined armies knowing that she could easily outwit the somewhat sluggish Gasher and the dense Yen. Thrett thought little of any plans and even less of his supposed allies for Thrett, ever a Beastum, trusted no one.

"Lusta the Bitch has devised a clever and sly scheme," Profundus announced to the gathering. "For, after we cross the river, we will then face the Elves and, perhaps, the Dwarf's main strength which will be massed to meet our onslaught. Crossing the bridge will be our main problem, for our warriors will be pressed together and unable to fight along a broad front. The advantage, despite our overwhelming strength, will be their's, may they all be cursed. Our losses might be excessive, though the outcome can hardly be in doubt. Lusta feels, and I agree, that a diversion, an attack upon their rear, would reduce our losses significantly."

"The plan is foolish," Gasher shouted, "for without the bridge we have no way of getting across the damned Rhus."

"Ah, but if we could get a small contingent, say twenty five stout warriors, behind the Elves they could create havoc in their ranks, seeding terror in their hearts. Is that not so?" Lusta asked.

"Of course it is so. But how do we get across?" Yen answered snappishly.

Lusta scratched a crude map of the Rhus in the sand. "Are there not many easy crossings north of the land of the Querques? And are they not unguarded, isolated and safe?" Lusta pressed on.

"Yes, many shallow, easy crossings, but once across the warriors would have no path to move southward through the endless mesquite thickets," Yen answered.

"But, look you, the small contingent of warriors need not move south; they could head westward to the foothills of the Pinus mountains, then along the ridges until they were behind the land of the Elves; then they would descend, following the main arroyos, and attack the Elves from behind, exactly where they would least expect an attack."

"Lusta's plan is sound except that it would take a very long time for even the swiftest of warriors to make so long a trek," Yen said derisively, for he held Lusta in great antipathy.

"But you forget, Yen, that we have a great deal of time, for building the bridge will be slow work and will be easily disrupted by our foes," Profundus observed.

"Would the warriors be mounted?" Gasher asked.

"No, I think not," Lusta answered, "for the horses would be of little use climbing the wooded ridges."

The discussion continued for many hours with Yen and Gasher opposing Profundus and Lusta, but as the hours passed the inherent virtues of Lusta's plans gradually won the debate. Gasher, bored with talk, left the meeting with "do as you wish" as his parting words, and lumbered off to his tent. Yen, slow but not dumb, finally agreed, wearied by arguing, and as the crossings in question were within the pale of the Querques, he, at last, offered to send twenty-five of his best warriors under the command of his bold nephew, Gore the Giant, so named for his massive size. In the end it was agreed that Gore and his warriors would leave at sunrise, that they would camp finally on the high ridges of the Pinus mountains overlooking the realm of the Elves, and that once there they would wait until the bridge was completed which would be made known to them by vast signal fires placed along the Rhus.

While Yen was making his arrangements with Gore, Profundus, Lusta and Thrett walked to the banks of the Rhus, stopping at a point where the channel narrowed as the current grew more fierce.

"Tomorrow, we will invite the Elves and their allies to meet with us here, for this is the narrowest place on the river for many a mile," Profundus offered. "We will await them here, and they can congregate on the opposite bank. The distance is such that we can shout across the Rhus. We will set the meeting for just after sunset, for the afterglow will silhouette them against the waning light, and you, Lord Thrett, will have twenty of your finest crossbowmen hidden in the brush. On my signal, they are to shoot down any and all who face us. With daring and skill, we will be able to slay a goodly proportion of their leaders. Is that not a brave plan?"

"Would it not be better, Lord Profundus, to invite them to our side?" Lusta asked.

"Better, certainly, but unlikely. After all, if we cannot cross the Rhus, the tiny Elves would hardly have a chance in the surging waters."

"But it has already been said," Lusta replied, "that the Elves are capable of great magic. Perhaps the rushing waters are no obstacle to them."

Profundus' visage reddened with anger. "There is no magic," he shouted. "They are but Elves and we are men. Speak no more of magic, the shield of fools."

* * *

Early the following morning, three scarlet warriors stood at the narrowed channel and sounded loudly on their war horns. The first shrill blare was answered with silence. The scarlet warriors again sounded their horns, and again silence ensued. Patiently, the scarlet warriors blasted their horns once more.

Then a voice was heard coming from the dense mesquite stand across the Rhus from the scarlet warriors.

"Who sounds these raucous horns? And for what reason?"

One of the scarlet warriors stepped to the edge of the river, cupped his hands to his mouth, and shouted, "Lord Profundus, Master of Greydome and all the grasslands, seeks an audience with the leader of the Elves."

The voice in the thicket replied, "I am Styrax, King of the Prosopian Elves. Speak on."

"Lord Profundus wishes to meet with the leader of the Elves and his allies this very evening, here, where we now stand, you on your side and we on ours. Lord Profundus will be joined by the leaders of the Querques, the Gluttas and the Shams. Lord Profundus wishes to avoid the horrors of war and would speak of peace with the King of the Elves. Do you agree to attend?"

"I agree. We will attend, Lord Profundus, as the sun wanes."

* * *

Early that evening, the attendants of Profundus placed four large throne-like chairs at the appointed place on the banks of the Rhus. With great care and skill, Lord Thrett positioned the crossbowmen deep in the brush that grew wildly along the edge of the river. Quietly, but eagerly, they waited. As the sun diminished, Profundus, Yen, Gasher and Lusta took their seats while Lord Thrett positioned himself just behind Lord Profundus. The sun approached the horizon.

"Gore and twenty-five of my fleetest and boldest warriors are moving northward," Yen reported to the others.

"Good! Now if this evening's pleasantry proves favorable, then I would say we are off to an auspicious start," Profundus said. "Let us hope that the dear, sweet little Elves will be on time."

"And that your crossbowmen are true," added Gasher who had little respect for warriors that were not under his command.

"And once we have slain their leaders," Lusta offered, "let us move the rest of our forces to where the bridge will be built, for I am growing weary of waiting on these little green creatures."

And as they waited, the sun slipped slowly

behind the distant Pinus mountains.

Profundus, ever anxious, called out, "Give them a blast on your horns—we haven't got all night and the light is fading."

The same three scarlet warriors advanced and sounded loudly on their horns.

They waited as silence answered them. Then, to everyone's shock and confusion, a voice from behind the thrones spoke out. "I am Styrax, King of the Prosopian Elves."

Yen and Gasher leaped from their thrones as Profundus and Lusta twisted their bodies around, and there, directly behind their seats, stood Styrax in his ceremonial gown.

Amazed at the sudden appearance of so small a creature, none spoke for a long moment. Then Profundus, rising from his chair, said, "Welcome! Welcome, King Styrax. Your sudden appearance here has surprised us; we were expecting you to appear across the river as it was arranged. Is there a crossing nearby?"

Styrax stepped forward, answering, "There are no crossings nearby."

"Then how did you cross?" Gasher burst out.

Ignoring the bulky Gasher, Styrax addressed himself to Profundus who was obviously the leader. "I have come to hear whatever you have to say. You have come with mighty armies; therefore, I assume your visit is less than cordial."

"Do not judge us too quickly, little king, for we intend no harm to the Elfin folk," Lusta said in a soft voice, a tone she rarely used.

"Then what do you intend?" Styrax asked, also speaking in a soft voice.

"We seek new lands beyond the land of Prosopia, even beyond the great Pinus mountains we see outlined in the waning light," Lusta softly answered as she stepped back from Styrax.

"King Styrax, do not be deceived by our martial splendor, for it is meant to impress those men we expect to meet beyond the mountains. We have no interest in Prosopia; in fact, we did not know of your people until we came to the banks of the Rhus. Where are your companions, your allies?" Profundus asked.

"I have no companions. I have no allies. I have no friends. I am King Styrax."

"But, surely, you are not alone," Profundus observed as he slyly stepped back a few paces from King Styrax, giving a subtle signal to Gasher and Yen to also step back. "We have only one interest in your land, my friend. You will allow me to call you friend, will you not?"

"Call me what you wish."

"Well then, King Styrax, all we wish is safe passage across your land of Prosopia, passage, that is, for our armies," Profundus continued, "and that is all we ask."

"And if I deny you that passage?" Styrax questioned as he watched his opponents quietly backing away from where he stood.

"Deny us passage?" Profundus' voice grew stronger and less friendly. "Deny us passage? Surely, you jest, for who are you, little Elf, to deny me passage?"

"I am Styrax, King of the Elves."

"And I am Profundus, Lord of Greydome and master of warriors who have no peers. And you are a puny figure wrapped in a pathetic robe daring to challenge your betters. Come, little Elf, use your wisdom if you have been granted any."

"I am Styrax, King of Prosopia, and you and your armies shall not pass."

"And who will stop me?" Profundus asked, his

face reddening in growing rage.

"I am Styrax, King of the Elves."

Profundus stepped further back, beside himself in anger, and shouted aloud, "Kill him! Kill the little green devil!"

A moment passed and nothing happened. Lord Profundus turned to Lord Thrett who stood there in amazement, for he too had expected a shower of arrows to pierce Styrax through and through. But nothing happened, as Styrax stood still with a faint smile on his face.

"Your commands have gone awry, Profundus," Styrax said loudly. "Perhaps, no one heard you."

"Kill him! Kill him! What are you waiting for?" Profundus screamed, his voice ragged with rage. "Call the guard, Thrett! Call the guard."

As Thrett was about to issue orders, Styrax boldly stopped him by saying, "Perhaps you will allow me to call. Guards! Guards! The Elves are upon us."

And instantly the air was shattered by a deafening brazen roar, as of no horn Man had ever heard, so loud, so frightening that Profundus, Lusta, Yen and Gasher were frozen where they stood. Again and again, the brazen horn roared forth, seeming to come from all directions.

Lusta was the first to recover her senses. She quickly drew her sword, screaming, "Kill the Elf! Kill the Elf!" But as she turned, sword raised, she found no one there.

"Where is he? Where is this cursed Styrax?" shouted Yen who now had sword in hand.

"Where are the crossbowmen?" Profundus shouted at Thrett.

Instantly, Thrett rushed to the cover in which his bowmen were concealed. Pushing back the dense and spiny branches, he found his men dead, enwrapped in silken nets with slender daggers in their throats.

"They are dead, Lord Profundus," Thrett shouted. "All dead, caught in silken nets and stabbed in the neck."

"Yahhhh!" Profundus bellowed, "Yahhhh! The damned Elf has outwitted us. He is in league with the accursed Shee. But where is he? Where is that green devil? I will tear his lying tongue from his head. Where is Styrax?"

Then, above the confusion, the voice of Styrax was heard from across the river. "Does Lord Profundus call for me? Does Lord Profundus cry out for his little green friend? We are friends, are we not, Profundus? Come, dear friend, join me here on my side of the Rhus. My hospitality can hardly be worse than yours."

And from all the bushes issued the sounds of merry Shee laughter.

Chapter Twenty-Seven

At dawn, Profundus summoned his allies, for their meeting with King Styrax had hardly been successful. His rage had been assuaged in deep thought and patient resentment. He now knew that the Elfin Brood was in league with the damned Shee, the fairy women who have always been a plague to Man. And though he was not certain, he felt that the Dwarfs were also in confederation with the Elves and the Shee, and he greatly feared the martial prowess of the Dwarfenfold.

"I have decided to move our entire force to the northern crossing. We accomplish little here, and the more we delay, the more time the enemy has to prepare his defenses. Do I hear any objections?" Lord Profundus spoke sternly.

"You are right, Profundus, we accomplish little here and the Elves have accomplished much." Lusta replied tauntingly. "Perhaps, my Lord, the Elves have mettle beyond our expectations."

"Damn the Elves! Blast their livers!" Profundus shouted. "King Styrax is a tricky devil, but his slyness only reinforces my belief that his armies are small and feeble. Though he tricked us—he and the cursed Shee—he did not dare to meet our warriors sword to sword. He is playing a delaying game, but we will not be duped."

Yen the Cruel spoke up, "My men will be ready within the hour. Have you given thought to the positioning of our armies?"

Profundus scratched a crude map in the sand with his staff. "Yen will occupy the lands north of the crossing. Gasher will concentrate his men to the east, guarding against intrusion from that direction. And Lusta will encamp south of the crossing. My scarlet warriors will guard the center and clear the area for the bridge builders. We must concentrate the larger catapults in the center to guard the crossing, especially during the building of the bridge."

As they rose to begin their work, Profundus added, "Each of you must send a detachment of skilled workers to the east toward Greydome where they are to gather great timbers for the bridge work. This must be done at once, for I will abide no more delays. Is that understood?"

Within the hour, Yen, Gasher, Lusta and Profundus had dispatched contingents of worker-warriors to collect the mighty timbers the bridge called for, and Lord Thrett accompanied them both to guard the timbers and to force the workers to move with haste.

As Lord Thrett was preparing to leave for the sparse forests of Greydome, Lusta rode up to him, reining on her steed to impede his progress.

"Do not delay, Lord Thrett, for I find little pleasure in the company of Profundus. The old fool wearies me."

"I will return as soon as I set the men to work," Thrett answered. "Be patient with our leader, for I fear he underestimates our foe. This Elfin King is not a fool."

Lusta smiled slyly as she spoke, "Do you expect Profundus to fail? Perhaps, you hope he will."

"I think little of him and his plans, after all, I am his servant."

"A position that must gall you, my ambitious friend." Lusta paused, not sure if she should continue. Then she spoke quickly and coldly, "He is old. His power wanes. His scarlet warriors look more and more to you for guidance. Think on this as you herd the timber-gatherers."

And as quickly as she came, she rode off.

Shortly thereafter, Yen the Cruel led his army northward along the Rhus, his warriors straggling carelessly after their leader. Gasher the Bold next led his forces forth moving slowly to the east of Yen and his cohort. Lastly, Lord Profundus the Guileful and Lusta the Bitch led their combined armies along the path taken by Yen.

* * *

Styrax was awoken from a deep sleep by Thuja.

"Styrax! Styrax! Wake up! The entire enemy is on the move."

"Where are they moving?" Styrax asked as he rubbed the sleep from his Elfin eyes.

"Ulmus has said they are moving northward, all of them including their weapons and war machines."

Standing and stretching, Styrax commented in a tired voice, "They move for the crossing, Thuja my friend, and Ulmus, ever alert, has done his duty. It begins, Thuja, it begins."

"What begins?" Thuja asked.

"The war begins."

Later, in council with Canna, Hebe, Thuja and the Wanderer, Styrax observed, "We must now prepare our forces to meet the onslaught. Thuja, you will attend upon Empress Saphiria in the Pinus mountains where she stays in the caves of the Nibelungen. Inform her that the Trolls and the Nibelungen are expected at the crossing and that there is no time for delay. Wanderer, you must inform the Shee, for only you know where they are. I will speak to the Elfin Brood, and we will move northward before this day is out."

Later that day, just at the first hint of evening, Styrax and Canna stood before their simple mesquite-thatched home. Styrax had sent Elfin messengers throughout Prosopia ordering all males and females of appropriate age to move northward toward the designated crossing. Unlike other folk, the Elves never moved in collective groups or troops, but moved singly or in pairs through the endless dense thickets that covered their homeland. Silently, but quickly, the Elves individually collected their weapons and began the trek, weaving their way to the appointed place.

Canna, looking about at her peaceful village, took Styrax's right hand in hers, saying, "We leave the peace we may never find again, my beloved."

Styrax drew Canna close to him, "How well I know your sadness, my love, for our happy land must now bear the weight of war and the curse of Man. Disharmony is upon us."

How still the village seemed, and silent, for all the Elfin children had been moved deep within the great mesquite thickets far from the Rhus. Now only the gentle breeze whispered through the boughs.

Chapter Twenty-Eight

Slowly did the armies of Profundus the Guileful and his confederates wind their way northward, for though the warriors were swift of foot and their steeds renowned for speed, their war machines and overloaded wagons coupled with thousands of stragglers, workers, women and a few children slowed their progress enormously, and it was nine days before these mighty armies came within sight of the northern crossing. Then, the positioning of the troops took another two days by which time Lord Thrett had returned with five wagons of stout timbers freshly hewn in the forests of Greydome. After unloading the burdened wagons, Thrett ordered his men to return to Greydome to acquire another load of bridging timbers.

On the opposite bank of the Rhus, the Elves had already gathered, though wisely they stayed within the dense thickets of mesquite to keep their numbers secret from the sentries posted by Man. King Styrax camped upon the very knoll from which he had challenged Graspar many weeks before, when he and Thuja had their first confrontation with Man. From this elevation, Styrax, while still hidden from view, could observe the entire emplacements of enemies. The Elves had reached the crossing in four days, only to find the Wanderer and the Shee already encamped amid endless Shee laughter. And two days later, the Empress Saphiria and the Nibelungen force in brilliant golden armor marched precisely into the Elfin camp. Knowing that his enemies were unsure of who was allied with the Elves, Styrax placed the Dwarf camp far back from the river and from the curious eyes of Man. The Trolls had yet to appear, but Styrax assumed they would come later as their journey was by far the longest.

Meanwhile, Gore the Giant and his hand-picked warriors, twenty-five in number, had crossed the Rhus far to the north in the land of the Querques and were progressing into the foothills that led to the great ridge and towering peaks of the Pinus mountains. As they were mounted on especially swift steeds, they made good speed until they found themselves climbing a long, sloping ridge line that led up to the crest.

Gore the Giant was a particular favorite of Yen the Cruel, for Gore knew not fear and his strength was that of three of the strongest warriors. His armor was massive and black, and he carried a battle-ax that inspired terror in his foes. He wore no helmet and his greasy locks hung down over his shoulders. His men were tested warriors noted for their relentless cruelty. Their plan was simple, to wait upon the crest until the signal fires were seen, then to descend upon the Elves from behind, slaying many and causing such unexpected havoc to the Elfin lines that Profundus and his armies would be able to surge forward destroying all before them.

Once upon the crest, Gore ordered his men to make camp. Quickly they found a clearing but no firewood, for the Dwarfs had gleaned all the deadwood in that part of the great pine forest. Without hesitation, the warriors took their axes and began to chop down small pine trees, and soon they were seated around a blazing fire that lessened the chill of the mountain air. Carefully, they honed their weapons, sharpening the blades to deathly edges. And as darkness fell, they slipped into the sleep of exhaustion, for the ascent had been long and continual.

One warrior had been selected to keep guard, and he sat near the fire adding logs whenever the blaze seemed to diminish. Soundly, they all slept, and even the guard tended to drift off, his head falling sideways on occasion, forcing him back into alertness. Toward dawn, he thought he heard a noise, the snapping of a twig, perhaps. He stood up and walked around the fire but saw nothing.

Suddenly, the camp was roused by the raucous screams of the guard, and the first warriors to rise thought they saw a huge cat-like creature bounding off into the dark with the limp form of the guard clamped within its huge jaws. Quickly, the suddenly woken warriors armed themselves and rushed about the fire, shouting and screaming commands which no one obeyed. Gore finally silenced the mayhem by smashing his ax against his shield, creating a deafening din.

"Silence! Silence!" Gore shouted as he continued banging his shield. "Control yourselves. What has happened?"

Many voices spoke at once until Gore thought he understood what had happened; a mountain lion had killed the guard who had probably fallen asleep on his watch.

"You act like terror-stricken children," Gore roared. "We have lost but one warrior who has been punished for sleeping when he should have been watching. That is it, nothing more. Go back to sleep. I will stand guard until sunrise."

In the warmth of the rising sun, Gore organized his encampment, sending two of his trusted warriors to scout the higher ridge for a safe, downward trail so that they could descend upon the Elves swiftly. Others he sent to hunt game, and still others were given the task of making temporary shelter and gathering more firewood which they gained by felling more pine saplings. As the others worked, Gore found the massive tracks of the beast that had slain the guard, and he was stunned for never had he seen paw prints so huge. That night, he swore, he would post four dependable sentries to ward off any further attacks by the monstrous creature.

Later, as the hunting party returned with numerous rabbits and a small deer, Gore walked to the edge of the crest. Far in the distance he could discern the mighty Rhus winding its way through the barren landscape. Then, carefully, he scanned along the ridge where he saw his two scouts probing the rugged cliff face seeking a safe descent. As he watched, the two scouts were forced to re-enter the forest in order to go around a soaring rock outcropping. Patiently he waited for the scouts to appear on the other side of the massive rocks, but though he waited and waited, they did not appear. An hour passed, and the scouts neither appeared on the ridge nor returned to camp, making Gore become restless and angry.

Impatient at last, Gore selected four warriors and set out along the edge of the cliff following the tracks of the scouts. As he approached the rock-outcropping, he ordered his men to unsheathe their swords as he unbuckled his fatal battle-ax. Cautiously, they worked their way around the rock formation only to find no one on the opposite side. Gore's eyes traveled along the continuing cliff, but he saw nothing. Then one of the warriors shouted and pointed downward. Far below lay both scouts, their bodies crumpled amid fallen boulders, lying in the grotesque positions of death. One warrior was attempting to descend the sheer face of rock, when Gore stopped him.

"Leave them be," Gore ordered. "They are dead and not worth bothering about. The fools must have slipped."

* * *

As evening fell, Gore commanded four of his best warriors to stand guard. He warned them to be especially alert to avoid another attack by the huge cat-like beast. Then sitting by the blazing fire, Gore and his men ate heartily from the young deer they were cooking on a spit. Darkness fell swiftly among the pines, and soon all, except the sentries, were fast asleep.

When they awoke the following morning, all were safe, but the horses were gone, their tethers neatly severed. The guards insisted that they had remained awake and alert but had seen and heard nothing.

The warriors quickly armed themselves, for they felt more vulnerable without their mounts. Some whispered to others of the strange deaths of their three companions, while others questioned the odd disappearance of the horses.

One warrior, bolder than the rest, spoke his mind, saying, "Without our mounts we can move but slowly. Three of us have died strangely in this haunted forest. Perhaps, we should return the way we came."

Gore, angry but disheartened, answered, "Don't

be a fool. Will you—yes, you—face the wrath of Yen and the rage of Profundus and Lusta? We have our task and must do as we were ordered. Yen does not accept failure."

"But without our horses we…" the warrior persisted, until interrupted by Gore.

"Silence, you idiot. We will proceed on foot. Speak no more of returning lest you deal with me."

Gore's words struck deep terror in the hearts of his followers, for none would stand against Gore the Giant and his fatal ax. Again, he designated a hunting party and a wood-gathering party, even as he assigned four new guards to watch the camp even though it was daylight.

Having felled all the nearby pine saplings, the wood gatherers were obliged to wander farther afield, and as they moved farther from the camp their numbers thinned as they spread out in search of firewood. Three warriors had moved into a steep ravine, cluttered with many young trees, and began to cut down the available pines. They had felled two young trees and were beginning to chop on another when a booming voice roared out from within the forest.

"You fell my children, accursed thieves. There is no escape."

The warriors leaped back, dropping their axes as they drew their swords, looking in terror at each other and then scanning the forest. Nothing was seen. Slowly, they backed down the ravine until they found an easy place to climb out. But just as the first warrior climbed out of the ravine, he was struck by the bole of a huge lightning-struck tree and knocked over backward into the dry wash, the trunk of the trees crashing down upon him, crushing out his life. The second warrior carefully raised his head above the edge of the ravine only to find nothing of danger in sight. He scrambled out and turned to assist his comrade when he spied a great cat, the largest mountain lion he had ever seen, rush down the ravine, pounce upon his companion, crush him in its huge jaws, and bound away carrying the limp body with him. In panic, the remaining warrior ran toward camp, but just as he came over a rise, he ran headlong into a green creature shaped like a Man but fully twice the size of Gore.

The giant quickly grasped the warrior by the head, lifting him up and saying, "I am Rhamnus," just before he crushed the warrior's skull between his massive hands.

When the hunting party and the other wood-gatherers returned, Gore was made aware that three more of his warriors were gone. Gore then began to know terror for the first time, though he masked it from his men.

"I know not what haunts this accused place," Gore said slowly as his eyes wandered about the campsite, "but from now on, no one is to leave camp. We will all stay together, hunt together, gather wood together and stay awake together. Whatever is out there is slaying us one at a time. If it wishes to continue, it must face us all. Is that understood?"

That night, the warriors built a larger fire than usual, and all stayed awake.

Shortly after the middle of the night, the air was filled with bestial roars of such magnitude that all were cowed and drew closer to the fire on which they heaped more and more logs, for none had ever heard such savage roaring that seemed to emanate from everywhere, echoing and re-echoing across the night.

Then from deep within the forest came a thunderous voice as of a hundred men: "I am Rhamnus, the Pinus Elf. You have slain my children. Now you must die."

Gore leaped to his feet, shouting, "Who speaks? Who speaks from hiding? Come forward. Face us like—"

Suddenly, a huge rock, easily the weight of a Man, flew by Gore, missing him by inches only, and striking two warriors standing behind him, instantly dispatching them. Another rock flew by, crushing another warrior, followed by another that missed everyone.

Again from the darkness came the thunderous voice: "I am Rhamnus. You must die."

And another huge rock came crashing into the warrior's camp, only this time the massive stone crashed directly into the roaring fire, showering burning wood, embers and sparks everywhere while effectively putting the fire out. In the darkness, all became panic as warriors slashed in all directions with their swords and battle-axes, often striking each other. From nowhere and everywhere, great mountain lions sprang upon the terrified and hopelessly confused warriors, crushing them within their slavering jaws and carrying bodies back into the blackness of the forest filled with agonizing screams.

Then all was silent as Gore threw fresh logs on the remaining coals of the fire, and as the fire came back to life he witnessed the gory scene. Four dead bodies, some crushed by stone, others torn by fangs, lay crumpled around the camp. Gore counted the remaining warriors, and there were only nine remaining, two of whom were badly injured.

"Tomorrow, with the first light, we will begin the descent. We few, whoever is left, will attack the Elves from the rear. Little good we will accomplish, but at least we will strike at enemies we can see, enemies of flesh and blood who will face us in the light. But, surely, we must abandon this damned place." Gore spoke as in a trance.

With dawn, Gore led his remaining warriors to the edge of the cliff where a great steep rock slide made a descent possible though extremely treacherous. Slowly, his men, one by one, assisting the injured, began to climb down the precipitous, loose rocks. They moved slowly knowing that a single misstep could start a rock slide that would quickly become an avalanche. One after the other, they carefully stepped from stone to stone. Gore was the last one, and just as he was about to start down, he heard the booming voice of terror behind him: "I am Rhamnus, the Pinus Elf."

Gore turned to face the green creature who towered over him. "Who are you?" Gore blurted out as he unbuckled his ax.

"I am Rhamnus, father, brother and son of the pines that you have slain."

"Then taste my ax, Rhamnus," Gore shouted as he rushed toward the massive figure of Rhamnus, raising his battle-ax as he lunged ahead. But his effort was futile, for Rhamnus simply raised his mighty staff and jammed it into the chest of Gore who was thrust backwards over the cliff edge. Gore's body struck two of the descending warriors who then fell against others until bodies and loose rock tumbled wildly down the unstable scarp. Slowly at first, then with acceleration, the entire rock slide began to move until the mountainside became a deafening avalanche, burying all before it.

Rhamnus walked to the edge of the cliff looking down on the carnage below. Carefully he picked up the ax of Gore, breaking the haft from the blade.

Chapter Twenty-Nine

Thus the awesome forces had gathered at the northern crossing. On the eastern side of the Rhus were the savage armies of Profundus the Guileful with Yen the Cruel guarding his northern flank, Gasher the Bold encamped to the east ever watching for marauding bands of men, and Lusta the Bitch guarding his southern flank. The scarlet five hundred remained in the center, both to protect Profundus from his enemies and allies, and to protect the bridge-builders.

Across the Rhus on the western side were encamped the forces of Styrax, King of Prosopia, but these forces were deeply hidden within the vast area of dense mesquite thickets that crowded to the banks of the pitiless Rhus, ever sweeping toward the sea. Hidden well back from the river were the golden-armored ranks of the Nibelungen, disciplined and fierce. And along the river but enshrouded in the twisted foliage were the numerous Elves and Shee, awaiting the first onslaught.

It was not long until Profundus learned of Elfin weapons, for until the present, he had no concept of that with which the Elves waged war. Once his soldiery had been properly encamped, Profundus turned his attention to the building of the bridge.

Carefully, he watched as the master-builders waded into the strong-flowing Rhus testing the gravelly bottom with long poles.

Thuja waited patiently in a mesquite blind just across from where the men were working. As he watched they drew closer, having reached the middle of the river. Deftly, Thuja raised his long blowgun, aiming with great care. The poisoned dart flew straight and true, striking the foremost Man directly in the neck.

The stricken Man stumbled backwards, crying out and his companions quickly carried him back to the eastern bank. Profundus ran up to the dying Man and quickly yanked the dart from his neck. He touched the point of the dart to his tongue delicately and then spat out the poison.

"So, our green friends use poison darts. No wonder the Beastums seemed to die of sorcery," Profundus thought to himself.

Thereafter, none of the bridge-builders entered the river without the protection of a massive shield that effectively blunted the sting of the Elfin darts. Thuja and the other Elves quickly learned the futility of wasting their missiles upon metal shields, and they were forced to wait and wait until a Man foolishly lowered his shield or the rushing waters forced the Man to suddenly shift his protection. Then, rapidly, many darts would fly, and the builders would be forced to cease their work as they carried another of their dying comrades ashore. Thus, though the shields protected the workers, they also hindered their freedom of movement and slowed down their attempts to find solid ground upon which to place the bridge's piers.

That evening as King Styrax held council with the Wanderer, Queen Fon-du-Fon, King Sard, Empress Saphiria and Vastar, they were alarmed as Rhamnus' Mordant rushed into their camp still carrying Gore's broken ax haft in his jaws. The great cat ran quickly to the fire, dropped the haft, looked momentarily at Styrax, and as quickly turned and bounded off into the undergrowth.

"Fear not! Fear not!" Styrax shouted, especially concerned that King Sard might draw his sword and foolishly attack the massive beast. But all were so stunned that the Mordant had come and gone ere they enraptured their senses.

"He is the beast of Rhamnus, the Pinus Elf I have spoken of," Styrax said as he picked up the huge haft.

"It is from a battle ax," the Wanderer offered.

"And an ax made by Man," King Sard volunteered. "See how massive it is, and so crudely wrought, certainly not the work of the Dwarfenfold."

On the haft were scratched twenty-five marks, each of which had been crossed out. Styrax studied the markings slowly as he remembered his huge kin from the Pinus mountains.

"The message seems to be that Rhamnus has slain many of the enemy, for each of the marks has been crossed," Styrax muttered.

"Of course," the Wanderer blurted out. "Of course, Profundus attempted to out-flank us by sending warriors to attack us from the rear. Let us hope that your friend, Rhamnus, has killed them all."

"I am sure he has," Styrax answered, "for each of the marks is crossed out. The fools had entered his sacred land, even as they seek to enter ours."

Solemnly but joyously, they drank to Rhamnus and their sudden good fortune, for had not Rhamnus acted, they would be in great difficulty as none were prepared for an attack from the west, the only direction that had seemed secure.

King Sard was the first to break the revelry of the moment with, "But what of the bridge, King Styrax?"

"They have made but little progress," the Empress offered.

"At present, we are at an impasse: they cannot reach us; we cannot reach them," Styrax answered.

"But they have a weapon that can reach us," the Wanderer broke in, "for they have their catapults, weapons of awesome destruction."

"But what good will it do them if we simply withdraw from the river's edge and camp beyond their range?" the Empress asked.

"That is the problem, Empress Saphiria," the Wanderer answered. "If we are driven from the river's edge, then they have free rein to build their damned bridge. We will no longer be in a position to continually harass them. And if they have free rein, the bridge will be completed very swiftly."

"But, then, what can we do?" King Sard asked in frustration.

And no one spoke for long moments.

"He-he-he, my friends, he-he-he," Fon-du-Fon said happily, "thus far you have asked little of the Shee. Do you think that we, he-he-he, are too delicate or too small or too unmanly to do a day's work, he-he-he? We are ancient people and have always been a bane to the likes of Man, he-he-he."

And no sooner had she finished speaking than she rushed off into the darkness of the night.

"Have we hurt Queen Fon-du-Fon's feelings? She has run away so abruptly," Empress Saphiria observed.

"No. The Shee have tough hides, Empress, and never seem to take offense from mere words," the Wanderer replied. "Fon-du-Fon will now gather her clan to prepare for what they call Shee-ness, the act of madness that alone can conquer faint hope."

Fon-du-Fon ran quickly through the night, her silvery body almost invisible in the soft light of the moon, for the Shee by nature are moonlight hunters. Finding a small group of Shee laughing by the Rhus, she instantly gave orders as the Shee scurried about, laughing the while.

Slipping into the deep thickets, they gathered dead wood into small bundles, each the size of a Shee. Then quietly, ten Shee and Fon-du-Fon carried each bundle to the river's bank. With great caution, each Shee slipped into the stream using the bundles for buoyancy. The rest watched as the first Shee paddled quietly with the current, moving slowly for the eastern bank of the Rhus. Then another Shee slipped into the water; then another; then another.

Softly emerging on the eastern side, Fon-du-Fon led them slowly up stream when they were stunned to see Vastar struggling after them, his long legs carrying him as the bundles had carried the Shee.

As Fon-du-Fon helped Vastar up the embankment, she whispered, "He-he-he, what does so ancient a Man mean by following the Shee, the people of the moon, he-he-he?"

Panting for breath, Vastar answered, "My task is not the same as the task of the Shee."

"He-he-he, but is your task for Vastar? Or for the Elfin cause, he-he-he?" Fon-du-Fon asked as she drew her slender dagger from its sheath.

"Fear not, Queen Fon-du-Fon, my treachery, for that is all I have, is intended for Profundus and in the Elfin cause."

Fon-du-Fon stepped back looking up into the care-worn and weary eyes of Vastar. She paused a moment, then whispered, "He-he-he, but you are one of them not us, he-he-he."

Vastar knelt down and spoke softly, "I am not an Elf, yet I honor them for kindness I have never known. I have been among your people, the Nibelungen and the Elves too long. For I am of the race of Man though I am ashamed to acknowledge it."

"He-he-he, then what purpose have you, he-he-he?" Fon-du-Fon asked. "For unless you tell me of your purpose, you will go no farther, he-he-he."

"Fear not, little Queen. My aim is to benefit your tribes, for that which has been dead within me for most of my worthless life has begun to breathe again. Here me, oh Queen of the Shee," and as Vastar spoke strength entered his voice and his eyes again seemed clear, "I have but one action left in my pathetic span. I will die, that is as it should be, but I will take my accursed brother Profundus with me to the fires of the damned."

Fon-du-Fon put her dagger back into its sheath as she studied the wrinkled fact of Vastar. "I will not deter you, old Man, he-he-he, and I wish you success. Be cautious and wait for the diversion we will create. Man has never been a mystery to the Shee, he-he-he."

Vastar accompanied the Shee until they drew within sight of Profundus' camp; then they parted, each to the allotted tasks.

Profundus' camp was carefully guarded by the ever-alert scarlet warriors, but though they had sharp eyes, they were hardly sharp enough to see the silvery forms of the Shee who in the moonlight could move as if they were not there at all. With infinite care, the Shee moved toward the wagons and catapults massed but a few hundred yards from the river's edge. Slowly, ever so slowly, they crawled beneath the wagons and slithered through the parched grasses until they had reached their goal, the catapults themselves. Dispersing, each Shee carefully pressed dry thatch against the inside of the massive wooden wheels. Then, each in turn struck tiny flints until the thatch began to smolder. And as quietly as they came, the Shee slipped away back to the river, regaining their withered bundles, and returning to the western side of the Rhus.

Meanwhile, Vastar, using his craftiness that had served him lifelong, had sidled closer and closer to the ornate tent of Profundus heavily guarded by scarlet warriors. He knew now that he must wait for the mischief of the Shee to manifest itself.

For many minutes, the camp remained peaceful, but then Vastar saw the smoke rising from the massed wagons and catapults in the field beyond the tents. He waited until the shouting began and warriors were rushing toward the smoke that was now tinged with flame. And as the conflagration grew, Profundus' camp was as if struck by panic, with screaming men shouting and rushing about with water buckets. Soon Profundus burst from his tent, enraged by what he saw and realizing immediately the fell blow the enemy had struck. One warrior ran up to Profundus reporting on the damage and what was being done to stop it. Immediately, Profundus ordered his personal guard to assist in fighting the numerous fires, screaming at them as they rushed off, "The catapults! The catapults! You fools, save the catapults."

In the mayhem, Vastar carefully crawled to the back flap of Profundus' tent. He slipped inside, hiding behind an arras that hung upon the rear tent wall. Soon, Profundus, shaking his head, reentered his tent. In disgust, he sat at his table looking out at the burning catapults and his panic-stricken warriors. Deftly, Vastar crept forward until he found himself behind his unsuspecting brother. Slowly, he drew his dagger; then, quickly he stood, pushing the point firmly into his brother's neck.

"Quiet, brother, quiet. It is I, Vastar, your brother in blood. Do not move! Do not speak! My blade has a fatal bite."

Profundus, in terror, moved not.

"I cannot describe my joy to stand thus with my knife finally at your throat. Years of anguish and loathing come to fruition soon."

"My warriors will kill you if you slay me," Profundus gasped out, sweat covering his forehead.

"That is of little matter, brother," Vastar answered, pressing his blade deeper into Profundus' wrinkled neck. "Remember me, brother. Remember all the evil you have become. Remember my wife as my blade pricks your throat. But most of all, remember the son you thought you had slain, for he is now the strength of your enemies."

Lord Thrett, returning from the now contained conflagration, was astounded as he approached the tent of Profundus, for through the entrance he saw his old foe, Vastar, holding a dagger against the neck of his new master. Rapidly, without being seen, he skirted the tent, entering through the rear flap as Vastar had done. Stealthily, he drew his short sword as he slipped up behind Vastar whose entire attention was upon tormenting his hated brother.

"I have dwelt with the Elves, brother," Vastar continued, "and no longer will I honor the cause of Man. We have become the very beasts we have destroyed; we have become the anathema. Seek thy peace, brother, for I am your doom."

Swiftly and mightily, Thrett's sword swept

through the air, decapitating Vastar instantly, the dagger falling futilely to the ground.

Profundus leaped from his seat, his hands grasping at his uninjured throat, sweat pouring from his face. "Ah! Ah! Is he dead? Kill him! Kill him!" he shouted, kicking wildly at the crumpled body of Vastar.

"He is dead, my Lord," Thrett said with disgust, wondering at that moment if, perhaps, he had beheaded the wrong Man.

After a moment, Profundus collapsed in his chair wiping away his sweat on the sleeve of his robe. He dared not talk as yet, fearing his ability to control his speech.

Lord Thrett looked down at the remains of Vastar. Stooping down, he wiped his sword clean with Vastar's long cape. As he stood and sheathed his sword, he said to the crumpled form, "I told you I would kill you when I no longer needed you."

Still breathing heavily, Profundus finally managed to speak, "Have you...are the fires still raging?"

"We have controlled them, my Lord. The men are busy now assessing the damage."

"What of...what of the catapults?" Profundus asked.

"We have saved eleven of the twenty, and two more can be salvaged. The rest are ashes. We have also lost all of the bridging timber though more is on the way from Greydome."

Profundus stood and walked about the tent, slowly gaining complete control of himself as his terror began to turn to rage. In fury, he asked, "Who is responsible for this? Who dares attack the camp of Profundus?"

Lord Thrett held up a silken net, saying nothing as he waved it in front of his master.

"Damn them! Damn all the Shee throughout all of eternity," Profundus raged on. "Where were the guards? How is it I am surrounded with treachery, by treachery and fools? Am I ever to be cursed by those damn Shee, little women who make fools of Profundus and his mighty host?"

Lord Thrett simply shrugged his shoulders as he left the tent to continue his work of undoing the damage that had been done.

Profundus ordered his warriors to nail the headless corpse of Vastar to a post with the grisly head planted upon a high spike. The post was to be planted along the river so the Elves would see the horrible remains and realize the futility of challenging so mighty a Lord as Profundus. But later, when he was alone, Profundus thought only of Vastar's words: "Remember the son you thought you had slain, for he is now the strength of your enemies."

Thrett was busy salvaging what he could from the ashes when Lusta came to him.

"It seems that our mighty leader Profundus has sadly underestimated our enemies, and they have struck a telling blow," Lusta said as she put her arm on Thrett's shoulders.

"We have lost seven catapults and all the bridge timber. I fear that the old fool is losing control of himself and even of some few of the Scarlet Five Hundred," Thrett answered angrily.

"Do not worry, my love. It works for us. If you sense malcontent in the ranks, then nurture it. You and I have little to lose and so much to gain."

Chapter Thirty

King Styrax and Queen Canna, the Wanderer, and Empress Saphiria and King Sard waited impatiently for Queen Fon-du-Fon to return. All were cheerful as they rejoiced in the martial success of Rhamnus, knowing now they had little to fear from the west, and knowing, deep in their hearts, though none spoke of it, that should they fail, Rhamnus and the Pinus mountains offered them a path of retreat to either the Nibelungen caves or to the shelter of Rhamnus' pines, both of which were a haven from the ravages of Man.

As they paced about the fire, the laughter of the returning Shee was heard, and soon Fon-du-Fon skipped carelessly into the camp. "He-he-he, the Shee are here," she shouted, "the children of the moon have again been victorious, he-he-he."

Styrax took her tiny hands in his, tears of happiness in his eyes, for since their first meeting, a profound bond of love had grown between them. "Has anyone been injured?" Styrax asked when he could control his voice.

"He-he-he, many have been injured," Fon-du-Fon answered happily, "many, many have been wounded, many others have been slain, he-he-he. But I speak not of the Shee, but only of Man, he-

he-he. The Shee are unscathed and triumphant, he-he-he."

Within moments, Queen Fon-du-Fon had recounted the raid of the Shee in which at least ten men had been silently dispatched, and though Fon-du-Fon, having quickly retreated after setting the fires, did not know how many catapults had been destroyed, she felt sure that at least five were burned beyond salvage and that most of the timber brought down from the eastern hills had gone up in flames.

"Has Vastar yet returned?" Fon-du-Fon asked.

"Vastar?" They all questioned at once.

Seeing their surprise, Fon-du-Fon realized that they had known nothing of Vastar's plans. In detail, she explained all that she knew. And the while she spoke, they all watched happily the chaos and confusion of their foes across the river as seemingly innumerable men ran wildly about with water buckets, screaming orders that none heeded and cursing each other, their enemies, the darkness, and the stars that witnessed the madness.

"You say that Vastar intended to kill his brother, Profundus," the Empress said. "But how do we know if he spoke the truth? After all, he is one of them."

"As I am," the Wanderer answered lightly.

"But we know you, Wanderer. We know your heart and you are now one of us," the Empress replied softly. "But hardly was Vastar to be trusted. My thought is that we should have executed him at once."

"In doing that, we would be acting as men do," Styrax said, "and what would we have gained if in defeating men we began to act as they do and became as they are? No, no, Empress, I cannot allow the crimes of men to become our crimes."

"He was free to do as he chose," Canna added. "He is an old Man, feeble in strength. If he slays his brother, so much the better for us. If he returns to their ranks, they have but small gain."

"Let us forget Vastar for the moment; this is hardly the moment for sadness," Styrax shouted happily as he jumped upon a huge bolder. "The Shee have had a mighty victory, and we should rejoice. Empress Saphiria, summon the Nibelungen! Queen Fon-du-Fon, call together the Shee! Thuja and Canna, sound the horns of the Elves. This very night we will carouse and celebrate our first successes against our foes. Tonight we shall sing and dance, eat and be merry, drink and laugh. Bitter times may lie ahead, but this night shall be given to merriment."

Within the hour, the Nibelungen, the Shee and the Elves were deep in their revelry. Dwarf wine, Shee liquor and Elfin Fool's Delight flowed copiously and plentiful supplies of favored foods were made available to all. Soon the Shee were singing their high-pitched songs accompanied by Elves playing upon their reeds and brazen horns while the Nibelungen chanted rhythmically. Thuja danced boldly in great leaps and bounds that contrasted marvelously with the delicate, swan-like dancing of Hebe. Though steeped in perpetual sadness for his lost tribe, Gaius Fortunas Duergar joined the dance by standing on the side while making tiny, shuffling steps. And, finally, to the amazement of all, Empress Saphiria danced a sprightly reel with her kinsmen, her stout figure surprising everyone with its lightness and grace, her bold and rich laughter harmonizing with the Dwarfish chanting.

Great fires were built along the western bank of the Rhus, for the Wanderer had insisted that their merriment be made evident to their enemies on the opposite bank. For on the far shore, the camp of Profundus was still a bedlam as the soldiery slowly began to douse the great fires started by the Shee. Men everywhere had formed long lines in order to pass river water to the scene of the great conflagration while still other men carried the dead and wounded to shelter. With great anger, the ranks of men heard the joyous music of the Elves and their compatriots wafting across the surging waters of the Rhus. A fell spirit descended upon the camp of Profundus, for proud men had tasted shameful defeat at the hands of little women but a third their size.

Lord Thrett was summoned to wait upon Profundus.

"I want all sentries doubled or tripled, if need be. This cannot happen again, for no one can make a fool of me. I am Profundus the Guileful, Lord of Greydome and Master of the Scarlet Five Hundred. Damn the Shee! I will uproot their entire tribe and feed their little bodies to the buzzards."

Lord Thrett, filled with disdain at the ravings of Profundus, reported, "The Shee have slain ten men, wounded seven, and have destroyed seven catapults and damaged two others, both of which can easily be repaired. All the bridge timber is gone."

"Tomorrow, you must send a contingent east to gather more timber," Profundus barked.

"It has already been done, my Lord. New timber is already being gathered," Lord Thrett replied.

"Meanwhile," a smile came to Profundus' wrinkled face as he spoke, "have a large fire set by Vastar's corpse, large enough for the Elves to see what awaits them. Have the horns sounded. I will speak with Styrax. See to it."

The Elfin revelry was interrupted by the massed horns of the scarlet warriors. All of a sudden, the

Elfin music stopped, and all eyes were turned to the river. Gradually, great flames began to erupt near the shore of the far side, and soon the Elves, the Shee and the Nibelungen were able to discern the limp body of Vastar hanging from a post, his head grotesquely impaled upon a spike jutting from the top of the post. Silence quickly enveloped the night as Profundus strode to the edge of the river.

"Styrax, King of the accursed Elves, it is I, Profundus, and I want to speak with you," Profundus roared.

Styrax stepped forward, facing his hated foe across the Rhus. "I am here, Profundus. Have you found the evening's entertainment to your liking?"

"Speak of your victory with Vastar," Profundus shouted back, "for soon you will be where he now is."

And in silence, the Elves, the Shee and the Nibelungen stared at the remains of Vastar, horrified by what they saw and even more profoundly shocked by the knowledge that brother had slain brother.

Styrax paused a moment; then he raised his cup on high, shouting loudly for all to hear, "Raise your cups, my friends. We drink a solemn pledge to the shade of Vastar. We vow to avenge his death and to destroy those who are responsible. Here me, Profundus! This night you have tasted of our anger. Do you hunger for more? Know then that the men you have sent to encircle us are all dead, destroyed by Rhamnus, the Pinus Elf. And now, Profundus, we return to our delights, for we have much to celebrate."

Quickly, the Elves, the Shee and the Nibelungen left the river, and as quickly their music once again filled the air, wafting across the turbulent Rhus and galling the still enraged Profundus.

Chapter Thirty-One

King Jasper had returned to Troll-Land with bitterness in his heart, angered by the Wanderer, his Empress, King Styrax and, especially, the Shee who in their careless manner had belittled the martial prowess of the Troll warriors. King Jasper felt that his allies suffered from timidity and had little knowledge of the nature of warfare.

Once at home, Jasper became a whirlwind of activity, for truly he longed for battle, for the din of sword on shield. Troll maidens cheerfully burnished the copper-toned shields and armor of the warriors who were diligently honing and rehoning their swords, battle axes, and spears. All night the forges roared and hammers resounded, echoing in the eerie light and dense smoke, and while the Trolls worked they chanted loudly the staccato songs of their people: "Hrumf, hrumf, hrumf, hrumf," counter-pointed with "Hoyoh, hoyoh, hoyoh, hoyoh." And amid the flying sparks and glowing embers, their strong, compactly muscled bodies sweated in rhythmic labor.

As the days passed, King Jasper grew more and more restless, for in the days and nights of preparation, he had conceived a mighty plan by which he and the Trolls alone would destroy the armies of Profundus, marching, after victory, in martial glory to the camp of King Styrax. For though Jasper was a fine leader and a loyal subject of Empress Saphiria, he had an insatiable thirst for glory and an implacable hatred for Man, the creature who in the mists of the past had driven the Dwarfs beneath the surface of the earth. In his heart he knew a senseless need to impress the Elves and the Shee, and, on a personal level, King Sard and the Nibelungen, forever the people of the Dwarfenfold were envious of, and constantly in rivalry with, other Dwarfs.

Finally, the preparations were complete, and an army of one thousand brilliantly arrayed Trolls gathered in their great hall. After much loud laughter and many toasts, King Jasper strode boldly to the dais, his voice roaring forth, "I drink to battle. I drink to blade on blade. I drink to the fallen bodies of men."

In the fervid excitement, the Trolls banged their short swords across their shields, creating sounds so powerful and deafening that the rocks themselves seemed to grind one against the other.

And King Jasper continued, "Are we not the trolls of yore? Are we not the masters of the spear? Does not Man still quail at the sight of Troll warriors?"

The Trolls roared back their answers, again banging their swords upon their shields while they stamped their feet. Slowly and softly at first, they began their warrior's chant: "Hrumf, hrumf, hoyoh, hoyoh."

And as the chant began to swell, Jasper shouted above the din, "But our allies all of them though they be friends would have us hiding in bushes, sneaking out to attack solitary warriors and lowly workmen, then skulking back into cover.

Is this our way? Is this the way of the Trolls?"

In mighty unison, the Trolls roared back, "No! No! Never!"

And the fatal plans were laid.

* * *

With the coming of evening, the Trolls set out in rigid martial order, but instead of following the usual route through tunnels and caverns, they marched boldly along the Rhus as it grew from a mountain stream to a mighty river. At the last shallow crossing, north of the land of the Querques, they forded the river and continued marching southward along the eastern shore. Within two nights of marching, for Trolls like all Dwarfs shunned the heat of the sun, they came upon the ruined and mostly deserted city of the Querques.

As the Trolls approached, their scouts reported that a small group of Querques were loading wagons of supplies destined, it was assumed, for the army of Yen the Cruel. Taking fifty warriors, King Jasper attacked without pause and without mercy. The Querques, taken by surprise, offered but feeble resistance, and the skirmish ended quickly with twenty Querques slain and two taken captive. The two remaining Querques were brought before King Jasper. In sullen terror, they were forced to kneel before the King, hoping for life but expecting death.

King Jasper surprised them, "Go to Yen, your hateful master. Take your horses and go. I spare you now so that you might warn your cowardly master that the Trolls are coming, lusting for blood and vengeance. Be gone! My patience begins to burden me."

Quickly, the Querques ran for their horses and rode south, the Trolls banging their shields and laughing as the Querques rode off. Yen's supplies were put to the torch, and the pathetic Querque dwellings amid the ancient ruins were razed. That night the trolls celebrated in drunken revelry.

For four more nights, the trolls marched on, ever following the Rhus southward, and on the fifth night, as they crossed a rise, they saw before them on a distant ridge what seemed to be thousands of campfires.

King Jasper had found Yen the Cruel.

Yen had brought his entire army of over five thousand strong north along the river until he found the battlefield he wanted. His army camped upon a long ridge that descended slowly toward the Rhus, ending in steep scarps that fell directly into the rushing river. As Yen looked down from the ridge, he saw a shallow valley of sere grass. On his left was the river; on his right the valley closed to a box canyon. His mounted warriors, he sent to the right, telling them to circle around the head of the canyon so that they were in a position to attack the Trolls from the rear. Yen was filled with expectant joy when his spies informed him that the Trolls were camped on the opposing rise and that they numbered but one thousand.

At dawn, the Trolls carefully formed their battle line. Shields in front, followed by a solid rank of spears and then another rank of stout axes. King Jasper stood in front of his warriors. As they looked across the valley, they saw the warriors of Yen the Cruel forming their battle line on the opposing ridge. King Jasper raised his spear and shouted, "Forward." The trolls in lockstep moved forward chanting, "Hrumf, hrumf, hoyoh, hoyoh" to the accompaniment of their swords banging loudly against their shields.

Slowly, the enemies approached each other in rigid lines. But as Yen's warriors came closer and closer to the ever-advancing Trolls, their undisciplined line began to disintegrate into a mad charge, disordered and confused. Soon the Querques crashed against the solid shield line of the Trolls. The Querque's swords, wielded wildly, caromed off the brazen shields as the Trolls marched forward, "Hrumf, hrumf, hoyoh, hoyoh." With great violence and rage, the Querques threw themselves against the Troll shields, but even as they did, the second line of Trolls, the spears, lunged forward, the deadly spear points shooting out from between the shields, piercing and slaying the foremost of the Querques. Again and again, Yen's warriors rushed upon the shields, only to be thrown back with grievous losses. And the line of Troll warriors moved ever forward: "Hrumf, hrumf, hoyoh, hoyoh."

Yen, watching on horseback from the ridge, waited until the Trolls had reached the center of the arroyo; then he ordered his servants to light a large, smoky signal fire. Within moments, his mounted warriors appeared behind the Trolls on the very rise from which the Trolls had descended.

King Jasper and his Trolls, having suffered but few casualties, continued moving forward, ever throwing the Querques back upon each other, causing such chaos in the disordered Querque ranks that many slew their own comrades in their wild attempts to break the Troll line. Forward, the Trolls moved relentlessly like an incoming tide: "Hrumf, hrumf, hoyoh, hoyoh."

Then suddenly, the mounted Querques charged with full force into the rear of the advancing Trolls, smashing the line in numerous places, allowing the Querque foot soldiers to break through. Caught off guard, many Trolls fell before the line of Troll battle axes could turn to face and repel the mounted Querques. Beleaguered, King Jasper screamed out his orders. Immediately, the Trolls fell back in orderly fashion, forming into a vast circle of shields around the Troll spears and battle axes.

The Troll's new formation proved a severe test for the Querques. If the foot soldiers charged, they were impaled on Troll spears. If the mounted Querques charged, the shields would part slightly as Trolls with axes rushed out, hacking the horse's legs from beneath them and slaying the warriors as they were tossed from their steeds.

Yen grew angry as his mounted charge was met and repelled, but quickly he revised his plan. Calling for crossbowmen, he ordered a thousand archers to surround the Troll circle and to shoot volley upon volley of arrows into the massed Trolls. Aiming directly at the Trolls, the first volley flew, only to crash ineffectively against the brazen Troll shields that no arrow could pierce. After many wasted arrows, Yen ordered his archers to shoot upward so that the arrows would fall from above. This volley had but slight success, killing three Trolls, but failed thereafter as half of the large Troll shields were swung into a position over their heads, thus blunting the force of overhead volleys. Gradually, the battle became a stalemate, for the Querques could not break the Troll circle, but the Trolls remained surrounded.

Realizing that he was trapped, even though his ranks were but slightly reduced, King Jasper ordered his circle of Trolls to move as a unit toward the river, for when they reached the Rhus, they could then face their foes with their rear protected by the rushing waters. The arroyo was now covered by the bodies of Querque warriors, and dead and wounded horses, neighing in agony. Again and again, the Querques rushed upon the wall of shields only to be pierced by Troll spears.

Yen was in a rage, for gradually his much larger, and seemingly stronger, army was being nibbled to death. But few Trolls had been killed while his losses were already beyond a thousand, and the remaining Querques were losing heart, some even deserting. Desperate, he launched his last attack, one that he held in reserve, hoping to succeed without it. For Profundus, when he was informed of the approach of the Trolls, feared that Yen's undisciplined soldiery would be a poor match for the highly disciplined and tested enemy. Yen was indignant at Profundus' doubts, but Profundus insisted that he take two catapults manned by scarlet warriors just in case the usual tactics of the Querques failed. Now, Yen was forced to use the catapults, for his warriors were failing and failing grandly. Finally, enraged at the Trolls, disgusted with his own warriors, and angry at Profundus for being right, he gave the signal.

The first catapult quickly moved into the valley, drawn by six horses and manned by eight scarlet warriors. Called a scorpion, this catapult was capable of shooting huge arrows, the size of small tree trunks. It was followed by a ballista, a much larger catapult capable of launching even larger arrow-missiles and weighty stones, and it was drawn by ten horses and manned by twelve scarlet warriors. With surprising speed, the catapults moved toward the battle in which Yen's soldiery continued to futilely assault the Troll's shield ring which foot by foot was moving toward the Rhus.

King Jasper was amid his warriors wielding both ax and spear. Perceptively, the Trolls, noted for their stamina and fighting spirit, were wearing down the now exhausted army of Yen. Maintaining their discipline and working in unison, the

THE ELFIN BROOD   313

Trolls not only continued their chanting as they fought but actually increased the tempo of the chant, thus increasing their effectiveness as their spears and battle axes continued to fatally reduce the ranks of men: "Hrumf, hrumf, hoyoh, hoyoh."

But as the Trolls were but half the size of men, they did not see beyond Yen's densely packed ranks and were unaware of the approaching terror the catapults represented.

Then the scorpion hurled its first arrow, tearing a gaping hole in the Troll ring of shields. Instantly, Yen's foot soldiers rushed into the gap, slaying many Trolls before the line could be closed. Then the ballista hurled a weighty stone which crashed fully into the Troll ranks, slaying many, especially the shield Trolls. With each fatal missile, the troll lines were further broken, and into each gap Yen's warriors rushed, re-invigorated by the sight of the collapse of the shield ring. The Trolls tried desperately to close their line, but no sooner had they closed one hole than another missile would tear apart another section of the line. Valiantly, but with growing helplessness, the Trolls fought on with ever mounting casualties and the gradual collapse of their disciplined order. Amid the chaos, King Jasper slowly began to realize the futility of his cause, and slowly he realized his end and that of the Trolls was approaching.

As the battle wore on, the trolls were reduced to half their original number, their dead lying carelessly amid the heaps of dead men. Then, King Jasper, uttering a piercing cry, ordered his Trolls to drop their shields, and to abandon the shield ring. Casting down their shields, they drew their short swords and lunged forward, attacking without plan or order. Yen's men wavered before the troll onslaught, but their lines did not break. And though each Troll fought with great skill and spirit, the much greater number of men began to make a final toll. Troll after Troll was hacked to pieces as more and more men joined the fray.

The Trolls were doomed. Pressed continually, they were driven in ever-shrinking numbers toward the Rhus, and there they made a final stand. The chanting had ceased. And those that did not die by the sword were forced into the savage waters of the Rhus where their heavy armor quickly pulled them under the surging waters. King Jasper was one of the last to fall. A sword thrust beneath his helmet severed his neck, and as he fell, the great cause of the Trolls was no more.

Yen looked down upon the carnage. The Troll army had been dispatched, but the cost to Yen had been catastrophic. For though a thousand Trolls lay dead upon the field of battle, over three thousand of Yen's warriors had been slain, his finest mounted warriors and his best foot soldiers. Bitterly, he realized that but for the catapults of Profundus, he would have seen his entire army annihilated before his eyes.

* * *

The morning following the Elfin celebration of the Shee raid, three Troll warriors, bereft of their armor, stumbled into the camp of King Styrax. Badly wounded and exhausted, they told their tale of woe.

Only the night before had the Elves, the Shee and the Nibelungen celebrated the glory of victory; now they were crushed beneath the disaster of defeat. Styrax and the Wanderer, though stunned and deeply saddened, realized the foolhardiness of King Jasper, and in their minds they recalled Jasper's frustration and anger when last they met in conclave. Empress Saphiria simply sat in the shade and cried bitter tears as she muttered softly, "Oh, the fools. Oh, the fools."

Black gloom descended on them all.

About The Author

Orville Wanzer was born in Brooklyn, N.Y. He has travelled extensively and has been a sailor, truck driver, and college professor, teaching English and Cinema. He has made two feature films and numerous short subjects and has been writing for most of his sixty odd years.

At present, Mr. Wanzer lives in a very remote area of New Mexico in the foothills of the Gila Wilderness. His life has been a long, often exciting pilgrimage away from his species, attempting to find in the natural world the harmony and peace he has never found amongst his own kind. When asked if he preferred wealth or fame, he answered that he preferred rain.

WATCH FOR THESE NEW COMMONWEALTH BOOKS

In Elfin lore, there are three distinct ages of the world. The first is the period in which Elves, Dwarfs, Titans, Fairies and Man lived together on this earth, a time known only through misty legends. The second age, understood primarily through the study of history, is the age of Man. This age is about to close, preparing the way for the third nascent age.

The Prosopian Elves have lived peacefully throughout the second age in the land of Prosopia. Man, who has destroyed his own homeland, has shown interest in Prosopia, and has prepared to capture these lands for his own use. With the help of the Dwarfs, Trolls, Nibelungen, Shee and others, the Elves, who normally avoid killing at all costs, will fight to save their lands from Man for…

Without extreme measures, Man's evilness will also destroy that which belongs to the Elfin brood.

The Elfin Brood

by
Orville Wanzer
